Bridge of the Paper Tiger

A Novel

John Chaplick

Cricket Cottage Publishing

For information about group sales and permission, contact Cricket Cottage Publishing, LLC, 4409 Hoffner Avenue, Suite 127, Orlando, Florida 32812 or call 407-255-7785.

Cover painting by Marie Schadt

ISBN: 978-0692459775
ISBN-10: 0692459774

Other Works by John Chaplick

The Pandora Files
An Enduring Conspiracy
The Rivergrass Legacy
Forbidden Chronicles of a Roman Centurion

Acknowledgements

No book, including this one, was ever written by its author alone. I wish to express my deepest gratitude to those special people whose help and patience made *Bridge of the Paper Tiger* possible:

My wife, Avis Anne, who took the time to edit each draft of my manuscript, and who managed to maintain a calm understanding while I sequestered myself away for far too long.

My two sons, Trevor and Kyle and their wonderful families who have always encouraged me no matter what I was doing.

My editor and critic Paula Stahel who, gently and firmly, helped turn a raw manuscript into an engaging novel.

My friend, beta reader, and critic, Ginger King, whose experience as an accomplished actress on stage provided a new dimension to the dialogue in the book.

My critique group members whose combination of objective assessment and warm encouragement helped me to develop my craft:

> Tracy Bird, Golda Brunhild, Gene Cropsey, Kathryn Dorn, Shaun Darragh, Elizabeth Griffith, Michael Hanson, Bob Hart, Vaughn Jones, Jeff Stark, Shaunte Westraye

My publisher, Jo Ann Robinson, and her dedicated staff at ***Cricket Cottage Publishing***

I wish to offer a special thanks to Marie Schadt whose cover painting represents an enticing invitation to the book's contents. Marie is a Tampa artist who has presented her work throughout Florida and parts of the southeast.

Chapter 1

The new director of the FBI's Boston Field Office downloaded the email from Washington and slumped into his chair. Jack Marshall stared at the gut-wrenching electronic announcement as though he hadn't read it right the first time. Saddam Hussein's weapons of mass destruction, which everyone agreed didn't exist a decade or so ago, had now surfaced in the form of a shipment of explosives to somewhere in Boston. Marshall shook his head and cursed under his breath. The memo made no mention of exactly where the shipment went, who received it, or its anticipated use.

Jack shoved the document aside, pulled Agent Mike Pallino's personnel file from a drawer, and turned toward the door to address his second-most pressing problem of the day. He motioned the waiting agent into his office without looking up. "Have a seat, Pallino. You're late."

Mike removed his leather jacket and pushed his sunglasses back on his head. "Yes, sir. Sorry. Traffic's a mess today."

Marshall closed the file drawer, looked up, and glared at his agent. "I thought I made it clear I didn't like mavericks. You operate as though you've never heard of the Bureau's procedures manual, Pallino. Hell, you're out there dressed like you don't even own a suit. Look, I follow the Bureau's operating guidelines to the letter, and I expect my agents to do the same." He pointed his finger at Mike. "I'll say this for the last time. You trample on standard procedure once more, and I'll have your badge."

Even after Jack pushed his second cup of coffee out of the way it vibrated enough to slosh a small puddle of caffeine each time he pounded the desk to emphasize a point. "I received a note saying you walked out in the middle of a mandatory training course. Damn it, Pallino, you don't walk out of an educational course because you happen to feel like it. The Forensic Science Research Unit is there for a reason. Especially for people like you who think we're still G-Men living in the 1920s. When are you going to drag yourself into the twenty-first century? This is a different kind of enemy we're up against."

Mike shook his head. "I've heard the sermon before, Jack. I mean, with all the holy sacraments about a new cultural landscape, cybercrime, and the need for unprecedented interagency cooperation. I didn't walk out on a whim. They weren't teaching me anything I didn't already know. It was a forensics seminar aimed at turning lawmen into lab rats. Why are they pushing this counterterrorism crap so hard?"

The director rolled his eyes. "They're pushing it because our country is under siege from a new source, and everyone on the Hill is convinced the FBI isn't equipped to handle it. My job is to change that. Beginning with you, Pallino."

"C'mon, Jack, our enemies will always be the same no matter where they come from. Firepower is the last line of defense against them, whether they believe in God, Allah, or neither. I'm not seeing the point here."

Marshall propelled his short, stocky body out of his chair and reached into a file cabinet. He extracted a brochure and shoved it in front of Mike. "Sit down and take a look at this," he snarled. "Explosives. Research Chemistry. Toxicology. Database Development. Infrared Spectroscopy." Jack perched on the edge of his desk and leaned toward Mike. "Now, if you can convince me you're at least generally conversant in all of these, I'll sign your waiver. If not, you get your ass back there and finish the course." He pulled a rumpled handkerchief from his pocket and wiped up the coffee spill.

Mike threw his hands in the air. "Okay, fine. I'll go back. Then you can call our Hartford office and explain why bookworm time takes precedence over their request for me to go down there and help out on a drug bust."

"I'll handle Hartford. You get going on forensics, and you damn well better get a passing score."

Mike extended his arms, palms up. "What's the big deal? Why forensics all of a sudden?"

Jack reached for the apocalyptic email and held it up. "You remember the weapons of mass destruction allegations that sucked us into a war with Saddam Hussein?"

Mike nodded. "Yeah, those charges faded into myth long before the war ended. So what about it?"

Jack slid off the desk and reclaimed his chair behind it. "Well, that was through our failure to find the arsenal, not because the weapons didn't exist."

He grabbed his coffee cup and downed the surviving contents. "Our sources in Pakistan just informed Washington that the weapons that didn't exist have now reappeared after more than a decade of careful concealment."

Mike cocked his head. "Like where?"

"Like here, damn it. Right on our turf. Word is that a load of innocuous-looking boxes labeled 'Ball Bearings' was shipped from somewhere in Pakistan to some privately held company here in Boston. No one knows what company. Washington will follow up with more details. Or so I'm told. Right now this electronic hand grenade they dropped on me an hour ago is all I have."

Mike took a quick glance at the offensive sheet of paper, turned back, and fixed his gaze on the director. "And I'm surmising the boxes contained something other than ball bearings, right?"

Jack returned the email printout to the cabinet and leaned back in his chair. "Enough HDX explosives to cripple a city. Maybe two cities, I don't know. The point is we have to find them, the people who plan to use them, and where they intend to use them. You'll finish that course day after tomorrow, and I'm making it your top priority to start working on this along with three other agents I'll be assigning. I'll make available whatever resources you need."

Mike hauled his six-foot-three, two-hundred-thirty-pound frame out of the chair and almost made it to the door before his boss caught him up short.

"One more thing, Pallino."

Mike turned as though he knew there'd be a caustic epilogue.

"I don't accept your premise that protocol is a navigational hazard. You keep that in mind starting today. Now get out of here before I lose my sense of humor. And start wearing a decent suit. Dark blue would be preferable."

* * * * * *

The minute he swung open his front door, Mike felt wrapped in an invisible blanket of solitude, the way he always did when Ellie was gone. He knew her engineering job required extensive travel. Still, spending evenings alone wasn't what he had in mind two years before when he'd rented a sailboat, taken her out on Nantucket Sound, and proposed.

Mike eased into his recliner, turned on the table lamp and tried, once more, to commit himself to *Chapter Three: Evidentiary Materials*. After four or five pages the vital concepts seemed to decompose in his mind, leaving only skeletal remains of words that had lost their meaning. He slammed the book closed, launched himself off the recliner, and poured a glass of wine. He tossed it down and poured another.

After he drained the last drop of Merlot from the bottle, Mike dropped onto the recliner and dozed off until the sound of the *Notre Dame Victory March* from his cell phone dragged him back into consciousness.

"Mike, it's Ellie. Were you sleeping?"

"Yeah, almost. You still in New York?"

"Yes, I'll be home tomorrow night."

"And out again the day after, right?" He sat up and rubbed his eyes.

"No. I won't have to leave for a couple of days. Mike, it's my job. You know that. You travel, too."

"Sure, I know. The place gets a little empty, that's all. I almost bought a dog today."

"I'm glad you didn't," Ellie snapped. "The last thing we need is an animal. You know as well as I do they have fleas, always seem to need shots, and they're messy. Are you still planning to go to Hartford for that job where they needed your help?"

He walked to the fridge and poured a glass of milk. If Ellie had agreed to have kids maybe he wouldn't want a dog so much. "No. Jack nixed the whole thing this morning. I'm back in that damned course again. By the way, dogs have fleas and make messes only if you don't take good care of them."

"Precisely my point. We don't have that kind of time."

Silence filled the next few seconds, as though neither could think of anything to say. Ellie broke the impasse. "Mike, are you still thinking of leaving the Bureau?"

"No. Maybe. I don't know. I'll see how it goes with this new director for a while."

"You don't like him much, do you?"

"I don't dislike him. I think he's a bureaucratic schmud, that's all."

"A what?"

"Schmud. A rule-book robot who can't brush his teeth without a set of written guidelines. The Bureau grows two kinds of agents— those who don't let the policy manual get in their way, and those who hide behind it."

"Oh. Well, you sound depressed. Did that dream about your father come back again?"

"No. Jack's lecture threw a cloud over my morning, the Red Sox lost eight-to-one in the afternoon, and the evening meal at O'Malley's Pub was lousy. What really bothered me, though, is I kept thinking I should have spent more time with Dad. He needed me at the shop during the summer when I was too busy with football practice. His repair shop died when he did. I should have been with him more and at South Bend less, that's all. I always thought spring practice should have meant summers off and spending time working with Dad in the shop. Coach didn't see it that way. Not for a team that had a shot at a national championship, anyway."

"Mike, it was your performance as a running back at Notre Dame that earned you second runner-up for the Heisman Trophy. You couldn't have done that fixing cars in your dad's shop. Get over it."

Mike stretched and yawned. He'd always suspected the Heisman Trophy publicity probably had something to do with his getting into the Bureau in spite of his dismal C+ academic performance. "Yeah, you're right. I miss you. What are you working on this time?"

"An angry client who claims we overran the budget without authorization on a building we designed for him. I'll take him out to dinner and get him settled down."

"Good. Have a safe flight back."

"I'll see you tomorrow night, Mike. Don't forget, there's plenty of nutritious food in the fridge. Stay away from cheeseburgers. And also the slice of pizza you hid behind the milk. They're junk food."

"Yeah, sure." He'd finished the pizza two days before. Now he felt sorry he hadn't ordered a burger at O'Malley's. It would have been hard to louse up one of those. Mike turned off the cell, tossed down the rest of his milk, and called it a day.

Chapter 2

Milton Pringle's walk down the long, carpeted hall past the firm's expansive audit and tax library only reinforced his feeling of being different. He paused to clean his horn-rimmed glasses and wipe his eyes. His peers, working on Potter, Moore & Bremer's more prestigious clients, routinely pulled late nighters in the library to research complex audit and tax issues. Milton couldn't remember ever having been in that room. The wall-to-wall shelves of Financial Accounting Standards Board Pronouncements and IRS Rulings represented a venue he'd never had occasion to explore — an exclusive neighborhood closed to all except the elite.

A last-minute tug on his jacket and tie and Milton felt ready to approach the managing partner's office armed with the most positive attitude he could muster under the circumstances. Four years with PM&B had taught him a summons to Paul Bremer's office could mean the end of a person's employment. Milton couldn't ignore the possibility it had something to do with his failure on the last two CPA exams.

"Go on in, Milt," Vivian said with a warm secretarial smile that never changed whether the visitor was going in to be knighted or executed. "He's waiting for you."

"C'mon on in, Milt. Want a cup of coffee?" Paul Bremer leaned over to pour himself one and held the pot over the cup he pushed toward Milton. Except for his Canali pinstripe suit and clean-shaven face, the lanky executive looked more like a twenty-first-century Abraham Lincoln than the managing partner of one of Boston's most prestigious accounting firms.

"No thank you, sir." Milton's mounting apprehension pre-empted his desire to do anything about the dryness in his throat. His mouth felt like it was lined with cotton. He tried to swallow. Maybe he should have taken the coffee. Not now. It would sound like indecision, another of the faults for which his father's criticisms echoed once again off the walls of his subconscious. He'd tried his best to please. The bar had always been raised too high.

"Sit down, Milt. I have some good news for you, and some not-so-good news." Bremer sipped his coffee, leaned back in his oversized swivel chair, and smiled in a fatherly way. "The good news is I'm giving you a crack at a new client. Metalcraft is a rapidly growing company. One, I might add, that looks like it might become rather important to our firm's strategic objectives. It'll be a much larger and more complex audit than anything we've given you before. I think you've earned the opportunity. This will be Metalcraft's initial audit, so I want you to do a first-rate job."

Paul leaned toward Milton as if to make a clear distinction between what he was about to say and anything he'd said before. "Now, what I *don't* want you to do is linger over details the way you have a tendency to do with your present clients. We're on a tight budget with this one, so spend your time on the major items, not the immaterial stuff. Got that?"

"Yes, sir. Thanks for your faith in me. You won't regret it." Milton shifted in his seat, glanced down at the floor, then forced himself to look directly at his boss. "What's the bad news?"

The senior executive's facial expression turned serious.

Milton felt the start of an old, unsettling sensation in the pit of his stomach. He could almost hear PM&B's one hundred-years' history of untarnished excellence screaming its silent outrage at his failures on the exam.

"Milt, the CPA exam results are out...unofficially. You'll be receiving your letter sometime next week. Since I'm a member of the State Board of Accountancy, I'm privy to the results early. I wanted to break the news to you myself so the letter won't be...well...so disappointing."

The sickening sensation meandered upward into the back of Milton's throat. His mind flashed back to the events which had buried his self-esteem in an unmarked grave, making him feel inadequate among all the Ivy Leaguers in the firm: his degree from a nondescript Midwestern university, any reference to which was tactfully avoided most of the time; those politely-worded rejection letters from the other CPA firms, including the one that suggested he consider a career other than accounting; at the top of the list — his monumental failures on the exam.

"So, you mean I flunked it again?" He looked down at his shoes and tried to ignore a developing nausea. The out-of-body feeling was there again. He wanted to *be* someone else. Anyone else would do at that moment.

"Milt, you scored awful close to a passing grade this time. You'll have to find a way to break through that barrier. I know you can do it. Look, I took a chance hiring you because I saw something in you other firms didn't. I still see it. You're as competent an auditor as anyone else around here. Do you know what your problem is on that exam?"

"Yes, sir. I can't seem to work fast enough to finish all the questions." He knew it had never been a question of speed. It was the panic he felt the moment he opened the exam. The kind that blocked rational thought and reduced decision-making into guesswork.

"Wrong." The executive downed another sip of coffee and returned to a stiffened posture against the back of his chair, as though his forthcoming pronouncement could be more effectively delivered from that position. "Your problem, Milt, is you shoot for a perfect answer on every question. That takes too long. You waste valuable time."

"Yes, sir. Thank you. I know I'll do better next time." Right away it sounded submissive and acquiescent. He couldn't think of anything else to say.

Bremer put down his coffee, walked around the mahogany desk with its vanadium sheen top, and patted Milt on the shoulder. "Okay, my boy, let's get it done. Now, I want you to begin the audit as soon as you collect the file from Vivian. The company's chief financial officer, Ali Fadhil, is a fast-track sort of guy. I told him to expect you. And by the way," Paul added with a broad grin, "when you arrive, remind him he still owes me ten bucks on the Red Sox game even if he is a client. Now go and make me proud."

Milt trudged back to his office determined to hold his head up high in spite of the bad news. Another failure. The word would spread like wildfire all over the office the minute the exam results were posted on the bulletin board. The other auditors and the clerical staff would smile politely at him without saying anything, although he knew what they'd be thinking: Milton Pringle bombed it again.

He'd be invited, of course, to the celebration dinner honoring all the firm's candidates who passed the exam. But, he knew he wouldn't go. The humiliation was bad enough without having it rubbed in. He slumped into his chair and tried to focus on the good part of Mr. Bremer's conversation— a new client, and a big one this time, instead of the little ones to which no one else wanted to be assigned.

14

"Mr. Bremer." Vivian's voice sounded softer than usual over the speaker phone. "Aubrey's here and wants to see you. I told him you were preparing for a meeting, but he says it's urgent." She lowered her voice to a whisper. "I'm sorry, but he says it has to be now and he's standing here seething."

Aubrey Moore, one year short of retirement, presided over the audit department, and every detailed function in it, with the same steel fist he'd wielded for the last thirty-five years. His short, muscular, barrel-chested frame hadn't changed much since his college wrestling days. Rarely did a completed audit survive Aubrey's critical review without half a dozen "to do" notes before it found its way into word processing for publication and release to the client. No one wanted to stand in the path of an angry Aubrey. Not even Vivian, who wore Bremer's rank like an emblem on her sleeve and usually didn't hesitate to stand up to anyone.

"That's okay, Vivian, send him in." The sight of a furious Aubrey barging into his office without stopping to close the door conjured up in Paul's mind images of a truck running a red light. With such a collision imminent, customary preliminaries were out of the question.

"Paul, what the hell's going on?" Aubrey's complexion swirled with alternating shades of red and purple. "Please tell me there's some earthshaking reason you felt compelled to take Tom Reardon off the Metalcraft job and put Pringle on it."

"Calm down, Aubrey. I knew you'd be upset, but it was necessary."

Aubrey arched his eyebrows the way he always did when the balance sheet didn't balance. "Necessary? Aside from fouling up my whole schedule, why is it necessary to remove a competent CPA who knows the cutting tool industry like Tom does, and put a brand-new client in the hands of someone like Pringle? Hell, Paul, the guy can't pass the most critical competency test in our profession, and he doesn't know a damned thing about the client's industry. Are we in the auditing business or not?"

"Relax, Aubrey. Breathe once or twice. We're also in the people development business. If we don't give Milton a shot at something other than our smallest clients, he'll never develop. As managing partner, I have a responsibility to produce qualified auditors as well as satisfied clients. You of all people must know that."

15

Aubrey placed his hands on Paul's desk, leaned toward him, and glared. "We also have a responsibility to the partnership to perform the kind of due diligence that avoids lawsuits. Paul, you were there. You remember when accounting firms lost massive lawsuits for not adhering to their own standards. Damn it, Metalcraft has never had an audit before this." His voice became loud enough that people in the hall stopped and turned. "Can you imagine the skeletons wandering around in that closet ready to invite litigation?"

Paul forced a laugh. "Lower your voice, Aubrey. It's under control. I'll keep an eye on Milton. Stop worrying about it."

Aubrey walked to the window that overlooked the Charles River and stared out for a moment. He shook his head and turned back to face his managing partner. "Fair enough, Paul, it's your call. I'll adjust the schedule. You better believe that, if Pringle screws that whole thing up, we won't have a leg to stand on in the courtroom. I'll see you tomorrow."

On his way out he threw another frown in Bremer's direction. Paul's smile acknowledged his acceptance of Aubrey's parting reminder about taking unprecedented risks.

Paul waited until Aubrey had huffed his way down the hall before he stood and took his turn staring out the window. He watched a team of Harvard rowers sculling their shell on a practice run while he thought about Aubrey's outrage. His Metalcraft decision had been a good one. There'd be no skeletons found in the closets there. He'd minimized that likelihood by assigning the auditor least likely to find them. He closed his files, laid the billing sheets on Vivian's desk for her to finish, and left for the day.

Chapter 3

Manus "Mac" McCleod's office hadn't changed since he founded Metalcraft, Inc. forty years earlier. Adorned only with samples of the company's various cutting tools, the cramped space left little allowance for creative decor. Its only window overlooked the loading dock, a testimony to Mac's belief that a CEO's job included keeping an eye on what was coming in and going out, rather than admiring a view.

"Come on in, Ali," Mac said. "I'd like you to meet detectives Saddler and McBride from the Boston Police Department." In sharp contrast to Ali Fadhil's dress pants, white shirt and tie, Mac's grease-stained blue jeans and faded denim shirt with rolled-up sleeves reflected his function-over-form approach to things. The aesthetic clash of Mac's hand-fashioned oak desk with the two metal folding chairs in front of it could have been attributable to the same mindset. Mac hadn't considered the seating capacity in his office until the two detectives requested a joint audience with Mac and his chief financial officer. Their arrival prompted the addition of another metal folding chair.

"Gentlemen, this is Ali Fadhil, my CFO, who oversees everything that has anything to do with money around here. He's my right arm. He views our company's future through the eyes of a twenty-eight-year-old, while I guide its present with the experience of a sixty-two-year-old. I've always been a day-to-day plant production guy. Never had time for the financial end of the business."

All four men took their seats, and Mac continued. "Ali, these men have some questions about that car accident a month ago that killed those two employees." He turned to the detectives and added, "We'd all assumed it was simply a tragic accident and never pursued it further." Mac turned back to Ali. "Since both of the deceased reported directly to you, I figured you'd be the best one to answer any questions. It'll only take a few minutes."

Detective Saddler's tone sounded almost apologetic. "We won't take up much of your time, Mr. Fadhil, just a few questions." The detective readied his notepad and offered a reassuring smile. "The medical examiner thinks their deaths were caused by head injuries incurred prior to the crash. Our mechanic thinks the brakes and steering mechanism might have been tampered with as well. Based on these reports and the report prepared by the deputy at the scene, we think we're looking at two possible murders here."

He glanced at Mac, and then turned to Ali. "In other words, it doesn't look like your typical crash death, although there wasn't much to go on because of the fire. We thought you might know something about their private lives that could help our investigation. For example, did they have any enemies? Might they have been on drugs? Did they gamble and owe money? Things like that."

Ali shifted in his chair while he contemplated the question. The hounds had, somehow, picked up the scent. Nonetheless, they would never find the fox. "I'm sorry, gentlemen," he responded after a brief pause, "I wish I could help. I really didn't have any close contact with either Shirley or Todd outside the office. I do believe they had a… shall we say…intimate personal relationship with each other, and were known to drink a bit after hours. Aside from that I can't add anything relevant."

"The curious thing, Mr. Fadhil," Detective McBride interjected with a frown, "is that the two victims were long-time employees of the company, with a clean record of competent performance and no indication of substance abuse. So, why would they all of a sudden get into a mess like this? And both at the same time. Doesn't that seem rather odd to you?"

The combination of McBride's stiff posture and steady glare conveyed its own message of dissatisfaction with Ali's responses so far. Ali's lips drew tight. He glared at his interrogator through narrowed eyes and spoke slowly. "Detective, the occurrence of any event so bizarre seems odd to me. Mr. McCleod and I were shocked. Metalcraft will support your investigation in any way we can."

"Well, Mr. Fadhil," McBride persisted, "we understand you personally hired two employees to replace the deceased a couple of days after the accident. Wasn't that a pretty quick turnaround? I mean, the job market being what it is and all."

Ali reached up to loosen his collar. The coldness in his voice betrayed an irritation he found himself unable to suppress. "The job market being what it

18

is, Detective McBride, I was able to choose from a ready supply of qualified people. Now, unless you have more questions, Mr. McCleod and I have a full schedule this morning."

"Sure, we understand," Saddler responded, clearly the friendlier half of what had shaped up to be a good cop, bad cop routine. "We'll be on our way. Here's my card if—"

"I'm afraid there's one more loose end here, Mr. Fadhil," Detective McBride interrupted. "I'd be interested in your explanation. The copy of our preliminary accident report, which we made available to you, personally, referenced our mechanic's suspicions regarding the unaccounted-for malfunction of the steering mechanism. Suspicions we subsequently found more evidence to support. You said nothing about it at the time, nor have you made any inquiries afterward. I would have thought such a startling reference might have sparked some measure of curiosity on your part, Mr. Fadhil. Would you care to comment?"

Ali ignored Mac's look of surprise and rose to a standing position in front of his still-seated adversary. "My full-time commitment to the operation of this company doesn't permit the luxury of pursuing suspicions, Detective McBride. That's your business. Now if you'll allow me to return to mine, I'd be grateful."

McBride conceded a reluctant nod, stood, and turned to face Mac. "Thank you for your patience, Mr. McCleod." He shot a skeptical this-isn't-over-yet glance at Ali on his way out.

Ali shook his head and pondered their comments while his eyes followed the two detectives until they were out of sight. Messy. The damn thing had been placed in the hands of professionals and therefore should have been clean. Nonetheless, the Boston police must have had no solid connection or they wouldn't be on a fishing expedition. Ali took a deep breath, straightened his tie, and checked his watch.

* * * * * *

Ali and Mac waited until the detectives had left and Mac's secretary had brought in a pot of black coffee before they said anything. Mac poured a cup for himself and one for Ali. "I'm concerned, Ali. The auditors are going to be here Monday. Are your people ready for this?"

The interrogation over, Ali leaned back in his chair and breathed a heavy sigh. "Of course they are. If there's a question they can't answer, I'll take care of it."

Mac shook his head and pushed a stack of invoices aside to make room for his coffee. "I know, but this is our first real audit. We've a lot at stake here. Without a clean, unqualified opinion from our auditors we can't get the bank loan. And, without the loan, we can pretty much forget about our planned expansion."

Ali put up his hand and smiled. "We'll get the loan, Mac. Stop fretting about it. I've helped you grow this company ever since you took a chance on me fresh out of Cal, and it's paid off. Relax. Our next step after the expansion will be to take this company public. You'll soon be even richer than you are now." He grinned, gulped down a swallow of his coffee, pushed the cup away, and glanced at his watch again. "Look, I have someone waiting for me in the conference room. I have to go. Can we talk about this later?"

Mac shrugged. "Okay. Just don't forget, Ali, you're my choice to succeed me as CEO here when I retire. My hope is that the expansion will encourage you to get more into the manufacturing part of the operation. You're a damned good financial executive, son. What you don't realize is that there's more to running this place than that. You need to get the feel of production. You know, roll up your sleeves and spend some time out there on the shop floor. Smell the grease. Feel the steel. Listen to the hum of the machines."

Mac walked Ali to the door, an unnecessary gesture designed, Ali figured, to allow time for an addendum to his lecture. Mac put his hand on Ali's shoulder. "You know why I come in every morning through the shop, rather than through the front lobby?" Ali opened his mouth to speak, then decided to let Mac continue. "Because I can tell right away whether things are running the way they should, just by the sound of the machinery. When everything's in sync it's like a big symphony. Bet they didn't teach you anything like that at the University of California."

Ali smiled. He knew Mac had never found time for a wife and family. The following week would mark the fortieth anniversary of Mac's marriage to Metalcraft, a union which spawned a reputation for excellence in the industry. A barren wedlock otherwise. For Mac, industry reputation had been enough. In the end, maybe the old man had it right.

"No, Mac, they didn't." Ali turned away, rolled his eyes, and walked out. The chaotic pounding of the machines assaulted his senses. The putrid odor of industrial paint, grease, and lubricating oil revolted him. He considered the shop a noisy, dirty place where poor people, like those he'd grown up with on the streets of Cairo, were content to squander their prime-of-life years for minimal wages. Ali despised them for selling themselves out because they couldn't do anything else. Above all, he resented the American system that exploited them under the guise of free enterprise.

* * * * * *

The dark-complexioned man paced back and forth in the conference room. A closely trimmed beard flowed from below his ears down around the sharp corners of his jaw to his chin, like a shallow stream seeking the path of least resistance. Behram Naji signed in at the desk under the name "Mr. Benjamin" on those rare occasions when he found it necessary to visit Ali. His pacing stopped the moment Ali appeared. Naji's menacing black eyes glared in unspoken disapproval of Ali's tardy arrival. Not given to small talk, Naji bypassed customary greetings. "I've replaced Ahmed Yasin as your mentor, now that he's assumed his new role in Iran's growing nuclear production network. He's assigned me to oversee your activities."

Ali shook his head. "I'm disappointed. I don't suppose this change is negotiable."

Naji ignored the remark. "The schedule's been changed. We've accelerated your timetable."

"Is this in response to the new U.S. sanctions against Iran?"

Naji nodded and sat down. "The paper tiger has now influenced four more nations to impose sanctions on our crude oil exports to them. Sheep afraid to disobey their shepherds. Additional sanctions on exports to Iran, of any commodities which could be used in our nuclear program, have been approved by the United Nations Security Council. These are more examples of its cowering to the United States."

"What's the new timetable?"

"Ahmed wants you to fly out to San Francisco tonight. You're to instruct Hakim and Saif to leave tonight also. They're to transport the material out there by truck, store it in a warehouse locker we've procured, and meet you there."

Ali shook his head. "Bad timing. I should have been told sooner. We're about to start an audit. This is the wrong time for me to be out of town."

21

Eyes blazing, Naji flew out of his chair. "Ahmed and I knew nothing of this audit. Damn you. Such an investigation could jeopardize the entire jihad. You're the one who set up the system specifically to avoid transmission interceptions by American authorities." He resumed his pacing. "And now you risk it all by putting the whole system on display for auditors. I don't understand this. I'm sure Ahmed won't either."

Ali stepped over to the conference room door, peered out, and closed it. He leaned against the edge of the conference table and responded with an air of confidence that seemed to further irritate Naji. "The bank mandated the schedule. To question it would only arouse suspicion. It's not an investigation. It's simply your average audit."

Naji reversed his pacing from clockwise to counterclockwise. He stopped, turned to frown at Ali in a manner that made it clear he found nothing comforting in that response, "And just how average do you think your auditors will be, Ali?"

Ali clasped his hands together. "I've made arrangements. The young man the CPA firm is sending out to conduct the audit is incompetent. There will be no mistakes at my end. Unfortunately, we can't say the same at your end." He raised his eyebrows and cocked his head toward Naji. "I've just learned your man apparently left some loose ends in the matter of those two accounting people. Now, that leads me to wonder about the competence of the two people you sent to replace them. Since the police aren't convinced it was an accident, they'll most likely get around to checking the backgrounds of those replacements."

Ali shook his finger at Naji. "Now, this presents a problem. I've successfully kept Mac McLeod out of my hair on this for three years. It's been easy because he trusts me implicitly, sees me as the son he never had, and doesn't want anything to do with the finances around here. Unfortunately, your foul-up caught his attention this morning while the police were interrogating me. It won't be long before he starts thinking he needs to trust me less and get into the records more."

Naji shrugged. "It doesn't matter. This will all be finished in the next week or so, as long as you follow the schedule. Then you will all be out of the country. Now, here's what I want you to do." He opened his briefcase and pulled out a manila envelope. "Ahmed and I have assigned a woman named Nahid Medah to work with you. You're to meet her this evening at the Hotel

22

Commonwealth bar downtown. You'll need to get started right away." Naji handed him the envelope. "Here's her resume."

Ali pushed away the manila offering. Competent demolition experts he needed. A female he didn't. Ahmed must have been nuts to think he'd work with one. Allah created women as lower-class creatures solely for the sexual satisfaction of the male, not to assume an equal status with him. "Forget it. Whoever she is, I don't need her. For two years I've bled this company drop by drop at my own risk to provide the funding for Ahmed's project. If these two experts are as capable as you say they are, I'm ready. I don't need a damned woman hanging on my shirttail."

Naji thrust the envelope toward him again and tapped it with his finger. "You'll need this one. She's Al Qaeda-trained, an accomplished assassin, and a highly capable civil engineer. Ahmed recruited her as part of a joint venture he established with the Taliban. Without her, you and your two men will be useless."

Eyes ablaze with anger, Naji leaned forward, his face close to Ali's. "Listen to me. Ahmed and I are growing tired of your arrogance. You've been living a comfortable existence in this country ever since Ahmed took you off the streets. People were fighting a war while you lounged around the campus at Berkeley, spilling beer and pizza on your expensive books…all paid for by Ahmed."

Still leaning against the table, Ali raised his head until his glare met Naji's. His voice slowed and turned cold. "Yes, and while your Iranians were cringing under the American sanctions and shouting their empty boasts about how they would destroy Israel and its American allies, I was converting Ahmed's dream into a reality." He stepped away from the table and shook his finger again at Naji. "In one week what I'm going to do in San Francisco will open the eyes of the Western world. Ahmed wants me to work with this woman?" Ali snatched the envelope from Naji's hand. "Fine. I'll do it if he says so. But she'd better be everything you say she is. I don't have time to wet-nurse an airhead."

Naji continued to glare at him, creating an awkward silence for the next few moments. "I've never liked you, Ali. You're spoiled, conceited, and ungrateful. Were it not for the place you hold in Ahmed's heart I would have been done with you long ago. Now hear me well. This jihad will be a critical component in our overall strategy of forcing American neutrality when we launch against Israel. You exist only to serve its purpose. Use all of your skills, and Nahid's as well. And under no circumstances are you to permit this audit to interfere. Do we understand each other?"

Ali extended his arms outward in a gesture of mock innocence. "Yes, of course. I haven't come this far simply to justify your doubts."

Naji shook his head. "Your first problem will be to find someone who can deal effectively with the auditors in your absence. Make sure you choose carefully."

As though there was little more to be said, the old mountain fighter and the young financier parted with an air of mutual contempt, each appearing to be satisfied he'd made his position clear.

Ali didn't offer to escort Naji through the lobby to the front door. Instead, he leaned against the table and stared out the window just to contemplate for a few moments after his visitor left. He would miss working with Ahmed, his old mentor. Ahmed had never been wrong about anything. The assignment to this jihad of an old mountain goat like Naji might well be his first strategic mistake. Naji should have been fired. No, executed.

* * * * * *

"Yes, Mr. Fadhil, you wanted to see me?" Phoebe Denton beamed as though it were an honor for a junior staff accountant to be invited into the CFO's office.

"I do, Phoebe. Come in and sit down. I realize you haven't been here long, although I've heard good reports about you, and Mr. McCleod seems to like your work. Regrettably, I'm going to be out of town when our audit begins Monday." He leaned back in his chair and shook his head. "This trip's come at the worst possible time, and I'm going to need a capable person to assist the auditor when he arrives. I'd like you to take that responsibility." He forced a condescending smile.

The young accounting clerk reached down to straighten her dress. She paused to catch her breath, as if to allow time to let the concept sink in. "Uh, yes, sir. Thank you. I'll do my best. You can count on—"

"Good. I know you won't let me down. Now, his name is Milton Pringle and, Phoebe, I want you to give him whatever information he needs, and no more. What I mean is, we have a responsibility to protect proprietary information as much as possible. So, I'm trying to say I want you to walk a narrow line between being helpful and being gratuitous. Do you follow me?"

24

"Yes, sir. Definitely. I think so. If he doesn't ask for something, I'm not to give it to him, right?"

"Exactly. And don't even suggest something he might want. Let him tell you what he wants." Ali rewarded her with another smile. "Now, Dave Bauer and Russ Bakish are waiting outside. Please send them in as you leave. And remember, I'll be only a phone call away if you need me. And Phoebe, this responsibility you're taking on will represent a strong recommendation for your future promotion if you handle it well."

She nodded, smiled at him, and flashed a triumphant grin at the two guys on her way out.

Ali knew Hakim and Saif didn't particularly like the names Russ and Dave. He was sure they would become comfortable with them, and no one had challenged the names or the other alterations in their personnel files.

"Come in, gentlemen, we don't have much time." He motioned them in with a wave of his hand and pointed to the chairs in front of his desk. "Sit down. Our schedule's been advanced. I want you to get that stuff out of the locker and into the truck *carefully*. You're to start out tonight for San Francisco. Drive responsibly and don't get arrested...no drinking, screwing, or anything else. Focus only on getting there and securing your cargo in the warehouse compartment we rented for you at Hunter's Point. I'll be there waiting for you when you arrive. Any questions?"

Hakim spoke up. "Yes, sir. What's the plan when we get there?"

"I'll let you know when it's necessary for you to know. Now go."

They shrugged, exchanged puzzled glances, and left.

Ali waited until they were out of sight, reached for his cell phone, and punched in the number for stockbroker Bill Kessler in the San Francisco office of Merrill Lynch.

"Hello, Bill, it's Harvey Morgan again in Boston." Ali had chosen the name from an obituary several years before when he began using some of Metalcraft's funds to build a nest egg of his own. Naji hadn't figured out that not all of the bank transfers went to fund the jihad.

"Good afternoon, Harvey. What can I do for you?"

"I'm sending you a check for two hundred thousand to be deposited into my cash account. I want you to cash out my investments and prepare a cashier's check made out to me for the balance in my account. I'll be reinvesting it in a business I'm starting. Don't worry. I'll reinvest the profits with you. Come to think of it, better leave fifty thousand in my account. We'll get together again soon."

"Of course, Harvey. I'll take care of it for you. I do have one question, though. I've been curious as to why you kept your investments in our Boston office for the last two years, and then decided to transfer them all to my office here. Don't get me wrong, I'm delighted to work with you, it's just that I wondered if there was a problem with our Boston office."

"No. No problem at all. It's just that I'm planning to launch another business and wanted to be working with a local office. I'll see you in a week, when I'll need to take the withdrawal."

Ali leaned back in his chair again and stared at the ceiling. He'd suppressed doubts about the upcoming operation more than once. He knew that many in the Islamic world would heap praise upon him for his role in the success of the jihad. Still, he would pay for his accomplishment by forfeiting a coveted position as CEO of a future blue-chip corporation. At any rate, he would walk away with an interest-bearing investment. The funds he'd siphoned bit-by-bit from Metalcraft through the jihad repositories and into his Merrill Lynch account had been consistent over the years. They had gone undetected. He'd made himself a wealthy man.

The very thought of it prompted a slight grin accompanied by a sigh of satisfaction.

Chapter 4

Aside from a general mandate to stay in top physical shape, Jack Marshall hadn't prescribed a specific physical conditioning regimen for his Boston Field Office agents. Mike Pallino and special agent Ted Krueger, both workout freaks anyway, lived out Jack's unspoken expectations to the limit. Although they used exercise equipment from time to time, they preferred the weekly long-distance jogging routine they'd established four years before, when breath control had been easier.

Krueger waited until they hit full stride before he posed the question. "Mike, rumor has it you're thinking of quitting the Bureau. Maybe it's none of my business, but is there any truth to it?"

Mike's heaving chest forced his words out in short bursts. "No. Thinking isn't doing. I'm not crazy about the direction we're headed, and my boss and I are never going to see eye to eye on procedure. No, I'm not ready to quit my job. I'll tell you what I am ready to quit, and it's this run." He stopped, wiped his head with a towel, and turned to begin a slow trot toward the spot where he'd left his BMW. "Ellie's home waiting for me to help her pack for an out-of-town trip. I have to get back. Let's do a rerun tomorrow."

Ted grinned. "Okay. By the way, I'm glad you're not leaving. We can't afford to lose a bulldog like you, no matter what the boss thinks. See you tomorrow."

Mike walked to his car, pulled a clean towel from the rear seat, and spread it over the back of the driver's seat to protect the upholstery from his sweat. He slid in behind the wheel, pulled out into the street, and accelerated to sixty in a few seconds. Maybe he could get in some time with Ellie before she left on another of her trips to God knows where this time. Between his travel and hers, their times together were becoming shorter and much less frequent. More than a physical conditioning routine, jogging had become a form of exorcism through which he could purge his frustrations.

* * * * * *

Ellie threw her hands in the air. "Mike, can you stop singing and get out of the shower? I used the time you were gone to get some work done and now I'll be late for my flight. It's my turn. Why do FBI agents run so many miles, anyway? I hear from the wives in other agencies their guys are content to run two. Maybe If you'd run fewer miles you'd take shorter showers."

The moment he stepped out she stripped off her clothes and slid in without noticing his admiring glances.

"Hey, Mrs. Pallino, do we have time to crawl in the sack before you get dressed?"

"Not anymore we don't. You should have thought of that before you jogged."

He knew Ellie could have had any man she wanted when she chose him. He remembered their first meeting at an FBI Christmas party several years ago as vividly as though it had happened yesterday. She'd arrived at the party with some staff weenie who proceeded to establish a new record for the number of Manhattans consumed before he zonked out on a couch. Mike hadn't brought a date. He'd become engrossed in the task of trying to decide whether he'd prefer to get drunk quickly on bourbon or slowly on beer.

He hadn't seen Ellie until she'd snuck up behind him and thrown her arms around his waist. In her long, slinky, almost-see-through turquoise evening gown, she'd mesmerized him from the moment he turned around. They alternately danced, drank, and talked the evening away. The next morning Mike's only clear recollections were that he wanted to marry her, had agreed to take her sailing, and promised to show her his Notre Dame football awards.

That most people wondered what she saw in him never bothered Mike. He'd heard that some of the guys he worked with were convinced she'd married him only to more quickly establish her U.S. citizenship. After all, if you're an Iranian, someone remarked, what better way to beat the system than marry a federal agent. Mike vowed to beat the hell out of whoever said that if he ever identified him.

He slipped into his clothes and looked around for his shoes. "Okay, honey. Not to change the subject, but you know, I'm thinking we ought to buy a boat and do some sailing and fishing."

28

"In your dreams. Now, what are you looking for?"

He knelt to scan the floor under the bureau. "My shoes. I'm serious about the boat. My income's not bad and, as a consulting engineer, you make more than I do. We can afford it." He stood and scanned the room for the missing shoes. "I think I first fell in love with you when we went fishing and you took the hook out of the fish without my help. Remember?"

"How can I forget? I hate fishing. Your shoes are under the bed. Please close up my bag for me and take it down to my car."

He slid into his weather-beaten boat shoes without bothering to put on socks. "You told me you loved fishing."

"I lied. Besides, you said you were quitting your job. We can't afford a boat if you don't have a job."

"Yeah, well, I'm only thinking about it." He closed the bag and flopped down on the bed. "I'm becoming fed up with the system. I'm a lawman, not a damned pencil-pushing spy catcher. Another thing, when are we going to settle down and have kids? Maybe a dog. You know, cook hamburgers in the backyard like other couples."

Ellie turned to face the mirror just long enough to apply her lipstick. "We've talked about this before, Mike. The kids can wait a few years. You know I hate dogs." She executed a sensuous movement into one of what Mike referred to as her deliciously sexy outfits, ran a brush through her long, dark hair, and tied it back in a bun.

Mike rolled over on his side to watch Ellie slip into high-heeled shoes while he contemplated his own feelings. How many guys think their wives' feet are sensuous? "Okay, so what do you have against hamburgers?"

She turned to check herself front and back in the mirror. "They're greasy, low class, and remind me of guys on motorcycles with tattoos on their arms. What do you have against French cuisine and sushi? Now, please help me with my bag and briefcase. I have to catch a flight to San Francisco and I'm running late."

He hauled his muscular frame off the bed and stretched his arms. "Sure, okay. What are those official-looking documents sticking out of your carry-on?"

"They're RFPs"

"I know you probably told me once before, but tell me again. What are RFPs?"

29

"Requests for proposals. We get them from prospective clients who need our services. We do a lot of business responding to RFP's. The more of them we win, the more money we make." She stuffed her laptop into her carry-on. "Can we talk about this some other time, Mike? I'm really late."

"Sure. Give me your car keys so I can load this stuff. Is this trip all about RFPs?"

"Yes. I'll be back in two weeks. I'll call you whenever I can. Don't eat junk food. We've plenty of nutritious food in the fridge. And stay away from O'Malley's. It's a place to get in trouble."

Mike walked ahead of Ellie out to her car, threw her bags in the trunk, and glared at the RFPs as though they were little munchkins that whisked her off down some yellow brick road and out of his life. He kissed her goodbye, watched her pull out of the driveway, and missed her already. He would have stared after her a few moments longer if the sound of his cell phone hadn't torn him from his reminiscing.

"Mike, it's Jack." The grumpy tone hadn't changed. "Word from Washington is that the explosives shipment was more than likely sent to a company that manufactures a product of some kind. You know, has machines that crank out stuff. Just thought I'd let you know. Might narrow down the search a bit. Keep in touch."

Mike walked back into the house and headed for the fridge, cell phone pressed against his ear. "Oh, that's great, Jack. Now we've narrowed the scope from five hundred companies to maybe three hundred. Is that the best they can do?"

"Afraid so. Look, no one said this was going to be easy. That's why I put you and three of my best guys on it."

Mike shook his head. "Tell me something, boss. How is it that I have the honor of being placed with your three best? I thought I was your token maverick."

"You are, Pallino. You're a pain in the ass. However, the way I see it, this apparent terrorist plot is going to be convoluted enough to need at least one unorthodox screwball like you on its trail. So get going. I'm guessing we don't have much time. Talk to you later."

Mike reached into the fridge and slapped a few slices of salami on a bun. He sat at the kitchen counter to dive into his cold concoction while he tried to assess what Marshall expected him to do. Jack wasn't a bad guy when you came right down to it. In fact, Marshall probably had the makings of a damn fine Bureau chief if he hadn't been a graduate of the Schmud School of protocol. Come to think of it, if the Washington office could have set its agents free from their procedural chokehold, one of them probably could have ferreted out the exact location of the explosives.

Chapter 5

Nahid arrived at Boston's Commonwealth Hotel before the scheduled time and went straight to the lounge in case Ali happened to be there early. With the late afternoon happy hour crowd now in full swing, the waitress suggested Nahid sit at the bar until a table became available. Even before she squeezed onto a stool that had just become available at the male-dominated mecca she became the center of attention. The pungent odor of cigarette smoke and male underarm sweat irritated her nostrils and resurrected ugly memories of two fat, drunken men ravaging her thirteen-year-old body when she was too small to stop them.

Her conservative black business suit, which would have been enough to conceal the attributes of most women, failed to obliterate her seductive curves. The bun that gathered her long, raven hair up into a neat swirl at the back of her head served only to accentuate her smooth, olive skin and large, dark eyes. Nahid's high cheek bones drew attention to the fullness of her mouth, a feature Ahmed had often remarked could stir any man's loins.

She ordered a dry martini and tried not to notice the two overweight drinkers on either side of her, both of whom had long since reached their consumption limits. She didn't like being there and she felt even less enthusiastic about the reason for her being there. She'd objected the moment Ahmed had assigned her to the project. High risk with insufficient payoff. Worse yet, no blueprints or architectural drawings had been provided to her...which meant she'd have to steal them before she could even begin the engineering part of the job. If that wasn't bad enough, the resume on Ali Fadhil conjured up visions of a financial nerd, not a jihadist. Ahmed must have scraped the bottom of the barrel to fill such an important role with a damned bookkeeper.

The ogler on her left took it upon himself to initiate a preemptive strike, which broke her train of thought. He slurred his unsolicited introduction. "Hi there, I'm Paddy Ryan." He ignored her failure to respond and continued. "How 'bout I treat you to a good Irish drink instead of that queasy stuff they just overcharged you for?"

Nahid looked away and sipped her martini. "No thanks, I'm fine."

In an obvious refusal to give up, he leaned over in front of her toward his drinking buddy on her right. "Hey, Danbo, what d'ya think this beauty would look like in a bikini instead of that business suit?" With breath that reeked of cigarette smoke and beer, the frustrated man made his final, desperate offer. "Look honey, you come up to my room and climb out of that monkey outfit and I'll show you some moves that'll make you happier'n you ever been. How about it?"

Nahid had reached the limit of her patience. "I'm out of here," she snapped. She whirled around in her seat, swung her shapely legs out, and stepped away from the bar, but not quickly enough.

The drunk grabbed her arm. "Whatsa matter, doll, you think you're too good for me or somethin'?"

"Take your ugly paw off me and go fondle your beer." Even before she finished the sentence, Nahid knew it was the wrong remark in the wrong place.

"Hey, bitch, no one talks to Paddy Ryan like that. Who the hell you think you are? C'mere!" Alerted by the commotion, the patrons sitting at the bar turned to see what was going on. Ali Fadhil entered the lounge in time to see Nahid's inebriated pursuer stumble off his stool and tighten his grip on her arm.

Nahid struck with lightning speed. She slammed her heel against the tarsal joint in the arch of her aggressor's foot, with her weight and lower body strength focused directly on the point of impact. At the same time the man's arch cracked, and before he could scream out in pain, she swung her free arm upward, hand open, palm up. The heel of her hand smashed against the underside of his nose with enough force to release a stream of blood. Before the man's body slumped to the floor, Nahid backed away and turned to find herself facing an angry Ali and a roomful of shocked patrons. Several of them had risen to their feet and started toward the bar, as if they thought there was something they could do for the bleeding patron.

"Nahid Medah, I presume," Ali whispered in a voice that sounded angry.

Nahid drew back instinctively to prepare for a counterattack from one of the drunk's companions. She surmised who the person was and ventured a reply. "Yes. You're Ali Fadhil?"

"Yes. Come with me. We're getting out of here. Now. Move."

Nahid hesitated just long enough to regain her orientation with a quick glance around the lounge. Several of the onlookers had moved in to assess the hapless Paddy Ryan's condition. Others simply stared at Nahid in amazement.

"No, no. Don't look back," Ali barked. "Look at me. Head straight for the door with me. Now."

A voice from the bar fired a parting shot with a pronounced Boston accent. "Hey, mistah. That's one tough broad you got theah. Bettah put yaw body ahmah on befaw you screw her."

"Ignore it, Nahid. Okay, we're out. Where are your bags?"

"In my car. Parking ramp. Fifth floor."

"Good. So are mine. Let's go, maybe we can still catch a flight."

Nahid stopped and turned to him. "Wait a minute. We're ticketed for tomorrow. What's up?"

"Your little demonstration in there just changed our flight plans. Follow me."

"Look, it was a reflex action. I had no choice. The guy—"

"Wrong. You *made* a choice. Unfortunately you made the kind that might land your picture on the front page of the *Boston Globe*. Come on, we need to move faster."

Nahid put her hand up. "Whoa. The elevators are over there. Where are you going?"

"Forget the elevators. We're going up the stairs."

"We're climbing five flights of stairs? Damn it, Fadhil. Ahmed said you were arrogant. He forgot to mention your wires aren't all connected. What's the point?"

Ali whirled to face her. "The point, Miss Nahid, is I want to minimize the number of people who get a good look at you in that conspicuous black outfit — if that's even possible after your debut in the lounge."

Nahid waited until they had completed three of the five flights of their marathon race up the concrete stairs. Suppressed memories of fat, drunken rapists leaked out again through the fragile seal the soused bar-fly had broken. She lashed out. "Look, let's get something straight. He grabbed me. I didn't—"

"Lady, I don't think you're getting the picture here." Ali spun around and glared at her. "You made one hell of a scene back there. And you did it with hands which, given your special expertise, are classified as lethal weapons in the eyes of the law. Now, maybe in Ahmed's training camps this whole thing comes off as heroic. Over here it could be considered a damned felony. And here's the real clincher. You managed to do it in full view of a room crowded with potential witnesses, any one of whom could easily identify both of us. You just compromised my entire jihad if that drunken fool decides to press charges. All right, where's your car?"

"Down there to the left."

"Okay, mine's at the other end. While I'm bringing my car to yours, I want you to change out of that outfit into something less…uh, noticeable. Then follow me to the airport. Maybe we can get a flight out tonight. Maybe I can even salvage this whole mess."

"Uh, we may have another small problem," Nahid said.

Ali stopped in his tracks, turned and frowned at her. "What kind of problem?"

"Well, the accelerated schedule hasn't left me time to get the blueprints I need. I know how to get them, but I'll need some time to, ah, solicit them from the guy who has access to them in the San Francisco Highway Department's files."

Ali looked at her as though he anticipated the worst was yet to come before he responded. "Are we talking seduction, here?"

"Yes. Once I've established a relationship with the guy I'll provide sexual satisfaction in exchange for the prints."

"And what happens when the guy wakes up from his exciting night, figures out what's going on, and tells the whole world you conned him?"

"He won't."

"He won't what? Won't tell, or won't wake up?"

"Drop it, Ali," she fired back. "I think you know the answer to that."

In the ensuing moment of quiet reflection they glared at each other. Nahid knew the seduction would be necessary. She knew she was the only one who could pull it off, and waited for Ali to reach the same conclusion. Without his full support the jihad might as well be cancelled. She felt like

35

contacting Ahmed right there on the spot and telling him this jerk he considered his adopted son should have been left behind a convenience store cash register and replaced with someone competent. Ahmed must have been crazy to entrust the success of such a critical attack to an overcautious money-counter.

He looked her over once more. "Okay, let's move ahead and grab the next available flight."

They caught a red-eye special to San Francisco and settled into the only two seats left — nowhere near each other, which came as a relief to Nahid. She leaned back in her seat, ordered a martini, and contemplated her options. If, by some remote chance, Ali managed to get the job done, she would press Ahmed to make good on his promise to promote her. If, on the more likely outcome, he screwed it up, she could still opt for the promotion on the grounds that she'd been smart enough to know ahead of time that it wouldn't work.

Nahid pulled a blanket over her to offset the chill of the cabin air conditioning, and polished off her martini. Within half an hour the dim lights and the drone of the engines lulled her to sleep...and dreams of an abandoned little girl who survived in the streets and grew up to show the world how successful she'd become.

Chapter 6

The undemanding receptionist job at Metalcraft fit Trudy Foster like a glove. Blonde, friendly, curvaceously plump in a way that was not seductive, Trudy impressed customers and vendors, except she couldn't perform any functions requiring a serious intellectual commitment. With her pasted-on smile she introduced Milton Pringle to Phoebe Denton, the skinny, dark-haired girl who came into the reception area to meet him.

Designer glasses — Phoebe's singular outward attempt to simulate fashion — clashed with her loafers to create an overall bookwormish appearance. Milton hoped she made up in personality what she lacked in looks. He reasoned she'd be the first girl he would have asked to help with his homework, and the last he'd ask for a date. Side by side, Phoebe and Trudy conjured up the image of a before-and-after beauty treatment advertisement.

"Hello Milton," Phoebe said with a look of surprise that suggested she'd expected something more impressive in an auditor. "Mr. Fadhil's our chief financial officer responsible for the audit, but he's out of town. He assigned me to assist you until he comes back." She managed a half-smile, reached down, adjusted her skirt with one hand, and shook Milton's hand with the other. "I'm new here in the accounting department, but I'll do the best I can to answer your questions. I have you all set up in the conference room. Coffee pot's down the hall."

On his first large assignment, Milton had hoped for assistance from someone with more experience. He and Phoebe looked at each other with expressions that conveyed a mutual disappointment.

"Thanks. If you don't mind, Phoebe, I'd like a tour of the place to sort of get a feel for what the operation is like before I start. You know, see the manufacturing area and then meet some of the other people in your department and so on. Would that be okay?"

She managed another one of her half-smiles. "Sure. Come on, let's take a walk."

During the few minutes required to make the trip down the long hall to the manufacturing floor, Phoebe filled him in on her background, even though he hadn't asked. She'd been valedictorian of her high school class, couldn't afford to enroll in college yet, and was taking evening classes in accounting while she saved enough money to pay the tuition. Milt figured that the unsolicited curriculum vitae probably came in response to a justifiable feeling on her part that he felt uncomfortable having to depend on her. In an effort to inspire a higher level of assistance on the audit, he offered to help her with her classes, if she ever needed it. She acknowledged the offer with a warm smile.

At the end of the hall they exchanged the tranquility of corporate administration for the chaos of a manufacturing world. The tour of the production floor took Milton into an environment he'd never seen before, where the shrill whine of high-speed drills boring through steel combined with the excruciating roar of cutting and milling operations. Massive machines gobbled up raw materials seemed to howl at a deafening pitch. The place looked like a metallic Jurassic Park inhabited by pre-historic steel creatures. Milton stared in awe at denim-clad operators manipulating the monsters with the touch of a button. He put his face next to Phoebe's to try to make out what she was saying, but heard less than half of it. At least she smelled good.

With his ears still ringing after twenty minutes of cacophony, he returned with her to the quiet of the more sedate office venue. He followed Phoebe into an administration area where neatly dressed white-collar employees performed the data entry functions required to keep up with the flow of materials coming in and finished product going out. He welcomed the relief, but missed the fascination of watching Metalcraft's product being fashioned from monolithic blocks of what looked like junk.

"Milton, c'mon, I'll introduce you to the people who'll provide information for your audit." Phoebe led him first to a grumpy, middle-aged woman who scowled at him. "This is Dorothy Denzig, who's in charge of our inventory accounting. Dorothy, this is Milton Pringle. He's starting our audit today, and he'll need your help in his review of inventory transactions sometime during the next few days."

Dorothy fixed a stern glare at him in the manner of a mother about to scold her child. "There's nothing wrong with my inventory, young man. I spend eight hours a day making sure the company's warehouse is neither over nor under-stocked. When that gets messed up, I take it as a personal failure and dash off a nasty email to the supplier."

"Miss Denzig, my audit is not a suggestion that there's—"

"It's Mrs. My man is dead, but I still go by Mrs."

Milton could see her sizing him up as if to assure herself he wasn't a threat. "Yes, well I'll simply need to confirm that your inventory is accurately stated on the financial statements, and that internal controls are sufficient to protect it."

Apparently comforted, she settled into a calmer tone. "Well, do whatever you have to do. If I have any free time I'll see if I can get you what you need. Like I said, I work a full day around here, and that doesn't include audit support."

Milton reached an easy conclusion that any help from Dorothy would be reluctantly provided.

Phoebe ushered him into another office where a delicately built young man with a jeweled earring in each ear and his face glued to his monitor screen managed to ignore both of them. "Milt, I'd like you to meet James Frobish, our information systems manager. James, this is—"

"I know who he is," Frobish said without looking up. "I've laid the printouts he needs on the conference room table. Anything else, he'll have to wait until the end of the day when I have some time. Good to meet you, Mr. Pringle. Right now I'm in the middle of a problem, so maybe we can talk later."

Milton and Phoebe exchanged glances, as if in mute agreement that they'd probably struck another dead end in their search for proactive assistance.

Marsha Boone handled accounts receivable. Although she couldn't have been over forty-five, she looked sixty. Years of chain smoking and other bodily offenses had made her complexion sallow and her bulging eyes red. She didn't light up her next cigarette until after she'd shaken Milton's hand. "I'll tell you right up front I'm willing to provide whatever information you need," she said, "but it will have to be after the week's sales have been billed and booked as receivables. And I can assure you my records are all accurate. We have almost no bad debts and we have an average collection period of thirty-five days. Best in the industry."

Milton smiled and gave Phoebe an unobtrusive thumbs-up.

Before they reached the next cubicle, Phoebe took Milton aside. "Now Milton, this is an important person for you to meet. She's Adele McDowell, whose age and background are apparently some kind of secret. You know, undisclosed private matters, and not anyone else's business." Phoebe lowered her voice to a whisper. "She's well past retirement age. She does the accounting for payables, cash, and payroll — in her own good time — not that she possesses any particular competence in these areas. Adele happens to be an old acquaintance of Mac, who gave her the job to supplement her insufficient retirement income."

Phoebe began the introduction with a smile. "Adele, this is Milton Pringle. He'll be doing our audit."

Adele shook Milton's hand. "Just so you know, young man, providing audit assistance is not part of my job description unless Mr. Mac specifically orders it."

Milton nodded agreeably. "Yes, ma'am. I simply have to review the company's transactions as part of the audit." The woman's hand shook and he recognized the signs of Parkinson's disease. She made a noise that sounded like a grunt before she offered a nod. Milton bid her goodbye and followed Phoebe into the hall.

"Well, now that you've met the key staff members," she said, "I'll leave you to your work." Phoebe pointed to the conference room. "Let me know if you need anything."

"Thanks." Milton stopped at the coffee pot, poured a cup, and settled down at the conference room table. Phoebe had managed to cover most of the table top with a well-ordered array of audit documents.

* * * * * *

Two hours into the audit Milton experienced an uneasy sensation that something was wrong. Nothing glaring, just enough to produce that gnawing feeling an auditor gets when the financial statements portray an end position at odds with the underlying transactions that brought about that position. He reflected on one of his early audit lessons: whenever the "what is" and "what you think it should be" don't agree, check them out.

He felt isolated in the secluded conference room, surrounded by volumes of corporate ledger printouts, historic financial statements, and legal organization covenants. His thoughts darkened. On his first large audit maybe

40

he wasn't competent enough to ferret out the secrets he began to suspect might be buried under mounds of documents. Paul Bremer wasn't one to make mistakes, and he'd singled Milton out for this audit. Still, Bremer might have overestimated the abilities of a junior staff accountant who couldn't pass the CPA exam. Maybe the firm should have sent a certified accountant after all.

"Hi, Milton." Phoebe poked her head in the door and rescued him from his thoughts. "Are you getting along all right?"

The isolation sensation melted away under the warmth of her perky, upbeat manner. He pushed the historic income statements aside, walked to the coffee pot, and refilled his cup. "Pretty much, but I do have a couple of questions. I notice the company's cash flow and profit dollars are increasing every year, but during the last two years they're both going down as a percentage of sales. I wonder why."

She cocked her head slightly and fired off a quizzical look. "What do you mean?"

"Well, I mean Metalcraft is selling more but keeping proportionately less in cash. Do you have any idea what's causing that?"

"No. Mr. Fadhil says we're growing like gangbusters. What difference does it make as long as the dollars are up? And I know cash is up, too."

"Yes, however, collections are growing at a much slower rate than sales and everything else. It could make a substantial difference. It's like the company's shipping out more product, but getting paid less for it. I mean the ratios aren't looking good. There's a chance the bank's not going to like this when it's making a final decision on your loan. Remember, the loan request is the reason the bank insisted on the audit."

"Milton, is ratio analysis a normal part of your audit?" Phoebe placed her hands on her hips and frowned. "Because I always thought an audit was limited to a check to make sure the numbers weren't falsified."

He tried to ignore the tone of irritation in her voice. "No, it's not routinely done in an audit. It's my own way of cross-checking."

"Well, I think you're overreacting." Phoebe's frown intensified. "Mr. Fadhil's a brilliant chief financial officer and he knows what he's doing. If there were anything wrong, don't you think he would have said something?"

Milton paused to reconsider what now appeared to be a geeky kid enamored with her boss. He decided not to push her — at least for awhile. "I don't know. When's he coming back?"

41

"In a couple of weeks. In the meantime I suggest you check your figures." She turned and stalked out. Her abrupt exit had the effect of underscoring all his other failures to impress members of the opposite sex. Even at O'Malley's, hailed by his counterparts at PM&B as a "target-rich environment," Milton had struck out on all of the various approaches he'd tried. This time it would be different, though. This girl *had* to come back. It was her job to assist him. He'd get another chance.

The isolation feeling returned again. Milt realized he might have ruffled a few feathers. Still, the recalculation suggestion wasn't a bad idea. He ran the numbers again, once on his laptop, and once more on his pocket calculator. Same result. Whatever the problem was, it had been well concealed.

Time to take a break and call his dad. He knew he had to face the ordeal sooner or later, anyway, so he might as well get it over with. Milton grabbed his cell phone, took a deep breath, and paused before he punched in the number, as though a dialogue with his father might be the only event that could make the day worse.

"Hello Dad, it's Milton. How are you and Mom doing?"

The voice at the other end sounded authoritative, as always. "We're fine, son. Your mother and I are enjoying my week off from work. How's the job going?"

"Well, I have good news and bad news, Dad."

"I hope the good news is about your exam."

"Well, sir, not exactly. But I think you'll—"

"What do you mean by not exactly? Did you finally pass it or not?"

"No, sir, I'm afraid I didn't. Mr. Bremer said I came within a few points and—"

"Milton, this is disappointing to your mother and me. You're either not studying enough or not preparing properly. Damn it, I passed the bar exam the first time, and I had counted on you to repeat that performance on the CPA exam. Are you giving this thing your best effort?"

"Yes, sir." It didn't seem to make a difference. No matter how hard he tried, the outcome would always be less than expected. Bad enough to have a father who never failed at anything. Worse that all those success genes never filtered down to him. "And I'm going to apply a new technique on the next attempt. I'm sure I'll do well on that one. By the way, the good news is they gave me a large audit client for a change. It's an indication that the firm must be impressed with the work I've done. I think things are starting to look up for me. I have to go, Dad. Give my love to Mom and tell her I'll call tomorrow."

Conversations with his father usually turned out to be brief, to the point, and completely uncluttered with warmth or informality of any kind. No exception this time. The dreaded confession over with, Milton packed up the laptop, stuffed the Texas Instruments calculator into his pocket, and left for the day.

Chapter 7

The firing range reverberated with the incessant crack of small-arms fire by the time Mike showed up. The place was almost filled with agents getting their required practice time in. Mike found a slot, stripped off his jacket, and checked his weapons over.

"Hey, Pallino," the firing range assistant barked. "What are you doing back here so soon?"

"I need the practice." Mike didn't need it, and he was sure Pete Sutcliff knew it. Mike grinned. "You were my first firearms instructor, Pete, before they moved you here. You're the one who always taught us there's no such thing as too much practice. Remember your spiel about agents living in a world where it's often firearm training that keeps them alive? Marksmanship, proper grip, controlled breathing and trigger control, you always said. An agent's only advantage over a well-armed and dangerous opponent — you damned near made us write it on the board once."

"Yeah, I know. But you've already met your minimum four sessions a year," Pete persisted. "Has your boss upped the requirement?"

"No, it's still four. I just don't like getting rusty. Set 'em up for me, please. I'm going to alternate between the .38 and the Glock."

Pete shook his head and grinned. "Yeah, I get it. You're here to let off some steam. What's eating you this time?"

Mike clenched his teeth and slammed the shells into the cylinder as though he blamed the .38 for his frustrations. "I don't know. Lots of things, I guess. I got a call yesterday from the Boston police. An auto accident a couple of years ago is now looking more like an assassination. Some local company is involved, and the investigating officer asked if I could lend a hand."

"What did you tell him?"

"I told him right now I'm sitting on my ass reading books when I should be in Hartford helping the DEA boys crash a heroin party. Either way, I couldn't offer any real help. So I figure if I can pretend that little center circle is someone's head, and fill it full of holes, maybe I'll feel better."

Sutcliff smiled. "You still favor head shots, don't you? I know Jack Marshall frowns on it, and I'm betting you support the idea just to irritate him."

As though he needed time to consider the remark, Mike turned toward the target, squeezed the trigger, and pumped a pattern of holes in the little center circle. He set the .38 down on the platform and picked up the Glock. "No, not really. The whole Bureau favors center-of-mass shooting. It's not only my boss. I'll tell you what, though. If you want to be guaranteed to stop your attacker immediately on the first shot, there are only two places to hit him: the brain, or upper spinal cord. Incapacitation by gunshot wounds to the torso is a damned myth."

Mike fired, reloaded, and fired again until there wasn't much left of the circle. As always, he focused on breathing while he squeezed the trigger, as though he were letting the shot come out as a by-product of the whole breath control process. When he'd fired his last round, he put the Glock aside and repeated the exercise with the .38 on a fresh target. His ammunition supply exhausted, Mike stared at the decimated piece of paper and lowered the weapon slowly, as if to emphasize his reluctance to finish.

"Nice shooting, Mike." Pete put his hand on Mike's shoulder. "Now, remember. I was your first instructor, and I told you a long time ago what the odds are against a kill shot to the head. If the target's moving, or you have to fire fast, go for the upper body. Yeah, I know what you're thinking. A mortally wounded opponent can still fire at you and kill you. Never mind. Go with the odds on this, Mike. In the long run a non-lethal body wound is still better than a complete miss to the head."

Mike grinned and gave Pete a gentle pat on the shoulder. He gave a passing thought to the possibility that Pete's comment about irritating Jack might not be too far off the mark. "You're right. I'll keep it in mind. See you next time around."

* * * * * *

Mike felt better, as though the firing exercise had emancipated him from his troubles. His frustrations had almost disappeared with his shredding of the target range circles. Mission accomplished, Mike drove to the marina to relax and smell the salt air. He parked the car and walked down to the dock, where he could stand and gaze at his dream.

He'd fallen in love the first day he'd set eyes on her. Twenty-five-and-a-half feet long with an eight-foot beam, the Contessa-26 model's long keel, cut away at the forward end, gave it additional stability in heavy seas. Rigged for single-person handling, easy to maneuver and dependable, the Contessa offered all the performance features Mike wanted in a sailboat. An experienced sailor who had never owned his own boat, Mike had taken a number of rented ones out off Cape Cod and maneuvered with the diesel until he passed the breakwater. Once in open waters, he'd raise the triangular white sail to complete the craft's metamorphosis from sluggish caterpillar to butterfly.

"See you're back again," the old marina owner shouted in his thick Boston accent. He approached from a rickety shed he called his office and flashed a broad grin. "Still thinking 'bout buying her?"

Mike waved at the scruffy old guy who looked like he hadn't shaved or bathed in a week. The man's skin stretched tight over his chiseled facial features, baked into a dark reddish tan by an unforgiving combination of sun and seawater. "Yeah, I'd love to put her through her paces." Mike's mind filled with images of billowed sails above a small craft bobbing on the water. He'd swing the bow about on a close haul into the wind, then turn the boat leeward again and allow it to run free with a favorable breeze on the quarter. Mike enjoyed the sensation of salt spray in his face, and the feel of the bow plunging down into each trough, then rising gently again on the next cresting swell. He was sure he and the Contessa would belong to each other...someday.

The old man spread his arms out and turned his palms up. "So why not do it today?"

Mike shook his head. "Twenty-five thousand is too high." He pointed a finger at the old man and grinned. "Make me a better offer."

He figured there had to be some reason such a seaworthy craft sat tied to the dock for so long without any takers. It could be the buyers were put off by the raked cabin bulkhead, which tended to let in rain and spray. The boat was old, and Mike could hear the soft creaking sound as it rocked in its mooring. After a morning of listening to the roar of his weapons, he welcomed the soothing sound of tide-driven ripples slapping gently against the Contessa's hull.

The owner's voice broke Mike's reverie. "Ya bettah buy it while it's still heah. Twenty-five's a dahn good price."

"I don't know. Maybe some day I'll take it off your hands."

"Well, it's one of only a few left ahfta the factory closed in 1990, mistah. Ya bettah do it soon."

Mike laughed. Soon wasn't in the cards. He pulled two soft drinks out of the dockside vending machine and gave one to the old man. They talked for an hour until the price eased its way down to twenty thousand. Still too high.

"I hear some sailors object to the wind and spray coming in on them through that bulkhead," Mike said, hoping the negative observation might drive the price down a bit further.

The man threw his hands in the air. "Ahh, I won't sell this boat to sissies like that. If you cahn't take the weathuh, then you got no business being out on the watuh. That's my feeling."

Mike broke into the first good laugh he'd had in several days. "Okay, old man. I quit for now, but I'll be back."

They shook hands on a promise to reopen the negotiations at some later date. Mike turned for one lingering glance at the Contessa before he walked away. Among the mélange of events in his life there were two loves that brightened it: Ellie, and his intermittent affairs with the sea. One of them seemed to be always travelling to some damned place on the edges, too seldom in the center. The other drifted in his dreams, close to his heart, still just beyond his reach.

He exchanged nods with a pretty girl walking toward him with a big black Labrador. He couldn't tell whether she was leading the dog or simply trying to keep up with the lunging animal..The dog pulled hard on its leash, moved toward Mike before he could sidestep, and sniffed mike's leg. Mike grinned and reached down to rub behind the dog's ears. He gave the tail wagging animal a friendly pat and felt a twinge of regret that Ellie had never shared his love for canine pets...or any pets at all.

"There must be something special about you," the girl said, "he doesn't usually take to strangers like that. Do you have a dog at home?"

Mike tried to force a smile. "No, I'm afraid not. Always wanted one, though."

She turned her mouth slightly down in a gesture of sympathy. "Oh, I'm sorry. You look the kind of person who should. Well, maybe someday." She

47

flashed an enticing smile, pulled the dog away, and continued her stroll toward the marina.

Mike watched her go and wished he'd thought to engage her for a few minutes in some appropriate conversation about her pet. She reminded him of Ellie, only younger and more innocent-looking than Ellie had been when she boarded his rented sailboat for their first outing. Someday he'd buy the Contessa and name it after her.

Chapter 8

Milton followed Paul Bremer's instructions to the letter. He wanted the Metalcraft audit to be his best performance ever. Paul Bremer trusted him and Milton wasn't about to let his idol down. Under a tight time-budget he didn't waste a minute and didn't dwell on any one of the forty-five ledger accounts. By the end of the third day he'd completed his tests of transactions, reviewed the major activities in each account, and examined supporting documents.

Something still didn't look right. It wasn't the kind of discrepancy that leaped out at him. Just a gnawing little aberration that wouldn't go away. Prompted by his mounting feeling of concern, he walked over to Phoebe's cramped little office space and asked her to join him in the conference room.

She scanned the once-neatly-stacked tabletop now covered with scattered papers and shook her head. "Milton, you've sure made a mess here. How do you know where all the documents are that I arranged for you?"

"I know where they are. This is the way I work. Phoebe, listen, I didn't mean to offend you the other day. It's simply that we need to go over some things. If you have a few minutes I'd like you to look at these figures."

She spit her chewing gum into the wastebasket, pulled up a chair, and plopped down next to him. After pausing to wipe her glasses, Phoebe leaned on her elbows, and peered at his spreadsheet printouts.

Milton had already figured out that feminine grace and agility of movement were not among Phoebe's attributes. Still, it felt good to be near her. He pointed to a row of figures. "Overall, I'm finding the records fairly clean. At least in appearance, management has met the Sarbanes-Oxley compliance requirements. You—"

Phoebe frowned. "The *what* requirements?"

"The regulatory procedures promulgated in response to the Enron fiasco. On the downside, though, the cash discrepancies I'm finding won't go

49

away. You can see the cash inflow is less than the amount Metalcraft billed the customers each time."

"Of course it is, Milton. We give three percent discounts to any customer who pays within ten days. That's pretty standard practice. So, what's the problem?"

"The problem is the company's policy specifically prohibits offering discounts. Who authorized this violation?"

"Mr. Fadhil did. He's really sharp about finances, and he knew it would stimulate more sales. What's wrong with that? I didn't know there was a policy."

"Well, there is, and the company's selling its products cheap when it doesn't need to. The plant supervisor told me his manufacturing operation is working at full capacity right now. The company can't handle any more sales. These discounts are just throwing money away. That's going to raise some red flags with the bank." Milton folded the spread sheets and reached for his coffee.

Phoebe took her glasses off, wiped them again, and rubbed her eyes. "Well, you'll have to talk to Mr. McCleod about all this. He owns the place. I don't know that much about it and I have to get back to work."

"Okay, I'll see you later. We need to talk some more. I'd like you to take this cash flow form with you and fill it out for me when you get time. You can pull the details from the company's receipts and disbursements journals." He watched her walk out, her face tight with the same impatient expression she'd showed the first time he upset her by challenging Ali Fadhil's numbers. Milton wasn't surprised. She was too new and inexperienced to understand the potentially damaging effect of what she perceived as nothing more than an effort to maintain good customer relations. He figured the shadow of suspicion he'd just cast on a boss she obviously idolized only complicated the issue.

Anxious to share his discovery with the man whose parting words had been "make me proud," Milton pulled out his cell phone and rang up his boss. It was a standing order at PM&B that, when in doubt, call one of the partners for a decision. Paul Bremer listened to Milton's summary without offering a reaction one way or the other.

"Milt, I agree these look a bit questionable, so make notes and we'll bring them up again formally in our management letter. We'll resolve all these issues during our closing conference with the client. In the meantime, I don't want you to slow down the audit for something trivial. Understand?"

"Sure, Mr. Bremer, but I think Metalcraft is going to have a problem with the bank when we finish."

"You let me worry about that. You just keep going, and make sure you don't get involved in so much detail you overrun the budget. Okay? I'll talk to you later."

Milton paced back and forth. He'd never known Mr. Bremer to be wrong about anything. He couldn't recall him being upset about anything. There was no problem Mr. Bremer couldn't solve. Milton didn't want to be the one to hand him his first unsolvable case. Maybe Mr. Bremer expected him to identify problems and clear them up before they rose to a level requiring partner attention. He stuffed his calculator in his shirt pocket and locked the financial records in a cabinet. While he polished off the rest of the coffee, Milton reflected on the events of the day: unanswered questions and no one seemed to give a damn. He shoved the laptop back into his briefcase, and headed for his one-bedroom apartment.

* * * * *

Phoebe marched into her office, slammed the door shut, slumped into her chair, and glared at the schedule Milton had given her. She was sure she'd already given him all the cash information she felt any auditor would have wanted. This offensive little document looked like one of Milton's own "cross-checking" things designed to trap her boss, or maybe make him look bad.

She considered tearing it up. Or telling Milton she'd lost it, or something. Still, Mr. Fadhil had given her specific instructions to provide whatever the auditor asked for. She wasn't about to disobey the man she was sure knew more about finance than Milton did, anyway. Maybe Milton's unnecessary form would simply confirm that unassailable fact.

Mac McLeod opened Phoebe's door and thrust his head in. "Hey there young lady, why the glum expression?" He stepped in and sat on the only other chair available, filling the space to capacity. "How are you doing filling Ali's shoes all by yourself?"

Forced to reconnect with the world before she wanted to, Phoebe turned the ugly paper upside down and managed a smile. "I'm fine, sir. Just getting some data together for that auditor."

Mac returned her smile. "Yeah, auditors can be a pain in the neck. You getting along with him okay?"

She shrugged. "I guess so. He's all right, I suppose. He's sure a lot different than what I expected, that's all."

"How so?"

"Well, I mean I sort of thought he'd be tall, handsome, and maybe kind of mysterious. Like a more experienced guy who really knew what he was doing and didn't have to ask so many questions that don't seem to relate to anything."

Mac stood and couldn't contain a laugh. "Ah, I get it. Well, has he asked any questions you can't answer?"

Phoebe hesitated. She didn't want to burden a CEO with questions she probably should have been able to answer. Then again, she knew she'd committed to bring Milton's so-called "discrepancies" to Mac's attention. "Well, yes sir. He seems to have gone off on a tangent about customer discounts. I tried to tell him there's nothing wrong, but he wants to talk to you anyway. I'm sorry."

"Ahh, don't be. I'll get with him tomorrow. You just keep him honest and we'll sail through this audit like a pig through hot grease." Mac grinned and walked out, leaving Phoebe alone with Milton's four-column worksheet, which had begun to look more like an indictment than an audit schedule.

Chapter 9

After a fitful night's sleep, which he blamed on Bremer's failure to provide any specific guidance, Milton took his time dressing and eating breakfast. He even drove to work slower than usual.

"Good morning, Milton. You're late." Trudy's friendly smile confirmed it was a teasing observation, not a chastisement. Milton waved and smiled back. He rushed past her toward the conference room where he hoped an overdose of caffeine would keep him alert all day.

Before he could bury his head in the board meetings minute book, Phoebe stepped into the conference room with the CEO right behind her. "Mr. McLeod's here to see you, Milt. I know you wanted to meet him."

The denim-clad figure stood next to Milton and put a large, muscular hand on the accountant's shoulder. "Hello, son, I'm Mac McCleod. It's good to meet you."

Milton struggled to push his chair back and stand up quickly to shake the top executive's hand. Caught on the carpet, the chair didn't move, and Milt could only manage an awkward lunge forward. To Milton, Mac looked more like a shop foreman than a CEO. His jeans were clean enough, maybe even pressed some time ago, but his shirt still bore remnants of grease stains that must have survived all efforts to wash them away.

"Don't get up, son, I only wanted to meet you and ask how the audit's going. Phoebe tells me you're encountering some difficulty." Mac and Phoebe each pulled up a chair on either side of Milt. "What kind?"

"Well, sir, I'm concerned the company seems to be offering increasingly larger discounts to its customers, and not taking any of the discounts offered by its suppliers. It's hurting your cash both ways."

The executive frowned. He paused to glance at Phoebe before he turned back to Milton. "Son, I don't know where you're getting your information. I can tell you we've never offered discounts to our customers. Hell, we make the finest product on the East Coast. Why would we offer a discount on something our customers are begging for?"

"I don't know, sir. I also wondered why the company isn't taking any of the discounts offered by its suppliers. It doesn't make sense."

Mac scratched his head. "Well, Ali knows what he's doing. If he gave a customer a reduced price he probably did it as a one-shot deal to promote something. As to not taking the discounts our suppliers offer, Ali says we make more by holding and investing the cash at some reasonable percentage rate than paying it out to get an early three percent discount from the vendors. So now you know."

"Well, sir, all I'm saying is your cash receipts and disbursements tell a different story."

"Hell boy, that can't be. Look, before this company's growth started to take off I had a young accountant in here keeping the books. We stopped giving discounts then. When the company outgrew that young man's abilities, I brought in Ali. I'm hell-fire sure he doesn't give 'em either. Look, I have to get back to the shop. You check those numbers again and I'll run your concerns past Ali." He stood, patted Milton on the shoulder, and was gone before Milton could think of a response.

Phoebe and Milton turned to look at each other without saying anything. Phoebe broke the silence. "Milt, I don't know what to say. I can't imagine why he said we don't give or take discounts. I've recorded the sales discounts to the customers myself. Just the way Mr. Fadhil showed me, although it seemed like we used an extra form we didn't need. I don't know, maybe we should ask Mr. Fadhil."

Milton wasn't sure whether he sensed the beginning of a bond between them, or simply a softening of her attitude. Either way, he felt he'd found his first ally on an issue no one else seemed to care about. At least she sounded like she trusted him a bit more.

He stood, pushed the records aside, and leaned against the edge of the table. "Phoebe, I'm convinced Fadhil has either rigged the information system, or has found a way to circumvent it. This company's hemorrhaging cash, and right now I'm worried about whether other assets are disappearing as well."

"Like what kind of assets?"

"Well, aside from cash, raw materials inventory, I guess, would be the easiest to misappropriate. Who checks on that stuff when it comes in from the vendors?"

Phoebe cocked her head as though she had to think about it before answering. "That would be the new receiving and shipping guy Mr. Fadhil hired a while back. He checks the incoming items against the purchase orders and invoices to assure the specifications are met and the prices are as quoted."

"Is that the only internal control the company has on inventory?"

"Oh no, Milt." Phoebe threw up her hands and shook her head. "There's always Dorothy Denzig. She keeps a running log of in-and-out inventory transactions. I think she spends half her time watching over those guys on the loading dock. If they forget to check stuff off against her log, or make a mistake, she screams at them. The loaders are all afraid of her."

Milton nodded. "I don't blame them. That woman looked to me like the Wicked Witch of the East. I think I have a printout of her log, so where are those documents filed?"

"The packing slips and matching purchase orders are stored out on the loading dock, filed by P.O. number on Dorothy's log, with a copy of the invoice attached."

"Okay, I think I'll go out there with her log and have a look. And hey, Phoebe, thanks for helping me on this."

"That's what I'm here for, Milt." She offered a smile that looked flirtatious enough to make him blush a little.

* * * * * *

Diesel fumes, slamming tailgates, and shouting truck drivers made the shipping and receiving dock a difficult place to examine documents. Half an hour was about all the record-matching Milton could stand. He completed his comparison of purchase orders with attached packing slips and invoice copies, except for six sets he couldn't find. The missing records, one of the loaders told him, were in Russ Bakish's personal locker.

"He's out of town, fella," the loader shouted over the noise. "You'll have to wait 'til he gets back."

As far as he could remember, Milton had always followed the rules. His father's rules, school's rules, the firm's rules, and a litany of accounting profession rules. It had become a part of his fundamental behavior code. He hesitated for a moment while all the punishments he could imagine for breaking rules danced, like red-eyed demons, through his thoughts. Defiance of authority had never been part of his DNA.

The demons had been there before, he thought. Maybe that's why he'd never become the son his father could be proud of. Maybe that's why his cautionary precision on the CPA exam cost him enough valuable time to flunk it three times. Well, enough was enough.

Milton Pringle took a deep breath, picked up a crowbar, and ripped open the man's locker. The foul odor reached his nostrils before the six missing packing slips caught his eye. He found them crumpled on the bottom, as though they'd outlived their usefulness. Maybe Bakish never got around to cleaning out his locker. Milt scooped up all six and attached them to his clipboard. On top he placed the one splotched with the sticky, foul-smelling powder he didn't recognize. No purchase orders or invoices, only the slips, which he figured were better than nothing.

A loader climbed down from his forklift, and came up from behind. "Hey, you. What are you doing in that locker?"

Caught off-guard, Milton could feel his face tighten like it did when his father used to punish him. He turned, stiffened, and blurted out the first response that came to his mind. "I'm conducting an official bank inspection of assets stored in unauthorized places."

The man stopped, looked apologetic, and waved. "Oh, okay. Guess we were both just doing our job." Embarrassed, the loader forced out a sheepish smile, turned, and remounted his forklift.

Milton felt surprise at his sudden assertiveness, and, at the same time, a twinge of shame for what he'd done. If challenged, he rationalized, he would explain his action as a necessary follow-up to the cash discrepancies he'd already found. That would sound like a credible audit procedure.

He blew some of the powder off the top slip, glanced around to see if anyone else had witnessed his indiscretion, and made his way through the din of the factory floor and into the quiet of the accounting offices. He handed his pungent collection to Phoebe.

She drew her head back and pinched her nose. "Phew! This stinks. That guy must have let something go rancid in his locker." She lifted the stained slip carefully, turned it over, and held it up to the light for further examination. The sight of her setting it down on a desk and pushing it out of sniffing range elicited a grin from Milton. Phoebe took a deep breath, placed her hands on her hips, and turned to face him. "Milton, I think we have a problem."

"How do you know? We haven't tried to trace any of the incoming items on Dorothy's log into inventory yet."

She shook her head and frowned. "We're not going to find any of this stuff in our inventory. Or on Dorothy's log. The items on these records come from a New York warehouse we never use. The content listing on one of them looks like some kind of ball bearings we don't even buy. There are no prices listed. I'm also seeing what appears to be an almost completely obliterated name of some foreign country, which I can't make out. Do you think you ought to inform your boss about this, and maybe even the police?"

Milton looked down at his feet, then up at the ceiling. He turned toward Phoebe without looking directly at her. "Well, I'm kind of in a box here. Mr. McCleod isn't really interested in this and neither is my boss. I don't want to get Mr. Fadhil stirred up about it until I have more evidence. I can't afford another foul-up."

"What are you talking about, Milt?"

He shifted his feet, turned slightly away from her, and looked down at the floor again. "To tell you the truth, Phoebe, I'm sort of on probation at my firm. I agree with you, there's something really wrong here. If I make a big deal of it, though, and it turns out to be nothing, I'm pretty much washed up at PM&B. Anyway, this looks like an interstate commerce issue, and that involves the FBI, not the police. I think I'm going to explore that avenue first just to see what my options are. How about coming with me? I mean, as a source of verification."

After a long silence she smiled at him in a reassuring kind of way. "We'll go together, Milt, as soon as I can set up an appointment at the FBI headquarters with someone who'll talk to us. I think a call like that would be more appropriate coming from an employee of the company than from you."

Milt nodded. "I'd like that. You know, when I started this audit I thought I'd offended you by challenging Fadhil. I thought you didn't like me much to begin with, and—"

"Milton, it's not that I didn't like you. I simply thought so highly of Mr. Fadhil until you made him look bad with all your unusual procedures. I mean, well, I guess I'm seeing now that he's not everything I thought he was. Not only that. I'm starting to feel a little afraid of what he's doing around here.

Oh, darn it. I guess I really mean I think you're a nice, honest guy and I like you. Anyway, I'll let you know as soon as I set up the meeting."

Convinced a bond between them had now been established, Milton found himself feeling a little better about everything the more he thought about it. He may get fired if this thing should blow up. Well, so be it. At least he'd found the first girl who ever showed an interest in him. Maybe getting fired wasn't the worst catastrophe that could happen, anyway. Maybe it was time he lived his life for himself and not for his father. Sooner or later he'd pass the exam. Then there would be a host of second and third tier accounting firms that would be glad to hire him. Perhaps he wouldn't even tell his father when he earned his CPA certificate. Let him stew for awhile. He'd get married and settle down. And he sure as heck wouldn't treat his kids like his father treated him. Milton smiled, packed up his stuff, and headed for a hamburger dinner at O'Malley's.

Chapter 10

Agent Mike Pallino couldn't conceal an unintended grimace of disdain when he extended his hand to greet Phoebe and Milton. They looked like a pair of nerds out looking for kicks. He felt like spanking both of them for wasting the agency's time. On the positive side, he'd set their appointment for late in the day so they could only louse up the tail end of it.

"Good afternoon, I'm Mike Pallino. You're Milton Pringle and Phoebe Denton, I presume. Come on back, we can talk in my office." He forced a smile and tried to entertain uplifting thoughts like taking the Contessa out to sea.

Phoebe looked at Mike as though she couldn't keep her eyes off him. His six-foot-three-inch frame seemed to narrow its way down from a pair of wide, sloping, shoulders through a barrel chest and a flat, hard stomach to what couldn't have been more than a thirty-two- inch waist.

Small and minimally furnished, Mike's office immediately drew visitors' eyes to a strategically placed credenza, more like a showcase than a piece of furniture. A photograph of Mike's wife, next to an even larger one of his Notre Dame Football team, appeared deliberately positioned to create a beauty-and-the-beast impression. A picture of the current FBI director hung on the wall next to that of J. Edgar Hoover, slightly above an array of plaques recognizing Mike's progress and awards during his training as an agent.

Mike opened the conversation. "Okay, what can I do for you? The message I received said it was something about interstate fraud and possibly a foreign point of origin. I'd like to know how two youngsters like you became involved in something like this. So, talk to me."

Milton frowned, as though he resented the "youngster" remark. "I'm the company's auditor and I'm required to get involved as part of my test of transactions. Phoebe works for the company's CFO and she's assisting me in my audit. I'm twenty-five, by the way, and Phoebe can divulge her own age if she feels it's anyone's business."

"I'm twenty," Phoebe snapped, "and I don't see how our ages are relevant. Milton knows what he's talking about."

Mike put up his hands and grinned. "Okay, okay, take it easy. I meant no offense. Let's talk about fraud. What's going on at this company you're auditing?"

"Well, sir, it may be more than what my preliminary findings are indicating," Milton said. "I'm beginning to suspect someone is stealing cash, and maybe inventory. However, there's also a possibility the company is importing some kind of foreign material with no accounting identification of what it is. I'm not through with my audit yet, and already I suspect there might be more than fraud involved here."

Milton handed Mike the packing slips he'd brought with him, and summarized the sequence of events with an obvious effort to avoid violating client confidentiality. Mike listened with intermittent condescending nods. He paused for a few seconds to examine the packing slips before offering an assessment. "Okay, if this story is true, it's a felony. Even so, it looks more like a police matter than an FBI issue. Have you shared all this with the local police?"

"We thought about that," Milton countered, "until the undecipherable reference to what looks like a foreign country, plus those two dead people Phoebe told me about, led me to think it belongs in federal jurisdiction. I'll bring the internal control weakness to my boss before the audit is finished, but first I need to consider—"

"Whoa. Wait a minute," Mike interjected. "Back up. What dead people?"

With supporting commentaries from Phoebe, Milton expanded on his audit findings and wrote down the names of the two deceased employees on a piece of paper. Mike inserted it into a manila envelope along with the packing slips. After he asked a few more questions about the audit, Mike stood and extended his arm toward the door with an ushering-out kind of gesture, a signal the meeting was over.

Mike took a deep breath and released it with an audible sound. "Okay, look, I think you two are chasing your tails on this, but I'll check it out and get back to you. In the meantime, I'd like you to write up a brief summary of the items you think are audit discrepancies and e-mail them to me. I want to know everything you know about the two deceased employees and who replaced them. I'll be in touch."

"Is that *it?*" Milton asked, eyebrows raised.

"Yep. I need to do some research on this before we talk again."

Mike walked Milton and Phoebe to the door and returned to his office. He slouched into his chair and thrust his feet up on the desk.

* * * * * *

With tickets to the Red Sox game that night, Mike hadn't planned to work late. In fact, he hadn't planned to work at all. Still, the more he thought about two dead employees and packing slips which should have no reason to be smeared with a smelly powder, the more the story those two kids related became an issue he couldn't ignore. The Congressional Joint Inquiry into the terrorist attacks of September 11, 2001 had singled out the FBI for inattention to domestic terrorist threats, failure to collect and analyze useful intelligence data, and reluctance to share information with other members of the intelligence community.

Mike leaned back in his chair and thought about the skeptics' argument that the FBI's law enforcement culture had become too entrenched. That, from the beginning, the agency was improperly structured to develop the counter-intelligence skills required to effectively combat terrorism. With that kind of pressure being brought to bear on the Bureau, an agent who neglected to follow up on a possible terrorist lead that was handed to him would be in serious trouble. Although Mike had tried not to obsess on it, he couldn't forget that Jack Marshall had assigned him to be on the lookout for a Boston corporation in receipt of suspicious shipments from Pakistan. Now it looked like he might be directly confronted with exactly that entity.

Mike stepped out of his office, gave the Red Sox tickets away, and shook his head. He still couldn't believe what he'd given up for two geeks, a dirty piece of paper, and an off-the-wall story. He heaved a despondent sigh and settled back into his chair for a long evening's work.

His first task amounted to a forty-five-minute series of phone calls to find the right person before the Boston police finally put him through to Detective McBride.

"What the hell's the FBI doing on this case?" McBride snapped. "This is a local issue."

"Not any more, it isn't," Mike shot back at him. "Your 'local issue' now has interstate fraud and possible terrorist implications attached to it. I want a complete fax of your findings as well as every document and related memo, including the report of your conversations with any Metalcraft employees. I want it tonight. We're looking at more than a possible murder here."

McBride hesitated for a moment before he responded with what sounded to Mike like an air of self-satisfaction. "My pleasure, Agent Pallino. I'll even add my own personal two cents because I want you to remember you heard this from me first. Regardless of what comes out of your investigation, you're gonna find a slick operator named Ali Fadhil — a damned foreigner, by the way — right in the middle of it. And for whatever it's worth, my gut feel is that Fadhil's replacements for those dead employees are as involved in this thing as he is. I'll get the fax off to you in the next hour or two. I'll offer my own services any time you want. Good hunting."

* * * * * *

By midnight Metalcraft's evening shift had closed down the production line for the day. The few late-working administrative employees had long since gone, and Milton found himself the facility's sole occupant. At the end of a day spent auditing inventory purchases and unpaid vendor invoices, fatigue had set in. He yawned and drained the last drop from the coffee pot.

The document-matching process had gone fairly well until Milt came to four vendor invoices with a few more numbers on them than all the others. Something didn't look right. Until now he hadn't noticed that the attached remittance advices also bore an unusually long set of numbers. He rubbed his eyes. There was no reason for the inconsistency. He put a note on Phoebe's desk asking her to pull copies of the checks sent out in payment of the suspicious-looking invoices.

Deep in concentration on his audit procedures, Milt didn't become aware of the movement behind him until the man's foot struck Milt's briefcase protruding from under a chair. Startled, Milt vaulted out of his chair and whirled around to find himself directly in the path of a large man who, having recovered from his stumble, was now almost on top of him. Instinctively, Milt jumped aside and began a dash for the door. His more-agile aggressor moved to block his exit. Thoughts of being killed because he happened to be in the wrong place at the wrong time during a burglary raced through Milton's mind.

The man's dark, heavily-bearded face showed no expression. There was no sign of anger or any other emotion, as though his mission was simply a routine business matter, nothing personal. With his intended victim now inexorably trapped, the larger-than-life man seemed to take his time. He moved forward, his black eyes fixed on Milton with a look of impassive determination to do more than just rob him.

Like the eagle about to swoop and sink his talons into the rabbit, the threatening figure epitomized all Milton's childhood fears and feelings of inadequacy. Milton's whole world became compressed into one brief moment of unbearable panic, followed by the strange nothingness of being trapped in a transition zone between life and death. Cornered, terrified, and aware of his assailant's physical superiority, Milton Pringle took the only action he could think of. Just as the dark figure thrust a massive pair of gloved hands toward his throat, Milton pulled his calculator from his shirt pocket and hurled it at the man's face. Given the man's proximity, even the relatively uncoordinated Milton couldn't miss.

The flying digital missile struck the attacker's left eye with sufficient force to slow him down. Milton dodged around him, accidentally stepped on his calculator, and bolted through the side door of the accounting offices and out into the parking lot. He jumped into his car, tore out of the lot, and didn't slow down until he reached the safety of his apartment. He left a panicked message with a police desk attendant who didn't seem to think the matter warranted immediate attention but agreed to pass it on.

The traumatic event produced two immediate consequences for Milton: one, a sleepless night filled with questions: Who was the man? Where did he come from? Who sent him? Why? And, worst of all, what's to stop him from trying again?; two, a strange sense of satisfaction that the credibility of what Agent Pallino had casually referred to as "Milton's story" had now been established.

* * * * * *

The evening's work those two kids had left with him a few hours earlier took even longer than Mike had planned. The contents of the fax from the Boston Police Department confirmed Mike's mounting suspicion that Metalcraft had been infiltrated. It provided no concrete evidence as to why. He stretched his imagination as far as he could to embrace some kind of rational tie-in with the imported explosives. In the end, all he had left were heightened suspicions.

Two beers, a large pepperoni pizza, and six hours later he decided to call it a night. He pulled into his garage, checked his email, and had barely drifted off into a sound sleep when the sharp intrusion of his phone jerked him awake. After a few seconds of groping for the phone he picked it up.

"Mike, are you there? It's me, Ellie."

"Yeah, what time is it there? Damn, it's two o'clock in the morning here. How are you? Where are you?"

"I'm sorry, Mike. I completely forgot about the time difference. It's only eleven here. Just checking to make sure everything is okay. What's going on with you?"

"I'm fine, except I like TV dinners and cheeseburgers better than all that nutritious stuff that tastes like cardboard in the fridge. Nothing much happened except for a couple of nerds who came into my office this afternoon. I guess it was yesterday now. They entertained me with a weird story about death and fraud at one of the local companies. I thought they were nuts until I just checked it out and found they may be on to something. Looks like some financial officer may have a lot of explaining to do. Other than that, it's pretty routine around here."

"What company is it?" Ellie asked.

"You know I can't discuss details like that. Are you winning any of those RFPs?"

"A few. It's a competitive business. Anyway, get off the TV dinners and cheeseburgers. Eat vegetables like broccoli and kale. Lots of nutrition, and they fight cancer. You've a great physique, Mike. It's your cholesterol that's going to hell. I'll let you go back to sleep. Call you later."

Given Mike's tendency to avoid green vegetables, the prospect of eating broccoli came across as less than pleasant. The thought of ingesting kale seemed revolting. He hadn't had a cheeseburger in a day and a half. He was hungry again and he was due. The dim prospect of having to make Milton Pringle a partner on this case turned out to be Mike Pallino's last conscious thought before he lapsed back into the sleep Ellie had interrupted.

Chapter 11

Paul Bremer's twenty-fifth-floor office bore all the management trappings necessary to make clients and other visitors feel as though they were in the presence of corporate success without extravagance. Upscale, but not ostentatious, the decor conveyed a subtle blend of importance and intimidation appropriate for the managing partner of an accounting and auditing firm.

He was, after all, the one whose mergers and acquisition expertise had brought PM&B into prominence throughout New England. To assure the firm's market position he surrounded himself with competent partners and staff carefully selected to expand the firm's client base. Paul's entire environment exuded an air of professional excellence.

"Mr. Bremer," Vivian's secretarial-sounding voice droned over the speaker phone, "Mr. Potter's waiting to see you. I told him you could set aside a few minutes if that's okay with you. He said he needs to talk about Milton Pringle."

Tax partner Trent Potter's tax returns were rarely questioned, either by the firm's clients or the dreaded IRS. The firm's audits, thoroughly cleansed by Aubrey Moore of any failures to comply with generally accepted accounting principles, were never challenged in court, by the Security and Exchange Commission, or anyone else. In short, none of PM&B's products had ever become the subject of professional criticism.

"Send him in, Vivian."

The question had already surfaced from several sources as to why, in such an environment of high standards, Paul had seen fit to turn Milton Pringle loose on a high-profile client like Metalcraft. Or why he had hired Milton at all. Now it was Trent who sat on the other side of the great mahogany desk in Paul's office to raise the issue again.

Trent closed his eyes for a moment and rubbed his forehead. "Paul, I'm concerned about your...ah...protégé, Pringle. Are you *really* sure he's the right one to run the Metalcraft audit? I mean, our accuracy when we do that company's tax return is completely dependent on the accuracy of Pringle's audit. And who's going to sign off on that? You?"

Paul leaned back in his chair and smiled. "Trent, he's doing fine. Yes, I'll review his work. As will Aubrey. Your tax product will be rock solid as usual. Stop worrying."

Trent shook his head. "Okay, Paul. Only I'm not the only one who's worried. The senior staff auditors are appalled at your choice of Milton to do that audit. A few of them see it as a message that perhaps competence doesn't count around here. Anyway, I just wanted to run the whole thing by you once more, and I won't bring it up again."

"Good. I'll address all those concerns at out next staff meeting. Anything else?"

Trent shifted in his chair and leaned forward. "Well, Doris and I are still concerned about you and Edna. I know your wife has cancer, and we wondered if you're both holding up all right."

Paul's expression grew somber and Trent flinched, as though he wished he could have withdrawn the question. "Trent, I'm afraid it's hopeless. She's slipping away day by day and there's absolutely nothing I can do about it. Or the doctors, either." Paul turned to wipe his eyes with the back of his hand, looked down, and shook his head. "She can't take any more radiation, and we've passed her chemo limits. Truth is, Trent, I'm going to lose Edna, and don't know what my life will be like without her."

Trent hesitated for a moment. "Paul, it's probably none of my business, but how are your finances holding out? I know you've drawn extensively from the partnership."

"Thanks, Trent. I've a project going that may put the finance issues to rest. We'll manage. Thanks anyway."

Trent nodded, forced the kind of smile that implied acquiescence without full agreement, and walked out.

Paul rolled his chair away from his desk a few feet, stared blankly at the ceiling, and contemplated. Milton would perform as expected. Things would be fine. There was nothing to worry about...except how to explain to Edna where the money came from. Maybe there'll be no need for explanations. With only a matter of weeks left for her, his precious Edna wouldn't be aware of the issue, or even care. Paul straightened up, then leaned forward, put his face in his hands and wept.

* * * * * *

Milton left an urgent message for Mike and headed for Metalcraft. No breakfast. New route. Change everything. Make it hard for the guy to track him. Take time off at lunch to find a new place to stay. From the moment he left his apartment until he entered Metalcraft's lobby, he never stopped looking over his shoulder. Last night's over with, he consoled himself, although Milton knew the memory of it would haunt his tomorrows for a long time.

Every corner he turned seemed to offer a new opportunity for his attacker to leap out and finish what he started. Each flickering shadow became a pair of professional hands with black gloves reaching for his throat. Milton found himself with no effective action plan in mind, and no safe harbor.

The call to Mike hadn't been necessary. Milton discovered Mike, Mac, and Phoebe already waiting for him in the lobby. Phoebe reached him first on a dead run. "Milt, are you all right? What happened?"

"Phoebe, we must have spooked someone. I was attacked and I'm sure the guy meant to kill me. Now I'm worried about your safety." He turned to Mike. "Mr. Pallino, what I told you is no longer just a suspicion on my part. This is—"

"You don't have to sell me on it, Milt. I checked with the local police. They're convinced the two deaths were premeditated murder, and they're preparing to help me on it as we speak. I sent the packing slip you gave me to forensics for analysis. From this point on, my involvement will be to work with you to resolve the 'who' and the 'why' of this whole thing. I'm going to need your help. First of all, please call me Mike. Now, can you describe your assailant? And how did you manage to escape?"

Milt drew a deep breath and slumped into a chair. "Mike, all I can say is that he was as tall as you, wore black, skin-tight gloves, and moved a lot faster than I could. He came out of the dark. At first he looked like a gigantic shadow. When he got closer, his face looked like he almost felt sorry for me, if you can believe it. He had dark hair and a thick beard. The only reason I'm alive now is I threw my pocket calculator at him. It caught him in the face, I think. By the way, I need it back. I think it's still in the room where I threw it."

Mike put his hand to his mouth as if to stifle a laugh. "Milt, I think you better start looking for a new calculator. Phoebe told me she stuck what's left of your old one in her desk drawer. She said she wants to keep it as a souvenir of her new hero." He turned to Mac with a wide grin. "What do you think, Mr. McCleod?"

Mac threw a hand up in the air. "Hell, I never cared much for any of this new-fangled technology. I'd have to say young Milton's found the best possible use for the danged stuff. Maybe we ought to throw all of that electronic mish-mash at somebody." His grass-roots summary drew a laugh from all of them.

"Okay," Mike said, "let's take a look at the room where all this happened last night."

Milton felt a reluctance to re-enter the scene of his terror. He could sense the flashbacks coming on the moment they stepped into the room. Other than a few overturned chairs and a smashed computer terminal lying on the floor, the place conjured up in his mind the same nightmarish scene he had escaped the night before.

Mac shook his head. "Son, I don't want you working alone again. You leave when we leave, got that?"

"Yes, sir."

"And call me Mac from now on. I have to take care of some business now, and Phoebe has work to do, so we'll leave this investigation with you and the FBI. Keep me informed at all times." Mac looked at Mike. "I never thought this would happen. Damn it, I'm developing increasing reservations about my CFO."

Mike sat on the edge of a desk and took notes while Milton paced the floor trying to review the sequence of the attack, one agonizing movement at a time. After Mike had extracted all Milton could give him he put his notes away.

"Okay, Milt, before we get into your audit findings so far, I need to ask one more question. Do you own a firearm?"

"No. Do you recommend I go buy one?"

"No, I'm going to do something completely against the rules. I'm going to give you one." Mike pulled a revolver from his coat pocket. "This is a Taurus thirty-eight caliber revolver. It's the safest, lightest, and easiest to handle for someone not accustomed to working with guns. I want you to come with me to the firing range tomorrow and I'll show you how to use it. I'll pick you up. I want you to keep the firearm handy in your apartment, only until we can sort out what happened last night and find this guy."

"Is it the kind you use?" Milt couldn't resist asking.

"No, the standard issue for us is a SIG Sauer, a Smith & Wesson, or a Glock. We have to qualify on the firing range every now and then with these and various other weapons. They'd be a little heavy for you, and you wouldn't like the kick. The one I gave you is lighter and more user-friendly."

He handed Milton the gun. "Hold it in your hand. I want you to feel the balance of it. Now, Milt, the law is a bit restrictive when it comes to shooting at someone, even in self defense. As bizarre as it may sound, it's against the law to shoot an intruder unless you're convinced your life is in danger and you have no other recourse. The 'stand-your-ground' law is still working its way through the legislature here. So, don't shoot if you can run and hide."

"Sure, Mike. I'll be careful. It feels light."

Mike's expression turned serious. "Okay. Now on a related subject, where do you stand in your audit? I mean, it doesn't take a rocket scientist to figure out someone doesn't want you to finish it. Simple logic says there's something in those accounting records valuable enough to kill for. Any idea what it might be?"

"No, except I'm finding some invoices with an odd-looking string of numbers on them. Phoebe's checking out a sampling of invoices today. What would you say if I suggested the numbers might be some sort of code?"

"I'd say you've been watching too much television. Anyway, I have to get back to my office to fill out the usual Department of Justice forms in order to get a case number for this, and request resource allocation to it. So, I'll leave you to the rest of your day. Let's meet back here tomorrow. In the meantime, I need you to apply all your auditing expertise to try to identify what there is about what you're doing that someone might want stopped. Now, I have to tell you this, Milt. Given these unusual circumstances, you don't have to continue with this audit if you don't want to."

Milton nodded. "I want to keep going until I finish it."

"Okay. Like Mac said, though, go home when the other people do. See that Phoebe does too. By the way, I took the precaution of renting you a new apartment. I'm sending a man to meet you here when you're ready to leave. He'll go with you, help you move, and he'll keep an eye on you. His name's

Sam Rausch. Do whatever he tells you to do. No ifs, ands, or buts. I'll see you later."

Not in the mood for coffee or much of anything else, Milton eased himself into a chair at the end of the conference room table and stared at the piles of audit documents. He wondered if any of them contained whatever information it was that prompted the attack on him. He'd been through every item and hadn't seen anything that could be considered a real threat to anyone.

Okay, he thought, let's review the sequence here. The financial numbers are what they should be except for the discount discrepancy and the failure of collections to keep pace with sales. Although those are problems Mr. Fadhil will have to explain, there was nothing in them that should incite an attack on Metalcraft's auditor. Still, there was the unaccounted-for stuff in Bakish's locker and the unusual numbers on the invoices. Mike said he'd check out the smelly packing slip. That left the invoices as the next priority item.

Milton reached for his cell phone to dial up his boss and fill him in on all that had happened. He stopped before he'd punched in all the numbers. No, better not, he thought. With all the trouble he was in already, one word about this and the firm would jerk him off the audit so fast he wouldn't know what hit him. He stuffed the phone back into his briefcase, pulled out the gun Mike gave him, and rolled it over in his hands. He'd never dreamed his first real opportunity with the firm would turn out like this.

* * * * * *

On the way back to his office Mike stopped at Matt's Tire Barn, partly to pick up a new spare tire, but mostly to chat with Matt Sullivan. The two of them had been friends long enough for Mike to sense there'd been something making Matt edgy the past couple of days.

"You okay, Matt? You've been acting like you have a burr under your saddle."

"Naw, it's nothing. I got that tire ready for you. Gimme your keys, I'll throw it in your trunk."

"Come on, Matt. We've been friends too long for that kind of bull. What's on your mind?"

Matt hesitated before he looked up. "Okay, something's been bugging me. I wasn't even going to say anything to you. Damn…this is so crazy I can't believe I'm even thinking about it. Aw, hell, never mind. It's stupid. Forget it."

"No, go on. I'm hooked now, so spit it out."

Matt hesitated again, looked away, and turned back to face Mike. "Well, you remember that blurb in the paper the other day about that tough broad who wore a tight black outfit and decked some drunk at the Commonwealth?"

"Yeah, I think I heard some of the guys talking about it. The woman took off with an unidentified guy, so the story went. What about it?"

Matt looked down at his feet. "Well, Bobby Driscoll and I were out bar-hopping that night. After a couple of stops we wandered into the Commonwealth lounge for one more before supper, and we saw the tail end of that thing. I never told anyone this. We'd had three or four by then, of course, so maybe things got a little blurry." He looked up. "Mike, I swear that woman looked…well…aw, this is dumb. Forget it."

"No, tell me. She looked what?"

Matt shifted from one foot to the other. "Okay, don't take this the wrong way, please. I've only seen your wife once, but this woman looked like Ellie. I mean, not just looked like her. This woman was a dead ringer for Ellie. Damn it! I didn't want to say this, Mike. I must have been out of it. I'm sorry. Forget I said anything, okay?"

Mike laughed out loud. It made about as much sense as Snow White attacking Attila the Hun. "Matt, you guys must have had a helluva lot more than three or four. Ellie wouldn't be caught dead in a bar. That is, unless they served roast duck and caviar. Ellie could probably kick a guy on the shins and run, but that's about it."

"I know, I know. I probably hallucinate when I've had a little too much. Look, please don't tell Ellie anything about this, okay?" He tossed the tire into Mike's open trunk and pocketed the cash.

"Okay, your hallucinations will remain our secret forever. I have to run. Pick you up for the Sox game at six tomorrow?"

"Yeah, sure."

"And Matt, no drinks until we get to the game. Got it?"

"Got it, Mike. See you."

Mike tightened down the tire in the trunk so it wouldn't slide around, and stared at it for a few moments while his mind recycled Matt's bizarre tale. Matt's black outfit reference revived Mike's last image of Ellie climbing into

71

her car wearing her most conservative black business attire. He shook his head and grinned. Ellie would laugh him out of town if he recited Matt's drunken illusions. He slammed the trunk closed, eased into the driver's seat of his BMW, and hit the accelerator.

Chapter 12

His itinerary from New York to Tehran took longer than Behram Naji had anticipated. He managed to make up some time on the drive from Tehran to Nantaz because he knew a short cut traversable only by Jeep. Accustomed to fighting in the mountainous terrain of Afghanistan, Naji made no secret of his preference for the rigors of a bouncing Jeep over the tedium of trans-Atlantic flying.

He pulled up to the barrier surrounding the fuel enrichment plant and waited for the guards to review his credentials. He'd been there before and the guards knew him. Even so, no one entered a maximum security facility without a thorough screening. After they motioned him through, he drove to the administrative lot and pulled up in front of the uranium conversion section of the facility.

He parked, sat in the Jeep, and looked around. The warmth of the noon sun brought back memories of travel through the mountain crevices of Afghanistan during freezing nights to avoid American surveillance craft during the day. Naji felt glad to be alive today and safe in Iran.

The scenery had changed since his last trip. A monolithic, heavily-guarded nuclear facility spread out over most of the space where a small suburban community used to be.

He dusted off his *shalvar* trousers tied at the waist, checked his *masih* designed shirt, and stepped out of the Jeep toward the warm embrace of a waiting Ahmed Yasin, his former commanding officer. Ahmed's long, thick beard, once as dark as a moonless midnight sky over the mountains where he fought, now showed signs of graying.

In their younger days, they had been together at the end of the Russian Campaign. Years later, they joined up again to counter the American offensive in Afghanistan. Ahmed had flirted with death all too often during both campaigns. It was only through the frequent intervention of Allah and the loyal Naji that the Mujahhidin managed to avoid the loss of such a capable leader.

"Behram, my good friend," Ahmed cried out, "I'm glad you're here!." He wrapped Naji in his arms. "How was your journey?"

"Long and tiring, sir. I see the facility has grown since my last trip. Congratulations on your promotion. I also see more gray hairs in your beard. Is that a by-product of your new role in our nuclear program, or is it the other way around?"

Ahmed smiled and they embraced again. Ahmed's heavy beard brushed hard against Naji's face. "Tell me, Behram, how are our two young protégés doing? Are they on schedule?"

"They are, although they share a mutual distrust. Ali, as usual, wants complete control and he's become convinced Nahid is there only because she curried favor with you. You know how he is. Not to worry. He'll soon recognize how essential her contribution will be. He's just arrogant, not stupid enough to reject her assistance."

Ahmed laughed. "I know. He's always been a bit difficult. Still, he's like the son I never had. I'm so very proud of him."

Naji's eyes narrowed and a grim expression gave his countenance a darkened look. "Yes, I know," he said through clenched teeth.

Ahmed continued as though he hadn't heard the comment. "What about this audit I heard is going to be conducted?"

Naji shook his head. "The on-going audit is becoming a threat, as I warned Ali it would. Worse yet, they had an unfortunate scuffle with some drunk at the hotel in Boston. No matter; they've managed to get through it all so far. I made the importance of our jihad unmistakably clear to Ali, as you ordered, Ahmed." Naji raised his hand in the air. "Still — and this is just between us — I have some reservations about the likely effectiveness of this whole project."

Ahmed grinned. "I'm sure you do, my friend. Come, let's get you settled in my quarters and we'll talk about it."

The luxury of Ahmed's lounge-and-bar suite at the top of the stairs presented a sharp contrast to the cold-gray steel of the conversion plant surrounding it. Always the wary soldier, Naji scanned the room quickly, looking for objects that shouldn't be there and places where recording devices might be hidden. Satisfied, he shook his head and eased into a chair he felt certain had been designed more for napping than for serious conversation.

74

Ahmed handed Naji a glass of his favorite pomegranate juice and took one for himself. "A toast first, and then you can share your reservations with me."

After they tossed down a few swallows of the *aab anaar*, Naji leaned forward, took a deep breath, and looked straight at his superior. "I don't wish to appear unsupportive, Ahmed. Please forgive me, I mean no disrespect. I agree the jihad will shake the foundations of America's comfort for awhile. I'm not convinced we'll accomplish anything of lasting value."

Ahmed leaned back in his chair, cupped his hands behind his head, and threw a mildly chastising glare at his subordinate. He released a heavy sigh. "Ah, some will view it that way. Although, from you I expected greater vision, Naji. Listen to me carefully, now. Iran's president has agreed to my proposal for a coalition agreement with Russia, China, North Korea, and certain key leaders in Syria and Pakistan. I've scheduled a summit meeting with representatives from these countries for early next week."

Ahmed sipped his juice slowly and pointed a finger at Naji. "If Ali can demonstrate our capability to strike a significant blow against the United States, these countries will be more willing to sign the agreement and throw the weight of their military and political influence with us. The Americans aren't naive. They already recognize these powers as their most threatening potential enemies."

Naji shifted in his chair. "Threatening, perhaps, but the Americans are confident. They fear no one."

Ahmed finished off the rest of his drink and leaned forward with a raised fist. "Ahh, yes they do, Naji. The United States is economically and militarily exhausted from twelve years of senseless war in the Middle East. The American people are now polarized politically. They've had enough of federal government. Some state leaders have even contemplated secession. Americans will see the withdrawal of the United States from its alliance with Israel as a small price to pay for avoiding a confrontation they can't win against a coalition of these countries."

Naji remained silent. He rose from his chair, walked over to the juice container and poured himself another cup. "You make a strong case, Ahmed," he said. "My question is, will these alliances help us establish the sovereignty of Islam? Or will we simply end up substituting one hated enemy for another?"

"Only Allah can answer that. Right now I want you to consider this. The most effective way to defeat a rich, complacent enemy is to terrorize him until he becomes a poor, frightened one. To this end we have accomplished much in the last few decades. Air travel, once an easy, convenient luxury, is now an expensive, highly inconvenient ordeal...as you recently witnessed. The paper tiger now restricts the freedom of its people in many ways while it waits fearfully for our next attack. And don't forget, the names of all Middle Eastern leaders were virtually unknown several decades ago. Now, many of them have become household words. Some say we have already won."

Ahmed sprang out of his chair with an agility that belied his age, and confronted Naji. "The face of the world is changing, Behram. You and I will live to see a whole new power structure. Ancient Greece came and went. The Roman Empire collapsed after a few centuries. Its glory receded into the Dark Ages. Europe later emerged as a great power that has since lost its position. Soon the United States and its Western allies will watch their dominance fade into the past as well. They will then look to Islam for leadership. We are living in a marvelous era!" He grinned, patted his anxious companion on the shoulder, and returned to his seat.

Naji sipped the pomegranate and leaned toward Ahmed. "Forgive me, I don't wish to appear negative. In fact, I feel better about all this after your explanation. My only concern is the complete dependence of it all on Ali Fadhil and Nahid. I realize the success of their jihad is the blow our coalition needs to see before its members sign. Still, there is no guarantee Ali will be successful. I've never trusted him the way you do."

Ahmed offered one of his comforting smiles. "Nothing is ever guaranteed. I assume you've made the appropriate arrangements with our Salvadoran allies in San Francisco?"

"Yes. I've made available to Ali enough money to recruit them."

"Good. Then you've doubled our chances for success. Tomorrow I'll take you on a tour of the facility. We received another consignment of nuclear fuel rods from Russia. As soon as we can integrate our propulsion capability into a long-range missile delivery vehicle, we will have reached our final nuclear objective."

Naji shifted in his chair again. "Yes, sir. Now, that raises another question. Won't our enemies react to all this?"

Ahmed put his hand to his chin and thought for a moment. "Ahh, yes. Well, the International Atomic Energy Agency continues to throw the

Nuclear Non-Proliferation Treaty in our face. We continue to ignore them. We will not yield to Western pressure. The lives of the Zionists will soon come to an end. It's only a matter of time. Come, you need some sleep. We'll finish our discussions after the tour tomorrow and then we'll send you back to New York. You'll need to be there to help Ali and Nahid get out of the country after this is done. First, I want to show you something. Follow me."

Ahmed pressed five numbered buttons on a wall-pad. The pad lit up and a heavy door opened. Ahmed switched on a dim light which revealed a nondescript little room distinguished only by the absence of everything except a wall map of the United States. Another button-touch and the map lit up.

Ahmed turned and grinned. "Now, Naji, tell me what you see."

Naji strained his eyes to adjust to the poor lighting. "I see a map of the Unites States peppered with little black dots. Since the dots are on the larger cities I presume they're nuclear bomb targets."

Ahmed beamed. "Wrong. Bombing will not be necessary once our coalition is in place and properly armed. The dots represent our power centers. Can you see the circles radiating outward from each city until they touch the circles of adjacent cities?"

"Barely. What do they mean?"

"They mean we will one day govern our hated enemy. Each dot represents the installation of a trained leader from one of our coalition nations. The American population in each set of circles will be governed by a set of dictates established by the coalition. The Americans' system of government — even their Constitution — will be replaced by ours." He paused as if he were waiting for a reaction.

Naji frowned. "You said bombing will not be necessary. Are you assuming the Americans will simply let us walk in and take over without a fight?"

"Not at all. Their military will want to prepare for all-out war. Their government will overrule such action once its leaders realize the futility of it."

Naji raised outstretched hands in a gesture of mock innocence. "Forgive me again, Ahmed. I'm not seeing the futility of it."

Ahmed wrapped his arm around his old subordinate once more and squeezed him. "Ahh, my friend. You've always been my right arm. My most trusted one. Strong, courageous, resourceful. Lack of vision has been your only weakness. Now, think about it. Picture the paper tiger flanked on one side by China, Russia, and North Korea, and on the other by all the Islamic nations led by Iran. For decades, each of these powers has nurtured the hope of ultimately squeezing or crushing the United States into submission. These anti-American forces, in the aggregate, have always outnumbered the Western powers in land, people, and resources. Together they could amass armies that would dwarf the American military and its allies. Yet, they've never sought to use that advantage to overpower their Western counterparts. Do you know why?"

Naji shook his head. "No, but I have a feeling you're about to tell me."

Like the Cheshire cat poised to devour the canary, Ahmed beamed again. "Technology, Naji. They lacked the technology. The Western powers, led by the United States, have managed to establish military dominance for one reason, and one reason only. They held the technological balance of nuclear power, even in the face of Russia's growing arsenal. Not so anymore. Russia and China already have it. North Korea and Iran will soon have it. One day all the Islamic powers will. Our long-range missile capability is progressing as we speak. The armaments landscape is changing, Naji. The paper tiger has historically refused to use its nuclear power aggressively. Our coalition harbors no such reservations, and the Western world knows it."

Ahmed pointed to the map again. "Now, revisit your mental image of the United States surrounded by enemies of equal nuclear capability…minus any reservations about using it. Therein lies the futility of war from the Americans' perspective. That is why the American government will elect to yield to a peaceful alliance with us under our terms."

Naji turned to stare at the map again, then turned back to face Ahmed. "I've always respected your strategic brilliance, Ahmed. I truly believe you're the only man in the world capable of reversing the international balance of power. My only concern is that your dreams may be ahead of reality."

Ahmed darkened the map, turned off the room lights, and ushered Naji out the door. "Why do you say that?"

"You're forgetting. This entire international scheme depends on Ali's successful attack. I respect your faith in him. I regret I don't share it."

Ahmed smiled. "I know. Your down-to-earth realism has always balanced my soaring dreams. Perhaps that's why we've worked so well together over the years. You may be right about him. Until we find out, let us savor the dream of a world-wide transfer of power made possible by my protégé's success. After all, Ali has been my left arm while you've been my right. Smile and be confident. With Nahid's help, the three of us together cannot fail. Come. You're tired. We'll talk tomorrow."

Naji tried to suppress the ugly thoughts that raced through his mind during the short walk to his sleeping quarters. He wanted to scream out his anger. So much of Islam's future depended entirely on the competence of a man he disliked so intensely and trusted so little. Instead, he smiled, embraced Ahmed once more, and settled in for the night.

Chapter 13

During his twenty years as a draftsman for the San Francisco Highway District, Phil Mosely had been promoted only once and endured three lateral moves in order to keep his job. Married to a woman who never let him forget he could have done better, Phil accepted his mediocrity and managed to make the best of it. Haunted only by the frustration of never having been able to bond with his now-grown son, Phil took life one day at a time. The paunchy, balding man's after-work activities consisted of bowling two nights a week in two separate leagues, and helping his wife, Constance, with her antiques business on weekends.

Phil almost always sat by himself during lunch on weekdays at the Highway District's cafeteria. This afternoon was no different, except for the presence of the most beautiful woman he'd ever seen sitting a few tables away. Entranced, he didn't even care if she caught him staring.

Nahid smiled in acknowledgment of his admiring glances. She paused and rose gracefully. Coffee in hand, she walked with the poise of a fashion model to Phil's table. She smiled again, this time even more seductively. "Hello, I'm Maureen Silar. I'm visiting from Brazil. May I join you?"

Still mesmerized by her sultry beauty, Phil struggled to think of something to say. "Why...uh...yes, please do," the startled man stammered. "I'm Phil Mosely, Miss Silar." He stood up to shake her hand. "I haven't seen you around before. Are you here on business?"

"Yes, and I couldn't help wondering why a good-looking man would be sitting all alone. Two questions ran through my mind when I saw you. Do you work here, and — pardon me, I'm not usually this forward — are you married?"

Her carefully-chosen attire featured a form-fitting beige outfit with a plunging neckline. The designer skirt was short enough to reveal her thigh in a way difficult for a man to forget when she crossed her legs. Phil couldn't remember having seen a woman so exquisite.

"What? Oh, well yes, but—"

"Never mind. I know what you're going to say. It's all right. So am I. Please don't misunderstand. I'm only in town for a couple of days, and…well, I'll come right out and say it. I was attracted to you and hoped we could…um…have dinner together tomorrow night. You know, just talk and sort of see where that leads us. I mean, right now you're the only one I've met in this city. It's a pretty lonely place."

Conservative pillar-of-the-church Phil Mosely could probably have barricaded himself against the advance of any other woman, even though he and Constance hadn't had sex in fifteen years. In fact, the thought of marital infidelity had never crossed his mind throughout his twenty-five-year marriage. Still, it had been a long time since anyone made him feel important, or in any way desirable.

By the time Phil shared his life story with her it was too late to return to his office. The two agreed to meet the next night at a secluded restaurant in Chinatown. They parted on yet another of Nahid's artfully crafted ego-lifting comments, which left Phil's heart pounding all the way home. The man who had become comfortable with his commonplace life now imagined himself the fairy tale frog who, kissed by the beautiful princess, had become a handsome prince.

* * * * * *

Phil knew it had been a long time since Constance had seen him pack a bag. His job hadn't required travel since his only promotion ten years before and yet, there he was, stuffing his overnight bag spread out on their bed. Her flabby arms folded above her protruding stomach, and her thick legs spread wide, Constance stationed herself in the doorway of their bedroom as if trying to decide whether she would permit him to leave the house or not.

"Phil, where on earth are you going? You haven't even finished breakfast. What are you doing?"

He continued packing without looking up. It was easier not to look at her. He remembered she'd long since decided that glamour was never an option, and personal fitness in the form of exercise and diet was a waste of time. Coarse, close-cropped hair clung tight to her head, accentuating the pumpkin-like qualities of her face. Mornings were the worst. He'd managed to desensitize himself to it all until he met Maureen. Now, the sight of his wife's unkempt appearance disgusted him beyond his ability to tolerate it.

"Dear, I have to go out of town for a couple of days," he said in an almost apologetic tone. "I'll be back day after tomorrow. I guess I should have mentioned it before. It's just a couple of days."

Constance let her arms drop into an akimbo position. "For God's sake, why? You never go anywhere."

Phil threw the last of his clothing into the suitcase and slammed it shut. "The District's putting on an educational seminar. Attendance is required. I'll be back in time to help with your antique show. Don't worry about it."

Constance threw her hands in the air. "Good grief, why do they bother to educate you if they're never going to promote you? And you know they aren't. Why don't you just stand up like a man and tell them they can stuff their seminars unless they're ready to give you a raise or something?"

"I happen to like my job, Constance. And whether you understand it or not, that's more important than money."

She rolled her eyes. "Yeah, I guess so. I figured that out when you turned down a chance to work for my father. All you had to do was say yes. Now, you're stuck in that weasel job going nowhere. Oh, never mind. It's pointless to even discuss it. Just call me when you get there." She whirled around and stomped out of the room.

Phil blew her a kiss and left without saying goodbye.

He put in his time at the office and tried to get his mind off the enchanting Maureen. She was everything Constance wasn't. How could two such different creatures have been made by the same God? The hours dragged by so slowly he began to think some supernatural force held them back deliberately to give him a chance to reconsider what he was about to do.

What if Constance found out? What if the folks at church found out? He could picture the news headlines: *Local Church Deacon Caught in Sex Scandal.* His bowling buddies might be the only ones who understood, and even they might not. Would the District fire him? Probably. So what? Constance was right. It *is* a weasel job. He deserved a better life. He deserved someone who could give him what he'd gone without all those years.

Five o'clock finally rolled around. Phil breathed a sigh of relief and cleared the top of his desk. He slipped out the door and headed for

Chinatown, toward an exhilarating new dimension in what had become a life of dull disappointments.

* * * * * *

In the darkened restaurant, the miniature lamp at their table provided the perfect lighting for a romantic setting. Nahid managed to turn her consumption of rice and Chow Mein into an enticing ritual of come-hither glances and seductive mouth curvatures with each bite. Phil responded to the growing ache in his loins by tossing down one drink after another.

"Tell me about what a draftsman does, Phil." She smiled and leaned toward him as though she couldn't consume another bite until she heard his answer. "It sounds so exciting to be building things in a large city."

"Oh, my job sounds more important than it is, Maureen." He ran a finger through what was left of his hair to fluff it out a bit. "Truthfully, my only really large task is my work on the Golden Gate Bridge. I'd like to take you up there, someday. I can show you some features few people know about."

Nahid reached out and caressed his hand. "Phil, I'd love to know more about the bridge. I've always been in awe of it. Now I'm simply in awe of you and what you do. I've never met a man like you before. I think you've underestimated your own importance" She kicked off one of her shoes and slid her bare foot up under Phil's pants leg. He smiled, savored the sensation, and made no effort to move his leg.

They prolonged the dinner over an engaging span of two hours, during which Nahid had no trouble weaving a tapestry of romantic allusions. Phil promised her he would do whatever was necessary to maintain a lasting relationship. His dream had become real, a just reward for his seemingly endless years of empty fantasy.

The after-dinner drinks and pleasantries consumed another two hours. Nahid insisted on paying the bill, and helped her inebriated devotee check into a secluded little hotel on the edge of Chinatown. The alcohol, Phil discovered, dulled only his senses, not his ardor. He craved his first sampling of Nahid's body.

Nahid knew her fish was hooked. Now he had to be reeled in that night to assure the next evening's transfer of the blueprint. With that in mind, she made certain their first night together proved to be a sexual experience unlike any Phil Mosely could ever have imagined. Confident that no further arousal was needed, Nahid slipped out of her clothes, dropped them on the floor, and settled her naked body into the most provocative position she could. All without losing eye contact with her gaping prospect. In one swift movement she drew him down on the bed beside her and made the rest look easy. Easy except for the difficulties responding to the clumsy sequence of grabbing, jerking, and bobbing movements typical of an amateur who hadn't had sex in years. She used all of her experience to make sure his satisfaction didn't come too quickly. The adventure came to an end when the little man screamed that he could bear the excruciating excitement no longer. After an hour of the kind of ecstasy that he gasped he'd even dreamed of, an exhausted Phil Mosely fell asleep in her arms.

By the next morning Nahid knew she had her mark so completely dazzled he would never suspect the possibility of a con. Without wasting any time she slid provocatively off the bed, stood, and turned her naked body to face him. She raised her arms above her head to fluff out her long, black hair in a movement carefully designed to reveal the fullness of her ample breasts and the soft curvature of her hips. She had Phil's full, wide-eyed attention. Satisfied he was primed to be taken, Nahid nestled next to him on the bed.

"Phil, I have a confession to make, and I hope you won't be angry with me," she purred. "I was reluctant to tell you because I wasn't sure you'd understand, and I didn't want to lose you. I know I should have been more up front with you about this. I work for an architectural firm in Sao Paulo. My firm has been trying, for some time, to build a structure like the enormous span you keep so expertly maintained here. It would—"

"Maureen, I don't do the maintenance. I'm just the draftsman on the project."

"Yes, I know. But you're very influential, darling. Such a bridge would bring economic development to a city where millions of people live below poverty level. Your office once offered to give us a copy of the blueprint of your marvelous Golden Gate Bridge, and that would have made construction of our bridge possible. Regrettably, pride wouldn't permit my superiors to accept that kind of charity."

Phil frowned. "I'm surprised the District made such an offer, Maureen. Those architectural renderings have always been jealously guarded. The ones we refer to as 'house drawings' are those that have never been shared with any of our subcontractors."

"I know. The offer surprised my firm, too. I think if your district hadn't seen the   tremendous value of such an international goodwill gesture, the offer never would have been made."

Nahid placed her hand on his knee and moved it slowly upward toward his vital parts. "Now, shamefully, the owners of my firm admit their mistake and have asked me to ask again in private. You know, one-on-one with someone in authority, like you, who has the compassion to be discreet so they don't lose face."

Phil frowned and moved into a chair.

Nahid slid onto his lap and stroked his knee before Phil could find expression for what she knew would be the beginnings of some serious misgivings. "If you could help me on this — just a copy, not the original — I would express my gratitude in any way you wish. And," she murmured while she caressed his neck, "I think we both know what pleases you most." She could tell by the flush in his cheeks and his heavy breathing that Phil Mosely had become too enamored to think abstractly enough to assess the possible consequences of what he was being asked to do.

Phil paused for only a moment. "I…guess there'd be no harm in a copy, if you say the District has already offered it. Your firm isn't going to use it anywhere here in the United States; so…sure, I guess I can get it for you, Maureen."

Nahid hugged him, described what she needed, and they agreed to exchange favors in a room she reserved under Phil's name at the Hyatt for their second evening together. She had chosen the Hyatt because it was large enough to reduce the likelihood that either of them would be noticed or remembered. The more people moving through the lobby, the less likely anyone would recognize Phil when he checked in. Nahid hadn't forgotten Ali's caution to use the back stairs for her own access to the room. Since there was no need for her to check in, there would be no indication she was ever there.

Chapter 14

Phoebe Denton breathed a sigh of relief, glad to see the end of a long, frustrating day. Twelve of the invoices Milton had given her to match up with receiving reports didn't seem to have any receiving reports. Worse, the invoices didn't match any of the incoming items on Dorothy Denzig's log. Just when she thought the situation couldn't get more confusing, she discovered the checks written to pay those invoices were all voided two days later with no explanation. One or two such reversals a year would be considered a normal correction of a simple mistake. Twelve, on the other hand, would require investigation — she knew that much.

Confronted with something she knew was beyond the realm of accident, Phoebe decided she'd deal with it the next day. With Ali still out of town and Milt on his day off, it would be embarrassing to take up Mr. Mac's time even if he were interested in accounting details — which Phoebe knew he wasn't. Time to go home and forget about things that weren't supposed to be the way they were. To add insult to injury, she forgot where she'd parked her car in the Metalcraft lot, which was not an easy place to scan for it. Many of the day workers hadn't left yet, and any empty spaces were being filled by employees coming in for a special evening shift Mac had called to handle an emergency order.

Engrossed in a search that took her wandering through rows of cars, Phoebe didn't see the dark green van coming until it screeched to a halt beside her. Two dark figures piled out of it and one of them grabbed her. Before she could catch her breath, he covered her mouth and lifted her off her feet. Her glasses flew into the air and she could feel herself being carried to the vehicle. The other man held the van's rear door open, like a dragon's mouth waiting to swallow her.

Recollections of childhood nightmares about being abducted flashed through her mind. Phoebe kicked, squirmed, and even tried to bite, but couldn't open her mouth. She felt the onrush of a claustrophobic sensation, heightened by the terrifying thought of dying with her mouth closed. She didn't want to die without screaming out something. She wanted to shout for her mother now more than ever.

Phoebe's would-be abductors didn't see the titanic figure approaching at a full- speed run from behind them, a shadowy silhouette against the pale early-evening sky. By any measure, Stitch amounted to a colossus who, in more memorable times, could run the hundred in slightly over ten seconds — almost a record for a man his size. His prowess on the football team of a nondescript college produced the entity's first and only undefeated season before his knees gave out and academic probation caught up with him. Unable to find work, he came to Mac McLeod, who took him in, made him a custodian and, fortunately for Phoebe, parking lot supervisor. Only Mac and the payroll clerk knew Stitch's last name. Others weren't even sure he had one.

In a single, swift motion, the six-foot-five, two-hundred-seventy pound Stitch wrapped a massive, powerful hand around each man's neck. He smashed their heads together, and caught the free- falling girl before she hit the ground. He drew the sobbing Phoebe gently into his arms and held her until she quieted down a bit. He retrieved her glasses, stepped over her unconscious predators, and helped find her car. The gentle giant patted her head, told her how brave she'd been, and waited for the still-shaking girl to regain her composure.

After the police finished their report and hauled the two thugs away, Stitch followed Phoebe home to make sure she made it safely.

* * * * * *

Phoebe's emotional outpouring in Mike Pallino's office echoed from one end of the hall to the other. "Why, Mike? Why? What could they possibly want with me?" Still agitated, Phoebe stood in front of Mike's desk and emoted loud enough to be heard by all the occupants of the first floor. Mike Pallino closed his office door to limit the disturbance. He took Phoebe's hand, led her to a chair, and told her to sit down. After he handed her a Coca Cola, he popped open one for himself, and passed one to Milton.

"I can't answer that with any degree of certainty, Phoebe. The police haven't been able to pull enough information out of them yet. My guess is they wanted to find out how much you and Milt knew about whatever it is they're trying to hide. I'd like to know myself. Milt, what's your take on this? You're the one who's into their record-keeping system."

Milton shook his head. "Mike, I'm not sure. I know it has something to do with cash, because Phoebe told me she found a bunch of unexplained voided checks yesterday."

Mike cocked his head and frowned. "Is that relevant to anything?"

Milt put his finger to his chin and thought about it for a moment. "I don't know for sure. I can tell you no company ever screws up that many checks unless its accounting system is badly fouled up. And this one isn't. At least not *that* bad. I'm going to—"

"Yes, and another thing," Phoebe interjected, "I found one check written for two hundred thousand to a consultant named Mr. Barnes. That one was *not* voided. It was sent to a post office box. We don't have anyone by that name on our list of approved vendors."

Mike raised his eyebrows. "Did you say *two hundred grand?*"

"Yeah, I'm going to have to look deeper into this," Milton said. "Right now, I'm concerned about Phoebe's safety. What's to stop whoever's responsible for this from coming after her again?"

Mike reached into his pocket and pulled out his keychain. He unhooked one of his house keys and gave it to Milton. "Well, Mac and this guy Stitch have agreed to keep a close watch on both of you during the day while you're at work. Still, I'm concerned about you being alone in that apartment, Milt. If these people, whoever they are, want you bad enough they'll find you. So, until we can sort this thing out, I want both of you to stay at my house at night. Even though it's against the rules, I'm saying to hell with the rules. Are you okay with that?"

Phoebe's attempt to conjure up a flirtatious smile at Milton looked clumsy but sincere, the first sign of a return to normalcy after her traumatic ordeal. "Well, I've kind of fantasized about that lately," she said, "but I bet Milt hasn't."

"You're blushing, Milt," Mike said. "Can we take that as a yes?"

Milton looked down at the floor while he shifted in his chair "Sure. That's okay with me."

Mike nodded. "Good. Milt, you can sleep in the guest room with me in separate beds. Phoebe can use my bed." He grinned. "If I'm going to break the rules I at least want things on the up and up. Okay, you two need to get back to work, or Mac will blame me for holding up the audit. Milt, I'll check on that $200,000 payment. I want you and Phoebe both to dig into that company's records as hard as you can and find out what the hell there is in there that prompted two attacks."

"We will, Mike. I'm reasonably sure it has something to do with those unusual numbers that appeared on the invoices and on some of the disbursements documents. I'm going to try another approach."

Mike looked skeptical. "Ahhh, yeah, okay. Just don't start wandering off into ya ya land with that. We're running out of time here. So try not to waste any of it."

Milton touched his forehead in a mock salute. "Got it, Mike. See you later."

Chapter 15

Their credentials alone were sufficient to guarantee reservations for any space they wanted at the best hotels in Beijing. For five of the most powerful political figures on the planet, such accommodations would have been appropriate. Instead, they opted for secrecy. In order to stay under the media's radar Ahmed had selected an obscure compound sequestered deep in the heart of Beijing's Shijingshan District, behind the tomb of Tian Li, the Shenzong Emperor's favorite eunuch in the late tenth century.

The group arrived on schedule and settled into their seats around an immense circular table. A small, delicate, continuously bowing lady set out the tea servings.

Ahmed stepped up to the podium and called the meeting to order with the help of his two translators. "Welcome, gentlemen, and thank you for joining me in this modest setting. I hope this room will one day become known as the crucible in which history's most dramatic transfer of power originated. Allow me to make the necessary introductions before we begin our journey. Beside me is Hassan Sharam, representing my country's distinguished president. Next, moving clockwise is our host, Ka Chuan Li, representing Hu Jintao, president of the People's Republic of China. He has promised us the best of Szechuan-style cuisines along with his own favorite blend of mint and jasmine bead tea, which is being served to you as we speak."

Li nodded and Ahmed continued the left-to-right sweep of his arm. "We are fortunate to have with us Russia's Sergei Petrov, special deputy to Vladimir Putin, and also North Korea's Kim Hwa, representing Kim Jong Un, president of the People's Republic of Korea. Unfortunately our Syrian and Pakistani representatives could not attend, but they have assured me their hearts are with us."

Ahmed paused to sip his tea while he scanned his audience. "We have all agreed, at least in principle, on the purpose of this meeting. Still, I must reiterate to assure we're all still in accord. We've long known that world dominance of economic and political power cannot continue to remain the private domain of the Western nations. Our countries must accept the challenge of wresting it from them. However, we know this cannot be accomplished all at once. It must begin with their long-term ally, Israel." Heads nodded in unison.

"My country will begin the process with a nuclear strike of sufficient magnitude to effectively eliminate any further Israeli activity in the Middle East. This, of course, brings me to the purpose of our meeting. We need to agree on how we intend to coordinate with each other on two subsequent courses of action. First, the forcing of United States neutrality when my country attacks their puppet ally. Second, how we will then proceed to the next step in our long overdue transfer of power from the Western infidels. So, I shall open the floor for further discussion of this matter, which I now place in your capable hands." Ahmed breathed a sigh of relief, took another sip of tea, and sat down.

Sergei Petrov's cold and expressionless eyes scanned the faces of the others, one by one, as though probing for signs of weakness. The dark shadow that remained of his beard combined with his sharply chiseled facial features to create an aura of permanent fierceness. Apparently satisfied with the results of his examination, he turned to Ahmed, and spoke in a tone devoid of emotion.

"I'm sure you understand that, before we commit to any action at all, Iran must prove the weakness of the United States by successfully attacking it without the use of suicidal methods. I, for one, will insist on your agreement to this stipulation."

"Before you answer," Ka Chuan Li interjected with his hand raised as if to prevent a premature response, "I wish to make it clear we are adamant in our opinion that suicide attacks, such as the one on New York's Twin Towers, are clumsy, and prove nothing as to either the strength of the attacker or the weakness of the attacked. Your strike must demonstrate the ability to cripple the United States from within, using methods which can be repeated again and again without importing forces from other countries." Heads nodded once more.

"Of course, gentlemen," Ahmed replied. He paused to offer a comforting smile. "Within the week you will all learn how efficiently my jihad can be carried out with no elements of suicide involved. We intend to make effective use of our adversary's many enemies within. We have no doubts about our ability to produce the results upon which your support is conditional."

"May we inquire," Kim Hwa asked, "as to exactly what kind of attack your people are planning, and where it will take place?"

Ahmed shook his head. "No sir. We cannot risk leaking information which might undermine the entire venture. I regret being unable to share this with you. However, I'm sure all of you understand the need for discretion in this matter, given that your subsequent cooperation is contingent upon its success."

Li stood, removed his jacket, and hung it over the back of his chair before he turned to address Ahmed. "On the assumption that your jihad will be successful, I wish to move our discussion to the next phase. Our ability to force the United States to disengage while you maul its cub does not come with a guarantee, Ahmed. It can be accomplished only if the United States can be made to perceive its neutrality as a proactive policy essential to avoid nuclear war on a much larger scale."

"Yes, and how do you propose to bring about this perception?" Sergei added.

Kim Hwa launched his short, stocky body from his seat without waiting for Ahmed's reply, pounded the table, and raised a clenched fist high above his head. "We do it by having the courage to issue the paper tiger a long-overdue ultimatum," he shouted. "The Democratic People's Republic has endorsed Pyongyang's proclamation that our supreme national task is to drive the U.S. out of South Korea and unify the peninsula under North Korean domination." He turned toward Petrov and Li. "The question now is, what kind of pressure can Russia and China contribute?"

The room went silent. Ahmed looked first at Sergei, then at Li, but said nothing. A moment later Li spoke with deliberation. "My country finds itself somewhat constrained in that we are economic trading partners with all of the Western countries. Furthermore, we are not yet economically or militarily prepared to attack the U.S. Such action must be deferred to a later date. My government, however, has committed to become East Asia's dominant power. This begins with a requirement that we end Taiwan's determination to operate as a separate and sovereign entity." He turned to Kim Hwa. "Such a commitment would then constitute our first contribution to your ultimatum."

Sergei nodded. "Good. Yet I believe your country has still another weapon in its arsenal of threats, Mr. Li. My understanding is that you hold paper in excess of a trillion in loans to the U.S. Am I not correct?"

Li nodded. "Yes. I see where you're going. For your information, our long range plan has been to call in the loans, forcing the U.S. to reduce its military spending in order to pay them. This would tend to weaken their defense capability. We could, however, make it part of our short range objectives in support of this coalition. So, what then, Mr. Petrov, would be your country's contribution?"

The Russian delegate reached down and pulled a dossier from his briefcase. He laid it on the table, and spoke without appearing to refer to it again. "Nuclear parity with the United States, leading ultimately to complete military supremacy, has always been our objective. Eventually, we expect Russia to become one of the top five world economies. For purposes of this ultimatum, I will urge my president to pursue, without delay, our objective of greater and more aggressive access to energy reserves in the Arctic and in the Middle East."

Silence prevailed again until Ahmed rose to deliver his summary. "Very well, gentlemen, I believe we have enough collective weight to force American neutrality. I will prepare a final coalition document to be distributed for your signatures. Contingent, of course, upon my country's successful demonstration that Iran can engineer an attack on the United States from within. Let us break for lunch, after which we will spend the rest of the afternoon addressing the next, and very vital, step toward our ultimate seizure of power from the West."

* * * * * *

The after-lunch discussion, no less emotional than the morning's exchange, covered a multitude of long range nation-specific aspirations never before voiced as a unified multi-national endeavor.

Ahmed turned his back to the podium and spoke from the floor. "Gentlemen, we must now agree more precisely on each country's particular contribution to the process of ending Western domination. We can—"

"It would be premature to formulate specifics at this time, Ahmed," Kim Hwa interrupted. "I suggest we wait until we know the outcome of your jihad in the United States, and that country's reaction."

Ahmed put up his hand. "Very well. I wish only to establish an outline for each of our planned efforts to contain Western power. I, for one, plan for my country's continued pursuit of its uranium enhancement policy…despite any temporary compromises our leaders might make in the interim. We will do it in the face of what I'm sure will be stronger import and export sanctions from our enemies. I would like to hear a brief summary of China's participation. What say you, Mr. Li?"

Ka Chuan Li stood and read from a document he pulled from his jacket pocket. "My country suffers from industrial pollution which is choking 400 of our 600 cities. All of them are experiencing severe water shortages as well. Our long range plan is to occupy the United States in order to access its abundant natural resources. The occupation, in addition to its governance advantages, will provide considerable relief from our environmental difficulties. As to your short-run coalition objectives, Ahmed, we will accelerate the call-in of our loans. This will deliver a crippling blow to the United States' economy."

Ahmed smiled, and turned to the North Korean representative. "And you, Kim Hwa?"

Kim glared at Ahmed, raised his dossier with one hand, and shook his fist with the other. "I have here an articulate proposal to combine my country's missile development process with Iran's. You tell your president this, Ahmed. His short-sighted refusal to share his missile technology with ours will only make it more difficult for this coalition to operate effectively." Kim pointed to his dossier. "These documents describe precisely how our two countries can attack the United States from East and West at the same time." He pounded his fist on the table again and leaned back in his chair.

Petrov waved his file of papers in the air and spoke from his seat. "I have been authorized to explore more formal alliances between Russia and each of the coalition nations. I agree with Kim Hwa, however. Until your attack on the United States has proved successful, Ahmed, such discussions would be premature."

A hush filled the room while Ahmed beckoned the serving woman to distribute pastries and to refill all the tea cups. He backed away and waited until she left and closed the door behind her before he stepped to the podium again. "Well, gentlemen, we seem to be in at least general accord, despite some individual reservations. I would like us to gather closer around the table to help me formulate a written outline of our action plan — such as we've covered in our limited discussions — for presentation to my president."

Within two hours Ahmed's assistant had entered all their scribbled notes into his laptop. The summit meeting concluded late that evening with Petrov's second reminder that everything depended entirely on the success of Iran's jihad in the U.S.

After the participants left, Ahmed and Sharam remained behind to relax and finish the last of the tea. The pensive look on Sharam's face caught Ahmed's attention. Ahmed nibbled on the biscuit the serving lady had placed beside him. "You're troubled, Hassan," he said. "May I ask why?"

"Not troubled, simply curious. After you and I return to Iran, our government will ask our opinion of all this. I share your confidence as to the success of your demonstrative attack on the United States. However, our president will go further and ask about the likely outcome of it. How shall I respond?"

"You may tell him this, Hassan. The world will see that the paper tiger's fear of our alliance has forced her to cower in her den while we cage and declaw her Israeli suckling. Then there will be no doubt the beast is no longer to be feared."

Hassan frowned. "Perhaps. Still, I feel we haven't given enough consideration to the possibility the tiger might become enraged and, despite the odds, emerge from its lair to protect the cub."

Ahmed paused, leaned back in his chair, and sipped his tea. He took another bite of his biscuit and shook his head. "Very unlikely, and I'll tell you why. The success of our jihad will be so swift, so easily accomplished that the American people will know we can strike again, frequently and at will. The beast is tired, troubled financially, and will know it's cornered by our alliance. Its people will not let it enter a war it cannot win. They've already lost too many young lives in the Middle East, with no popular gains to show for it. The tiger's failure to establish a self-supporting Iraqi government becomes more evident with each succeeding Al Qaeda attack. This assumes, of course, that the involvement of ISIS doesn't unite the world against us. At any rate, the beast is finished, Hassan, and my protégé's successful jihad will prove it."

Hassan nodded without saying anything more. He packed up their files and cleaned the room. Ahmed finished his tea and contemplated while he watched his assistant tidy up and make preparations for their return trip to Iran. The meeting had produced less than he had hoped for, but more than expected. The coalition would be formed, of that Ahmed felt certain. Notwithstanding their doubts and reservations, the meeting's attendees proved their commitment to the two phases of its objectives.

The major problem, Ahmed knew, would be the third phase of the power shift — the phase of which he had carefully avoided any mention during the meeting. The very thought of it continued to produce anxiety for him, as it had from the beginning. In terms of population, land size, and weaponry, Iran would always find itself dwarfed by both Russia and China. The power of these two nations, a distinct advantage in the formation of a coalition, would ultimately become a barrier to his attempts to position Iran as its leader in subsequent international operations.

"I believe we're ready to leave," Hassan said. "Our driver is outside waiting."

Ahmed patted him on the shoulder and smiled. "Then let's be on our way." There would be plenty of time to sort out the obstacles in the third phase.

Chapter 16

He'd registered under a fictitious name. Because all of Phil's personal items had been removed, the San Francisco police needed the better part of a day to identify the naked corpse. The medical examiner's report listed strangulation as the cause of death. The absence of any finger marks on his neck suggested his killer had throttled him from behind using a professional chokehold against which the less-than-robust Phil Mosely had no defense.

The tedium of Phil's life and his fantasy of a better one ended together in Room 417, where one of the Hyatt's cleaning ladies found him. In response to police questioning about the circumstances surrounding his murder, a bitter but resolute Constance issued her tearless proclamation that it was the insignificance of her husband's life which killed him.

Nahid left no fingerprints or any other trace of evidence she'd ever been in the hotel By the time Phil Mosely's body had been identified she'd progressed well into her briefing session with Ali and his two explosive experts in Ali's room at the Westin. On their knees, they gathered around the blueprint spread out on the floor. They listened as she went over each step of the procedure.

"Place your charges here, here, and here." She pointed first to one side of the structure, and then the other. "The timers should be set for thirty minutes to allow you time to get out of there. Tomorrow you'll also instruct and supervise some people needed for additional firepower. It's essential you make sure all of them do it right. Ali's already rehearsed the sequence of events with you. Are there any questions?"

Ali stood, hands on his hips, and stared down at the X's that marked the placements of the charges. "Why do we need such an extreme explosive instead of dynamite or something more standard and more available?" he asked. "The receipt, storage, and transfer of this stuff created a significant risk of discovery."

Nahid rolled up the map. "The structure has been reinforced to resist earthquakes and high winds, Ali. We need to make sure the steel will separate at critical stress points."

"Why are the charges placed *under* the span?" Ali persisted. "The guys are going to have to hang over the edge to attach them. The process is going to take some time. It'll slow us down. That increases the risk of getting caught."

"That's where the vulnerability to stress is optimal," Nahid replied. "Placing the charges at those points increases the likelihood the explosions will break off larger sections of the span. This is all on the assumption Hakim and Saif supervise the Salvadorans properly. It will be dark when we do this, so everyone will have to move carefully."

Saif ventured his first question. "What if we're seen by someone?"

Nahid stood and breathed an impatient sigh. "Ali has been observing activity for the last few days. He's scheduled this for when the vehicle traffic is minimal, with no pedestrian traffic. There's a National Guard patrol assigned, so we'll approach during the fifteen-minute break in their surveillance when their shift changes. Your chances of being seen are as small as we can make them. Anyway, we can't begin until the wind dies down, which isn't predicted for another few days."

"Where will you be?" Hakim asked.

"Ali will start at one end and I at the other. If we all work together efficiently, there will be plenty of time to set the charges and escape free and clear. The Salvadorans will hide us until arrangements can be made for our return to Iran."

Ali and Nahid waited until Saif and Hakim had returned to their rooms before they slumped into a couple of comfortable chairs. In deliberate defiance of Muslim custom, they opened a bottle of Napa Valley wine. For a few minutes they simply leaned back and stared at the rolled-up blueprint without saying anything. Ali savored a few sips of the wine before he broke the silence.

"Look, I know you don't like to talk about it, but I need to know how it went with the man you seduced to get the prints."

Nahid sprang up from her chair, walked over to the phone, and started to pick up the receiver.

"Whoa," Ali barked, "what are you doing?"

"I'm calling room service to send up some food."

"Please don't do that. I want you to stay as invisible as possible. There's food in the fridge. Right now I need to know about your evening with your victim. We can't afford to leave any traces."

"I never leave evidence." Nahid opened the fridge, pulled out a roast beef sandwich, and returned to her chair. "It went well except for the memories it brought back." She heaved another sigh, glanced out the window, and began a voracious assault on the sandwich.

"Memories? Like what?"

She paused to swallow. "Ahmed may not have told you. He rescued me from…ahh…let's say, a bad situation. I was raped when I was thirteen by three fat pigs, drunk and big as horses. I can still smell their alcohol and cigarette stink. I hated men after that. It didn't take me long to discover my physical assets could earn me more money than I could get anywhere else." She poured herself another glass of Napa Valley's finest and polished off the rest of the roast beef, wiping her lips carefully with a napkin.

"In martial arts I eventually found an outlet for my anger and a control for it at the same time. Manipulating men and stealing from them were a few more of the talents I'd accumulated before Ahmed found me. He provided a home for me — more like a sanctuary, really — and set about channeling my skills."

Ali poured another glass from the bottle. "Channeling them where?" he asked. "And what did Ahmed get out of all this?"

"After I completed his training I told him I would commit myself to Al Qaeda on condition that I be given a position of authority. He finally agreed, although it was difficult for him because of the lowly status of women in much of our Muslim world."

Ali chucked the uneaten portion of his sandwich into a waste basket. "So, when does this promotion come?"

"As soon as we complete this jihad. I have Ahmed's word on that."

Silence filled the room again before Ali continued the dialogue. "You did well, today, Nahid. The blueprint was critical, as was your knowledge of structural engineering. We all have some bad memories."

Nahid kicked off her shoes, curled one leg under her in the chair, and stretched out the other, allowing her skirt to slide up enough to expose her leg's curvature from the thigh down. She smiled. "And what are yours, Ali?"

"My what?"

"Your unpleasant memories. You just admitted we all have them." Her question was purely rhetorical, more for conversation than anything else. She'd long since hardened herself to other people's feelings. Their expressions of joy or sorrow rolled off her like rainwater from a roof. She leaned back and sipped her wine slowly as though she didn't care whether Ali answered the question or not.

Ali stood, stretched, and hesitated, as though trying to decide whether or not he wanted to answer the question. He walked to the window, stared out at nothing in particular, and returned to the couch. "I guess mine would be begging."

"Begging? Where?"

Ali was slow to reply, and she could sense he didn't want to talk about it. "On the streets of Cairo. My father was a cripple. We were destitute. He supported my mother and me by begging on a street corner where a constant stream of tourists passed. They were mostly wealthy tourists from Western world countries. I was only seven. My father demanded my presence beside him, mainly to enhance the appeal to Americans who were suckers for kids. I learned the value of money listening to the clanking of coins in a tin cup."

Nahid cocked her head to one side and smiled. "And after that what?"

Ali stretched out his arms again and yawned. "Right then and there, on the streets of Cairo, I swore to myself I would never be poor again. Not long after my parents died, Ahmed found me. I was fifteen. By then I was buying and selling dry goods and other merchandise for an old man who ran a profitable business. He taught me how to make money and, even more, how to manage it."

"So then Ahmed took you in and paid for your education in the United States?"

"Yes. You're not the only one whose skills were useful to Ahmed." Ali opened another bottle of wine and poured two glasses.

"What brought you into Al Qaeda, Ali?"

Ali paused to take a sip. "At first it was Ahmed's teachings. He became my mentor. Until he sent me to the United States, I accepted everything he told me as gospel — Allah, the prophet Muhammad, what they stood for. It was all about driving the infidels out of the Muslims' holy lands. Particularly the Americans and their military bases. When I actually witnessed the American way of life firsthand, however, I was appalled. What I saw was an unstable culture, surging forward out of control and running roughshod over the rest of the world. Even its own people. I saw investors making fortunes in real estate and the stock market without actually producing anything, while people like my father lived barely above starvation. At that point I decided to embrace the way of militant Islam."

Nahid nodded. She and Ali continued to share experiences until the second bottle ran out.

Ali stood, stretched his arms over his head, and yawned again. "It's been a long day, Nahid. In the interests of minimizing your exposure to outside investigation, I didn't reserve a room for you. It's best you sleep here tonight. It's a king-size bed." He removed his shoes and stripped down to his waist. "Plenty of room for both of us."

Nahid felt more comfortable with him after they'd shared their past. On the assumption that Ali felt the same, she slipped out of her skirt in a graceful movement designed for enticement. She sensed Ali hadn't found an outlet for his physical desires since the project began. With an eagerness that she found somewhat surprising, Nahid contemplated the prospect of exploring the extent of Ali's sexual prowess while exercising her own.

They tossed their remaining garments aside, and wasted no time joining together under the sheets. Ali caressed her feet before he began, slowly working his way up. No stranger to the art of making love, Nahid responded expertly to each of his movements. All of their senses came alive. For hours they relished the excruciating excitement of their sexual encounter. They postponed the inevitable relief as long as possible, savored its delight, then drifted off into the kind of sound sleep that only wine, exhaustion, and complete sexual satisfaction can produce.

Chapter 17

Submerged in Milton's paper trail, Mike Pallino felt as uncomfortable as he did trying to work with Jack Marshall's protocol. Mike saw himself as an in-the-field lawman, not a desk jockey, a fact he made no attempt to hide. He viewed all forms of paperwork as navigational hazards — uncharted reefs on which the strewn wreckages of expediency could be seen throughout the Bureau. Now he felt like he was drowning in a sea of audit documentation.

Still, he knew his instincts had never been wrong. They'd been telling him for the last twenty-four hours to set up camp in Metalcraft's conference room, to get as involved as he could in Milt's audit. Mike made every effort to obey the blind impulses, but the pained expression hadn't left his face since he began working his way through the piles of Milton's audit trail.

He inched his way around the elongated conference table and flipped through each little pile of accounting documentation in no particular order. He asked Milt a few questions about the significance of each stack's contents, grimaced, and moved on to the next one. Before he'd made it halfway around, Mike stopped, shook his head in frustration, and glowered at Milton.

"Milt, I'll confess I was a long way from the top of my class at Notre Dame. In fact, my commitment to football kind of kept me pretty close to the bottom. Even in my wildest nightmares I never saw so much damned paper spread out all over the place as I'm seeing right now." Mike ceased his document reconnaissance efforts, took a seat next to Milton, and pulled a small notebook from his shirt pocket. "Now, as a change in subject, but I've uncovered a couple of items that might interest you."

Milton grinned. "I can use all the help I can get. What do you have?"

"Well, for starters the two guys Fadhil hired must be fictitious. They're not recorded anywhere else under the names Bakish and Bauer. As to that post office box Phoebe gave me for the mailing of that mysterious two hundred thousand, it's registered to a Paul Bremer. Does any of this ring a bell?"

Milton lowered his head and looked down at the floor.

"Milt?" Mike waited. Milt looked confused, and seemed to be struggling for a response.

Milton put his face in his hands. The words came slowly. "The bell that's ringing says he just might have sold me out."

"What are you talking about? Who sold you out?"

His face still in his hands, Milton continued. "My boss, Mr. Bremer. I'm afraid he figured I was too incompetent to uncover whatever it is they're hiding. That's probably why he blew me off when I told him about my concerns the other day. Mike, it's starting to look like he gave me to whoever's trying to get into this company. Or rather, sold me."

Mike had to allow time for Milton's remark to sink in before he responded. "Come on, Milt. That's a little harsh, not to mention a real stretch of the imagination. That money sent to the post office box is probably just a prepayment of the audit fee."

Milton straightened and turned to Mike. "No, Mike. No one ever prepays an audit fee. Nothing happens until the auditor's time sheets are sent in. Then the reviewer adds a few hours, marks the dollars up, and sends the sheet to billing before an invoice can be sent out to the client. I haven't submitted any hours yet. And my time sure as heck isn't going to be anything near $200,000. I can tell you that."

Mike could see the tears welling up in the eyes of the young accountant he'd come to see as a partner. Mike's expression softened into a blend of sadness and sympathy. He recognized, for the first time, the measure of respect which had emerged from the initial contempt he'd held for the man he'd once considered a nerd. He reached over and put a sinewy hand on Milt's drooping shoulder.

"Milt, if what you say is true, that guy Bremer is one despicable scumbag. And he may be in a hell of a lot of trouble if we ever get to the bottom of all this. These guys must have something big they want to hide, if they're willing to spend that kind of money to do it. Look, I'm truly sorry about you being used like that. Right now, though, Bremer's main crime is the somewhat lesser one of being an accomplice in a felony. We have to proceed from there and move forward on this. I'm going to need your help, big time. Are you okay with that?"

Milton turned away and looked down at the floor again. "Nothing's really okay, Mike. The only guy in the firm I thought had any faith in me just proved he didn't."

Mike shook his head. "Yeah, and by now he must realize he's underestimated you, big time. It also looks like he proved he's one hell of a crook."

Milton turned back and raised his hands in the air. "Guess my employment at PM&B is pretty much coming to an end. At least I won't be out of a job until this audit is completed. Anyway, you're right, Mike, we need to move ahead. I pulled those invoices with the strange-looking numbers on them for you to look at if you want. They go back a couple of years. I want to try something with them when you're through."

Mike pondered for a moment before he spoke. "Milt, my wife gave me a brief explanation of RFP's. Are you familiar with them?"

"Sure. It's an acronym for request for proposal. My firm responds to a lot of them. Why?"

"I'm not sure. Do your firm's RFP's have numbers on them?"

"No, the only numbers would be the request for the size of the job, and that's usually left up to the respondent to decide. What are you thinking?"

"Oh, I don't know. Just thinking out loud, I guess. You were starting to say you want to try something. Try what?"

Milton's expression brightened and he cupped his hands together in front of him. "Well, I thought I'd dig in to see if there's a match-up between the invoices with the long numbers and the discount scam I think I've uncovered."

Mike frowned. "What scam?"

"Look here, Mike." Milton pushed two documents forward on the table. "Metalcraft sends out invoices to each of its customers for the full amount of the customer's purchase, offering no discount. But Metalcraft's copy of the invoice, which the customer never sees, offers a three-percent discount if the customer pays within ten days. The accounts receivable is recorded at the discounted amount on Metalcraft's records. The customer then pays the full amount within ten days and Ali deposits the money in an offshore bank account from which I still haven't received any statements. Ali tells Mac he gets better interest rates there."

Mike nodded with a look of understanding. "Okay, I think I can predict what's coming next."

"Right, Mike. The offshore bank keeps the three percent, then forwards the ninety-seven-percent balance to Metalcraft's regular business bank account. There it gets recorded as a collection on the discounted sale and shows up as a normal deposit. Everything looks fine because that deposit matches Metalcraft's copy of the discounted billing to the customer. The customer never knows the difference, and each transaction is too small to raise suspicion at Metalcraft."

Milton gulped down another swallow of a once-hot coffee and leaned toward Mike. "For example, a $2,500 billing to a customer is recorded as a sale discounted at three percent to $2,425. When the customer pays the $2,500, Ali scams seventy-five dollars, and the balance of $2,425 is recorded as a collection and deposited into Metalcraft's regular bank account. It matches Metalcraft's copy of the customer's invoice, and everything is in perfect balance. Neat, huh?"

Mike frowned and scratched his head. "Okay, I get it. Fadhil skims off three percent. Fine, that's fraud. But I'm not seeing how he makes any real money on three percent. I mean, seventy-five bucks just isn't that much in the overall scheme of things."

"True, Mike. But it's really big if you do it on two hundred customers a month at an average billing of $10,000 per customer. Big money in total, but no single transaction is large enough to attract any attention."

Mike raised his eyebrows and looked at Milton. "I'll be damned. So this is why commercial crime pays if you can get away with it."

Milton grinned. "Now, it gets worse. Look at this." He shoved another document under Mike's nose. "Ali's doing the same thing when it comes to vendors who offer a discount if Metalcraft pays within ten days. Phoebe says he told Mac that Metalcraft can earn more than three percent by investing the money for ten days. Therefore, it's better not to take the discount, he says. So Metalcraft transfers the full amount from its regular bank to the off-shore bank. The off-shore bank keeps the three percent, pays the vendor's bill within ten days, and no one suspects anything. Get the picture?"

Mike nodded and smiled as though his distaste for numerical concepts had suddenly begun to dissolve. "Yep, and I suppose if you do it to all your vendors who offer discounts, it amounts to one hell of a lot of money. True?"

"True. You're becoming a forensic accountant, Mike. And now you know how badly Metalcraft is getting screwed at both ends every day."

Mike shook his head. He thought about Jack Marshall and the forensics the man had been trying to cram down everyone's throat. "Okay, this Fadhil's a crook, and he's a smart one. Now, explain something to me. Why hasn't this been discovered before?"

"Probably because this is Metalcraft's first audit. Mac isn't interested in figures. He trusts Fadhil. No one else around here knows enough about the company, or the numbers, to figure it all out. If the audit doesn't catch it, then the scam goes undetected. Cash as shown on the company's records is reconciled every month to cash on the bank statements. But no one ever reconciles cash to sales, as I did, or ever checks up on discounts."

Mike pushed his chair back, stood, and released a sigh. "Well, we've made progress, but there are still a couple of unanswered questions. Why is someone on the outside paying $200,000 — and maybe more — to hide something? And why is that something important enough to prompt an attack on both you and Phoebe? I'm not seeing why an outsider could care one way or the other about Fadhil's fraudulent enterprise. Anyway, Milt, this riddle is falling right into our laps, and I have a sneaking suspicion we're running out of time. Any ideas?"

"No. The only idea I've come up with so far just crashed."

"What idea was that?"

"Well, those long numbers bothered me. So I thought maybe they represented some kind of code. You know, like maybe an alphanumeric system where the letter 'A' represents the number one, 'B' equals two, and so on."

Mike nodded. "And what did you find?"

"Nothing but garbage. So I guess I'm back to square one. I'll keep on trying, though."

Mike put his hand on Milton's shoulder. "Look, Milt, it's not for me to tell you how to do your job, but this code stuff is really out in the twilight zone. I think we need to concentrate on the missing cash, and I'll check again on that packing slip you found. Are you with me?"

"Sure. You're probably right. I tend to get too wrapped up in details anyway. At least that's what people tell me. Check on that bank that won't respond, will you, Mike?"

"You got it. Keep plugging. I'll see you later."

On the drive back to his office, Mike thought about Jack Marshall's charge to be on the lookout for explosives allegedly shipped in to some

Boston corporation. For the first time Mike realized he'd become so engrossed in Milt's audit that he hadn't made any serious effort to connect Jack's reference with the powdery packing slip or the attempt on Milt's life.

Milt's nasty little disclosure about discounts, Mike realized, had brought the concept of forensics into a clearer perspective. Fraud is one thing. Storing the spoils from it in offshore bank accounts is quite another. And how many two hundred thousand-dollar payments had there been? Why hadn't Ali Fadhil taken off with the scammed money long ago, instead of hanging around? Maybe the money wasn't his. And if not, what was it for?

Mike pulled out his cell phone and punched in Ted Krueger's number in Forensics.

Chapter 18

Under Ted Krueger's direction, the Forensics Division of Boston's FBI office had developed one of the Bureau's few strong practices in the subtle art of applying scientific knowledge to criminal problems. Aside from the reputation of the office, its director had meticulously honed his own natural talents in this unique science, which forged technology, patience, inference, and abstract logic into a legal application. Formerly a law enforcement agent, Krueger had reinvented himself.

Now that Milton had nudged him into an interest in forensics, Mike could feel his resistance melting a bit. He'd made finding out more about the crumpled packing slip his top priority. Early for their meeting and unable to find a coffee pot or a magazine anywhere, he pulled up a chair outside Ted's office. All he could see were preoccupied people scurrying up and down the hall like a colony of ants. Mike was about to ask one of them where he could get a doughnut and coffee when Ted came out and shook his hand.

"Come on in, Mike. We need to talk."

"Good. I'm interested in anything you can tell me, starting with who those people are running back and forth like they're all late for something."

Ted forced a half-smile. "Lab types. They're busy trying to reconstruct a crime scene from insignificant-looking scraps of evidence, like this smelly piece of paper you brought me. Sit down. I'm afraid you're not going to like this." He pulled a file from his drawer and laid it on top of the desk with the kind of careful deliberation that might have been expected more for an antique vase than a stack of paper.

"I'll like it if you can prove murder and fraud with it," Mike said. "Any chance you could round up some coffee while we talk?"

Ted didn't look up. "I don't think we have time for that, Mike. I'm afraid this isn't about fraud, or even the murder of those two employees. I wish it were that easy. I think you have a mega-problem on your hands here."

Ted's face tightened. "Brace yourself. We couldn't pinpoint the exact location, but we figured, from its markings, that your packing slip came from somewhere in Pakistan. We made out what we think are the letters *mV*. Now, although that designation could have several very innocuous meanings, one possible usage is as a unit of measure for anaerobic conditions necessary for the preservation of explosives."

Eyes wide, Mike leaned even further forward in his chair and placed his hands on the edge of Ted's desk. "Explosives? What I don't like about your idea is that Marshall's got me on the hunt for boxes of what he called HDX — supposedly shipped to some company here in Boston. I'm hoping you're going to tell me one of your other meanings is more likely."

Ted looked down at his report and flipped forward a few pages. "I'm afraid not. The odor came from some kind of polymer, or plasticizer, used to stabilize highly sensitive explosives." Ted finally looked up. "Mike, we're talking about a very powerful explosive, polymer-bound so it could be shipped to this company of yours for subsequent use somewhere, probably in the United States. Jack may well have had it right when he said HDX. I think you damn well better get your fanny in gear and find out what that company did with this stuff."

Mike slammed his fist on the desk and sprang out of his chair. "Ted, that shipment came in weeks ago! Hell, it could be anywhere by now. How in the name of the Almighty could something like that ever get into this country in the first place? Don't we screen things coming from places like Pakistan?"

"Frequently, yes. What you're forgetting is that this was, or at least appeared to be, a legitimate purchase by an established corporation, and signed for by an authorized employee. Sometimes that kind of shipment gets through. Anyway, you'd better get on this right away. If the locker you're talking about was filled with this material and isn't anymore, then I'd say someone's about to make a big bang somewhere."

Mike returned to his seat, tilted his head back, and stared at the ceiling. "Great. That's just great." He turned back to face Ted. "Okay, about how big a bang would you say? I mean, are we talking about some kind of suicide bomber blowing up a commercial aircraft here?"

"No way to tell for sure, Mike, because we have no idea how much of this stuff was in storage." Ted stood and handed him a copy of the forensics report. "But if I had to read the tea leaves on this one, I'd say whoever's responsible has something bigger than an airplane in his crosshairs. I'm thinking maybe a city. Don't you have any other clues?"

Mike stood, spun around, and threw his hands in the air. "No. Damn it, Jack said the same thing about maybe a city or two. Hell, we've been focusing on *fraud*, for God's sake! Well, I'll tell you something. If any clues exist they're most likely buried somewhere in that company's accounting system."

Ted scowled. "You have to be kidding. A potential disaster this big lurking in an accounting system? What are you talking about?"

"Here's the deal, Ted. Someone's paying the auditor's employer two hundred thousand to assure the clues *won't* be found. Worse yet, they're sending out assassins to kill the auditor and his assistant just in case they *do* happen to find something."

Ted slapped his forehead. "Jeez, Mike, then I'd say you'd better dig into the company's system in one hell of a hurry. My guess is you don't have much time. If I were you I'd arrest the auditor's employer and then put some real heat on the auditor to come up with something. Is that the Pringle guy?"

"Yeah. In fact, he had some offbeat idea about a coding system. Now I'm thinking maybe he wasn't so far out in left field after all. I'm on my way to meet him now. Thanks. Keep your fingers crossed that we're not too late. Make me five more copies of that report and send two of them to Marshall. When he sees this the bad guys won't need any explosives."

Within an hour Mike had alerted the CIA, Homeland Security, and his boss at the Boston Field Office. Each of them asked the same critical questions: what's the target, who's responsible, and when? That Mike didn't have an answer to any of them raised everyone's emotions a few notches from controlled fright to panic.

Mike made the safe assumption that Jack Marshall's patience with his unorthodox style of doing things hit its limit with this sudden announcement about Milton's explosives.

Marshall's voice barked in Mike's ear. "Damn it, Mike, how many times have I told you to bring your investigative skills up to date? You've put the whole forensics issue on the back burner for years. Now, out of the blue, you come up with this sudden revelation. I need to know where and when this apocalyptic event is going to occur, assuming we can get there in time to stop it from happening at all. And you're telling me the only clue you have is buried somewhere in a damned *accounting system*?"

"Jack, the accountant and I are putting a full court press on this right now. We're reasonably certain the point man on this is a guy named Ali Fadhil, the CFO of Metalcraft, a company that makes precision cutting tools right here in Boston. We just haven't deciphered the coding yet. What I need is a couple of your computer sleuths to get out there and help us on this, like ASAP."

"Fine. I'll have 'em out there in an hour, along with a couple of agents to arrest Fadhil. I want you to get back and work with them to break that code. And I mean *now*. Then point out this guy Fadhil to our men as soon as they get there…and make sure you don't spook him beforehand."

Mike shook his head. "Forget it. Fadhil went out of town a few days ago. No one has any idea where he is, including the CEO. You're going to have to initiate a search for him. I'll have the CEO fill you in as soon as I can. I'm on my way to the company now. I'll call you when we find something."

* * * * * *

"Mike, where have you been?" Milton yelled. "I've broken the—"

"We have big problems, Milt." Mike entered, sprinting through the conference room doorway much like he had as a running back when he found an opening in the front line. His voice shook with an uncharacteristic anxiety. "We have a potential disaster on our hands. I think I was wrong about steering you away from that coding stuff. We need to get right back on it. You're going to have to bear down on those numbers you were looking at the other day. Now here's what I want you to—"

"It's done, Mike. I worked all night on it. That's what I was trying to tell you." Milton pumped his fist in the air. "You're not going to believe this. My alphanumeric coding idea was wrong, like I told you. The actual code is a modified betanumeric system where A equals two, not one, B equals three and so on. The numbers on the invoices received by Metalcraft combine with every *other* letter in the product description narrative to form an encoded message to Ali. Then, after Ali reads the message, he sends his reply, also coded, on the payment check, then voids the check and makes a reversing entry in the check register for the check, which he knows will never be cashed. The good—"

Mike's brow furrowed. "He makes a *what* entry?"

111

"A reversing entry. As in cancelling out the check that was recorded in the check register. The good news is I broke the code. The bad news is you're not going to like the message I just decoded. Look here, I'll show you one phrase so you can see how it works."

Milton shoved a document in front of Mike. "Look at this invoice for supplies. The vendor number, and I'm inserting the dashes, is 8-13-6. The product reference number is 8-21-3-10-8. The product description is *Bonding ADE cradle*. By the way, ADE is an industry acronym for air dried epoxy. I had to look it up. Now watch this on my laptop."

Mike leaned over to read it.

8 O 13 D 6 N 8 A 21 E 3 R 10 D 8 E
G o l d e n G a t e B r i d g e

Milton leaned back in his chair and folded his arms across his chest. "The rest of the message refers to some kind of compound designated HDX. Can you tell me what's going on here? And what's HDX?"

Mike slapped his forehead. "Whew! Yeah, I sure can. It's starting to look like some terrorist group has targeted the Golden Gate Bridge. The word 'jihad' keeps coming to mind. HDX is one hell of a powerful explosive, like the kind we learned was taken out of Iraq before the inspectors arrived. The militants apparently needed to repackage it here before they moved it to San Francisco. This Ali Fadhil guy has been into more than just fraud. We need to find him...fast."

Milt raised his hands palms up. "How do we do that?"

"You and I are going to San Francisco, pronto. Right after I alert my boss and the San Francisco field office. By the way, nice work. You're the best damned auditor *I've* ever seen."

From the glow on Milt's face, Mike assumed it had probably been a long time since anyone complimented him about anything.

* * * * * *

The cell phone discussion between free-wheeling Mike Pallino and by-the-book Jack Marshall became predictably contentious in a matter of seconds. Mike preferred expediency over protocol and had every intention of keeping Jack out of the loop until it was all over. Still, his boss probably needed to know in case additional help became necessary, and Jack's was a protocol world.

"Mike, what the hell do you mean you're taking an accountant with you? No way. You know the rules. We don't put non-agents in a hostile situation. If anything happened to this guy, the Bureau would hang us both out to dry. In fact, the White House wouldn't like it either. So forget it. Now, our San Francisco office is all set for you as soon as—"

"To hell with the rules, Jack. He's coming with me. It's imperative he be there. This guy's not just any accoun—"

"Imperative? Give me one good reason why it's imperative to expose a damned accountant to the line of fire in what may turn out to be a national disaster. Just one will do."

"Fine. I'll give you several. First, he's the one who broke the code and may well have prevented a disaster our intelligence gurus never saw coming. I'm going to need him to decode more of those invoice-based messages before our plane lands in San Francisco. Second, he's already *been* exposed. He successfully fought off one of their assassins without any help from us. Which brings me to my third reason. He might be the only one able to identify one of these characters. End of story. He's coming. And if the Bureau doesn't like it they can shove it. I'll call you when we get there."

Mike squeezed the off button on his cell phone and headed for his last stop before he set off for the airport.

Chapter 19

The abandoned shipyard at Hunter's Point earned its reputation as the armpit of California. Especially at night, but even in broad daylight, a comparison to Dante's Inferno might have been appropriate. A deactivated Navy shipyard, it was alleged to be San Francisco's toxic waste dump, a legacy of nuclear and chemical pollution. Once a beehive of repair and refitting activity for the ships of the Pacific Fleet, the abandoned facility had become a breeding ground for violent crime, drug trafficking, smuggling, and gang warfare.

As instructed, Ali, Nahid, Saif, and Hakim waited at the end of a desolate pier at the far end of the yard. The damp night air stung their nostrils with the odor of waste oil, dead fish, and salt spray.

Nahid shivered while she glared at Ali, who could tell she was nearly at the limit of her patience. "Ali, who is this guy who insists on meeting us on a damned pier in this godforsaken hellhole?"

"Carlos Ramirez," Ali replied. He rubbed his arms and shook a bit himself. "He's the leader of the local *Mara Salvatrucha* gang. They're violent and effective. That's why I chose them for this job."

Nahid continued to press the issue. "So why do we need him? Or his gang?"

"His gang has the weapons and the people we need to help us do what needs to be done. They come with a strong hatred of the American establishment in general, and law enforcement in particular. So they have an incentive to partner with us on this. Naji made the connection and set it up through the New York MS-13 cell."

In what had begun to seem a futile effort to keep the chill off, Nahid rubbed her hands together and rhythmically slapped her sides. "Okay, I get it. MS-13 is their gang designation. So what does *Mara Salvatrucha* mean?"

"La Mara was originally a street gang in El Salvador. Some of the guerillas became known as *salvatruchas*. When they fled to the United States during the Salvadoran civil war they took on the name."

Ali turned away from her and looked into the empty darkness toward the distant sound of an engine. "Okay, I think I hear Carlos coming. Treat him with respect, Nahid. Females don't occupy a high status in his system."

She kicked an empty beer can into the water. "In that case I dislike him already."

Carlos Ramirez pulled his K-1200 Harley to a stop in front of them, dismounted, and offered a cordial greeting to Ali. A dark, stocky man with sharp facial features that looked like they were hewn from a block of wood, Carlos spoke almost perfect English with a slight Salvadoran accent.

With lips tightened and eyes narrowed, Nahid scanned the man's sleeveless leather vest, white tee shirt, red bandana, and pants with split cuffs. The tattoo on his arm read 'Salvadoran Pride.' She made no effort to hide a look of disdain.

Carlos crafted a polite and almost imperceptible bow. "Please accept my apologies for the inconvenience, my friends. My *guerreros* and I must be very careful, you see. There are many who would gladly kill us if they could. I had to make sure you were not part of a trap, so I watched you from a distance before I exposed myself."

"We understand, Carlos," Ali said. "We wish to avoid the police and all federal agencies as much as you do."

"Ah, Mister Ali, it is not the police, or even the *federales* that we fear. It is the *Sombre Negra*, or 'Black Shadow' in your language. These are the death squads and, if we were ever captured and deported to El Salvador, we would be killed in a most unpleasant way. Anyway, enough of that. Come, follow me that we may discuss our business. My *cholos* in New York tell me you have a proposition for me and my *mareros*. It involves a very large sum of money, yes?"

Ali nodded. "A large sum indeed, Carlos."

"Good. Your car is parked behind this warehouse as instructed, is it not?"

"Yes. We'll follow right behind you."

Carlos led them along a dark, debris-strewn trail around empty dry docks, between abandoned cranes, old warehouses that sagged on the verge of collapse, and junk piles of obsolete ship-fitting equipment. A cold wind blew in from the bay and whistled a mournful eulogy as it passed through this remote graveyard of rusting ghosts.

The journey lasted barely long enough to allow time for Nahid to fire a few questions at Ali. "All right, Ali, translate please. What do these terms mean? And where did you learn this weird language?"

"You forget, I went to college here and, at Ahmed's insistence, I studied it. 'Cholo' means fellow gang member, 'guerrero' is their word for warrior, and 'marero' is a reference to the Honduran gangs known as 'Sea Wind.' 'Mara Salvatrucha' is actually an international gang."

"Okay, I get it. I suppose all that graffiti on the wall where we parked is theirs."

"Yes. That's the way they mark their territory."

Nahid shook her head.

Carlos led them to the gang's headquarters in what seemed like the most remote warehouse on the Hunter's Point peninsula. Again, they weren't prepared for what they saw. Thirty or more *mareros* armed with knives, sniper rifles, and AK-47 assault rifles formed a semicircle. Hakim and Saif looked at each other and moved to seek refuge behind Ali. Nahid remained expressionless. Several of the men stared at her, laughed softly, and turned away.

Carlos smiled at her. "Please excuse my *cholos*, Miss…is it Nahid?"

"Yes." She glared at him and shifted her gaze just long enough to throw an angry glance at the men behind him.

"Forgive me, Miss Nahid. They laugh because they realize they must carefully guard their hearts," Carlos explained. "You see, they have pronounced you a beautiful *ratera*." He smiled again, turned, and walked back to the semicircle. With his back to them, it was difficult for Ali and his little group to tell what was going on. The gang leader appeared to be negotiating with his men.

Nahid turned toward Ali for another translation. "*Ratera?* Please don't tell me he just called me a rat," she whispered.

"No. They called you a beautiful *ratera*. It means thief. That's why they had to guard their hearts. Relax. It was intended as a compliment."

Nahid rolled her eyes and shook her head again.

A few moments elapsed before Carlos turned away from his men and walked back toward Ali. His smile had disappeared and his tone became authoritative. "I have pulled these men away from their money-making enterprises so we might share in the decision whether to accept or reject your proposal. This offer, we are told, is so generous we can't refuse. Very well, speak. Why do you want our help, and what are you willing to pay for it?"

Ali glanced toward the men as if to check that they weren't about to attack him, and then turned to face Carlos. "I'll say it as plain as I can. We need you and your men to strike at the heart of the same establishment that has on its agenda the elimination of your *Mara Salvatrucha*. Our target is the Golden Gate Bridge. We intend to send it plunging into the waters of San Francisco Bay in several large pieces. We have the explosives and the expertise to do it. However, we'll need the help of your men, as well as their firepower."

Ali leaned in closer and lowered his voice. "Our plan is to use four teams of two on the Frisco-to-Marin side, and the same on the reverse direction. Your men will form these teams under the direction of Hakim and Saif, here. We'll also need a semi tractor-trailer to block the entrance to vehicular traffic at each end for thirty minutes while the two teams place the charges. I'm authorized to pay you one million dollars upon completion of the job."

Carlos showed no reaction. He sat on a stack of pallets, glanced in the direction of his men, then turned toward Ali. "Tell me, Mister Ali, why you need so many people to do this thing."

Ali had anticipated the question. He settled down on an empty crate. "The bridge, approximately nine thousand feet long, is suspended on cables strung between two seven- hundred and forty-six foot towers, each anchored by a sixty-thousand ton concrete and steel structure. After the September, 2001 attack on New York's Twin Towers, the California Army National Guard's 1st Battalion, 143rd Field Artillery Regiment was assigned to patrol the bridge in order to assist the Golden Gate Bridge Authority's police force. There are three lanes of vehicular traffic, plus a walkway in each direction, all busy with traffic most—"

"You still haven't told me why you want so many men, Mister Ali," Carlos said.

Ali shifted uneasily on his perch. "Well, I'm saying this is one well-built monster of a bridge, earthquake-reinforced, and constantly under a regimen of preventive maintenance. It's a carefully guarded American icon. Once we block the entrances and begin setting our charges it won't take the authorities long to figure out what's going on. They'll probably discover one or two of our placements even before they're detonated. Even so, they won't be able to neutralize all eight charges in time."

Carlos frowned. "And I ask again. Why so many men?"

"We'll be doing this at night. The odds of blowing away a significant portion of the structure are decidedly in our favor. We need six of your men to place the charges along with my two experts. We'll also need a driver for each of the trucks, and four or five more at each end of the bridge to provide covering fire."

Carlos leaned forward, placed his elbows on his knees and rested his chin on his fists. "And what if my men cannot get off the bridge in time?"

"Thirty minutes should be ample time. We'll have the element of surprise on our side. We estimate ten minutes to lower each man down eight to ten feet over the side to attach the explosives. It'll take only another two minutes to set the charges. That will make it impossible for the authorities to access the charges easily."

Carlos tilted his head slightly to one side. "And what is your function, Mister Ali?"

Ali rubbed his hands together and shivered. "I'll drive one SUV from Marin to Frisco carrying one of the teams. Nahid will do the same from Frisco to Marin, carrying the other. We'll drop off the teams at the locations she designated. Your teams on the bridge may carry with them whatever firearms they want; as long as Nahid agrees they won't get in the way."

Carlos paused as if to ponder the offer for a moment, then stood and walked back to his men who were milling about with a noticeable air of impatience. He motioned them to close in tight around him.

"What do you think, Ali?" Nahid whispered. "Does he have to get their approval? Can't he make the deal himself and order them to go along?"

"Maybe so, but I'd rather he have unanimous agreement so no one develops second thoughts and backs out up there on the bridge. It's a scary place at night, and we'll need all of his men."

The conversation among Carlos' men grew louder. Hand gestures became more frequent, and it looked like emotions were playing an increasingly dominant role in the decision process. Their argument reached a high-decibel crescendo, then silence. No one moved, and nothing was said until Carlos began what appeared to be a summary of the discussion, as if to assure there were no misunderstandings. He nodded as he spoke, then turned away from his men and walked back to Ali.

118

"My *guerreros* have agreed to your proposal, Mister Ali. However, one million dollars is not enough. You must understand that we have many business enterprises, all of which make good money with less risk. For example, an initial investment of two thousand American dollars in cocaine can be combined with two cheap household chemicals and produce ten thousand dollars worth of crack. We can turn it over four times and make forty thousand in one day, risk free. Our fee for murder is often in six figures. So you see, Mister Ali, one million for the high risk you propose is far too cheap."

Ali remained silent for a moment, even though he had expected the reply. Ahmed should never have trusted that damned Naji to structure a financial deal with these people. This arrangement was screwed up from the start, and now the only option would be to make the best of it. Ali responded as though he'd expected such a response from Carlos. "What would you consider a fair price?"

"My *mareros* are the best. They can assure your big bridge will become half a bridge. And they will accept the very high risks. But not for less than three million dollars. One million paid before we begin, and the rest immediately after the bridge is no more."

The counter-offer presented a problem. Ali had set aside two million in anticipation of such an outcome. To obtain approval from Naji for more would take time — time Ali didn't have. The million-dollar shortfall would have to be dealt with later. Right now there was a bridge to be blown. Ali walked away, paced back and forth, and turned to face the gang leader.

"You drive an unmerciful bargain, Carlos. Still, I believe you did it in good faith. I accept your arrangement and assume, therefore, that we have a deal."

"Good. We do, Mister Ali. However, there is one more small condition which must be met before I make my men available to you. You may consider this...ah...payment for the business we lost tonight by agreeing to meet with you."

Ali cocked his head and frowned. "And what would that condition be?"

Carlos signaled for one of his men to come forward. The moment the man stepped toward them Ali concluded this was the ugliest human specimen he'd ever seen. The man's wide grin pushed aside enough of his dark, unkempt beard to expose a mouthful of shiny, gold-capped teeth. Well overweight, even for his almost-seven-foot height, the abundantly tattooed

119

giant exuded a body odor discernable before he came within fifteen feet of Ali's small entourage. Nahid raised her hand to her mouth and gasped.

"This is Miguel Flores, my right-hand man, so to speak," Carlos said, extending an arm toward his *marero*. "He will make all the arrangements for the trucks and firepower you need. Miguel is a very good man, although his outward appearance has not endeared him to many women. Naturally, he is hungry for love, as we all tend to be sometimes. Now, Miguel has very much admired your beautiful engineer, Miss Nahid. So, the condition we have decided is that he will sleep with Miss Nahid for one full night, having sex with her to the extent of his pleasure."

Ali understood the thoughts he surmised must have been racing through Nahid's mind behind the look of shock on her face. He tried to picture a thirteen-year-old girl being raped by obscene men much like Miguel. Images that this repugnant mountain of a man must be conjuring up for her paraded through his thoughts.

Hakim and Saif looked appalled. "Mr. Fadhil," Hakim whispered, "this kind of treatment of her by outsiders is not permitted by al Qaeda. We cannot allow this."

Ali ignored the remark and turned to face Nahid. He expected her to unleash a violent refusal which, he feared, would insult the sexually excited Miguel and might end any hope for help from Carlos and his men.

Arms now akimbo and face drawn tight, she turned to fasten her glare first on Carlos, then on Ali. Her lips pressed hard against each other. She drew in a deep breath and, with an angry expression, exhaled as though it were fire through her nostrils. To Ali's amazement, she suddenly broke into a wide, enticing smile. She walked toward Miguel with a deliberately accentuated sway of her hips, wrapped her arms around the muscular colossus, and kissed him. Miguel grinned from ear to ear, patted Nahid on the head, and strode back to his *cholos* with a triumphant look on his face.

Nahid smiled at Carlos. "We accept your terms. I only hope he's large everywhere."

Carlos chuckled. "Okay, we have a deal, Mister Ali. What do you wish to be our next move?" They shook hands.

"Tomorrow evening we'll meet here," Ali replied. "We'll go over all the details with you and your men. Two nights after that we'll all make history by doing what the world never dreamed could be done. Pictures of that bridge plunging into San Francisco Bay will be remembered by the world forever."

Carlos ushered everyone out and turned off their makeshift system of dim lights. The darkened warehouse became, once again, another of the shipyard's abandoned ghosts.

Ali turned away from Hakim and Saif, still shaking their heads, and waited for Nahid to calm down before he tapped her gently on the arm. "Thank you for not squashing this deal. Now tell me why you ignored your intense disgust for men like him while you practically leaped into his arms."

Nahid glared at Ali again. "I ignored nothing," she snapped, "including my intent to kill him if he's not gentle. I had no choice. If I backed down, you'd have to find some other way to salvage our arrangement with them. I would appear weak — in which case they might not be willing to follow my orders without question up there on the bridge. I can't have that. This way they'll know if they don't obey me, Miguel will kill them. Get the picture?"

Ali smiled and gave her a friendly squeeze around her shoulders with his arm. "Lady, I'll have to admit that damned Naji was right when he told me you were essential to the success of this operation. Well done." They walked arm-in-arm back to their car and waved to Carlos who smiled back at them and revved up his Harley.

* * * * * *

Despite Ellie's frequent travels, neither infidelity nor any other breach of trust had ever become an issue in their marriage. Mike believed in Ellie. Still, the events of the past two weeks had cast some shadows on his mental portrait of her. They took shape in his mind as flashbacks, fuzzy images, none of which alone could be construed to be significant. Yet, taken together, they wove a dark tapestry which now cried out for further investigation. Mike began to consider the recent sequence of Ellie's activities from a new perspective. He could no longer dismiss them as coincidental.

He knew her Iranian origin didn't distinguish her from thousands of other immigrants. On those rare occasions when he thought of it at all, he simply wondered if all Iranian women possessed a natural charisma comparable to Ellie's. The unexplained RFP numbers would have gone as unnoticed as random numbers in the telephone directory had it not been for Milton's coding discoveries.

Ellie's trips to San Francisco never seemed relevant to anything until the city's great bridge became a target. Perhaps, in retrospect, he should have taken more seriously Matt's hallucination about the resemblance between Ellie and the lady in black at the downtown bar altercation.

He shifted his weight from one foot to the other. The closer the elevator brought him to the floor on which her firm's office occupied half the space, the more guilt he felt about violating her privacy. By the time he'd walked down the hall and stood in front of the door marked *Faraday, Ennis, Graham & Wilson-Architectural Solutions*, Mike managed to put lawman ahead of husband. This was part of a federal investigation, not a test of marital trust.

He smiled at the young receptionist who looked up at him from her computer screen with one of those automatic yes-may-I-help-you expressions. The problem, he suddenly realized, would be to gain access to Ellie's office files without making it look like an official search. Ellie would surely find out sooner or later. If this turned out to be a wild goose chase she'd be furious. It would be he who had broken the trust. If not…well, he didn't want to think about it.

Mike glanced around the reception area. The walls were decorated with plaques denoting her firm's architectural accomplishments. He figured this was the kind of professional place not likely to employ someone like Mike Pallino, who graduated at the bottom of his class with a major in the easiest social studies curriculum he could find.

He turned back to face the receptionist. A credible lie would now be necessary to explain the reason for his visit. "Good afternoon, I'm Mike Pallino, Ellie's husband. She called me from out of town asking me to pull some files to be faxed to her. I know where her office is. Would it be okay for me to go in? I have identification if you need it."

The receptionist surprised him with a welcoming smile. "That won't be necessary, Mr. Pallino. You and I met at the Christmas party. I was the one who had one too many and you stopped me and made me drink some coffee. Remember? Go right in. Call me if you need anything."

"Thanks. I won't be long." He couldn't place her. He'd made it a point to attend Ellie's company parties because she attended his. Yet he never remembered much about the people there. Maybe the receptionist wasn't the only one who had too many that night.

It took longer than he'd planned to find the file where she kept her RFPs. Ellie classified them as 'Lost,' 'In Process,' or 'Completed.' Only a few were marked with the same kind of numbers he'd seen on Milton's invoices. He grabbed as many of them as he could find and stuffed them into his briefcase. Mike assumed Ellie had taken the most recent ones with her, making the relevance of the ones he pulled up questionable.

He walked out past the receptionist, thanked her again, exchanged smiles, and made his exit. Once out, he paused to consider his marital options while he waited for the elevator. If it turned out his suspicions were completely unjustified, his explanation to Ellie would have to be one hell of a masterpiece of rhetoric. What would he say to her? "I had to search your office, dear, because you wore black, ran off to respond to funny-looking RFPs, and my drunken friend swore on his sixth or seventh cocktail that you beat up a bar-fly?" Mike knew that dog would never hunt. He might even lose Ellie. If his suspicions were right, then he'd already lost her anyway. A perfect Catch-22.

All the way down to the lobby Mike thought about it. No matter how hard he tried, he couldn't recall ever having found himself in a no-win position like this one. He threw his briefcase in the front seat of the car and headed for the airport to meet Milton.

Chapter 20

Preston Anderson stormed into his assistant's office, red-faced and waving the little document in the air. "Damn it, George, those FBI clowns have done it again. An email, a damned email is what I get from the chief of the Bureau. He now tells me a bunch of terrorists plan to blow up the Golden Gate Bridge. He ends my message with, 'My agents are on it.' You know what? In all my years babysitting the CIA, the DOD, and the NSA, I've never figured out what the hell 'on it' really means."

George Buckley had been assistant to the director of Homeland Security long enough to know Preston had a low threshold of tolerance for ugly surprises. Coordination of the anti-terrorist information-gathering efforts of other agencies had become an uphill battle even without the news of Mike Pallino's potential catastrophe in San Francisco.

A West Point graduate with twelve years in the CIA behind him, Preston possessed the brains, experience, and toughness to handle the job. Still, information-sharing between egocentric agencies in the intelligence community became the kind of nightmare that demanded every ounce of his capability.

"Now listen to this, George. As if that's not enough, I get a call from Jack Marshall in charge of the Bureau's Boston Field Office telling me it's actually Boston that's on it. Why Boston? You're gonna love this. Apparently the point man is some accountant who broke the terrorists' code while he was auditing a Boston corporation. That means the aversion of a national disaster now rests in the hands of a doggoned bean counter." Preston rolled his eyes and threw both hands in the air. "A David with green eyeshades sent out to fight Goliath! How damned incompetent is that?"

George rose from his desk and put his hand on Preston's shoulder. "Look, Pres, I know this whole thing's a couple of columns to the left of weird. I also know that, with your blood pressure, you need to calm down, or

San Francisco's going to become the least of your worries. Now, I received the same message you did. I've already dispatched some CIA agents, as well as a few of our guys, like I know you would have wanted. They're on their way out there now."

Preston shook his head. "George, what in the hell are a few FBI agents going to accomplish? All I'm seeing is a disorganized mess."

"Pres, I know you want everything to be run through the Terrorist Threat Integration Center. I know how you want DHS to have more control over TTIC. Look, there are two major problems with that. One, DHS simply doesn't have the analytical capability to handle this kind of task. Two, the FBI and the CIA are still in the best position to sort out intelligence input data whether we like it or not."

Preston slammed the email down on the desk and whirled to face his assistant. "Yeah, and that's problem number three, George. The FBI still hasn't made the transition from a law enforcement body to a counter-intelligence agency. Oh yeah, I know they've established an Office of Intelligence. And guess what? Half of them are still operating under the old J. Edgar Hoover G-man philosophy, and the other half wouldn't recognize a terrorist plot if they tripped over it. Case in point: a damned accountant figured it out for them. And still the CIA is geared toward secrecy in its foreign operations with absolutely no legal domestic jurisdiction, and no incentive to share intelligence information."

George perched on the edge of his desk and looked up at his still-pacing boss. "I realize that. The problem is that our whole defense mechanism has historically been focused on threats beyond our shores. Homeland protection has been the domain of civil law enforcement agencies operating pretty much independently. We've made substantial progress since 2001, but this whole thing isn't going where it needs to be overnight."

Preston pulled up a chair, sat down, put his elbows on his knees and rested his chin on his cupped fists. "The President doesn't see it that way. And frankly, neither do I. Overnight has come and gone. We need nationwide coordination enough to cover three hundred million people, fifty states, three thousand sixty-six counties, and God knows how many municipalities. And you know what? We're still arguing over what our infrastructure is."

George stepped over to a six square-foot pull-down map of the United States. "Look here, Pres. We have seaports all over the perimeter of this country." He swept his finger in a one hundred and eighty degree arc around the shoreline of the country. "The numbers people in our statistics group tell me we docked two hundred and thirty thousand ships and five billion tons of cargo last year. Want to know why our infrastructure is in question? Less than three percent of that cargo gets inspected."

Preston Anderson drew a deep breath, stood up and walked over to the map, released it back up out of sight and sat down on the edge of George's desk. "Then I suggest we make an investment."

George raised his eyebrows. "An investment?"

"Exactly. We invest in new capabilities. Like efficient mechanisms for allocation of intelligence and counterterrorism resources."

"Fine, Pres, you've just redefined homeland security. Now, how do we pay for it?"

"Hell, I don't know. All I know is if we don't we're as vulnerable as a squirrel in a rattler's den. Right now we can't even set up a successful internal computer system. The FBI just blew a six-figure expenditure on one that still doesn't work. I tell you, George, if we don't get our cyberspace act together we're going to have Golden Gate Bridge jihads all over the place pretty soon. Cyberspooks, terrorists, and white-collar scam artists have raised the bar on criminal activity, and we're simply not prepared to deal with it."

George put up his hand. "Well, maybe we aren't. We can't do anything about that right now. We're calling in all the resources we can from our San Francisco field office, and we've sent out the most knowledgeable agents we can from this end. We'll have to hope it's enough."

"Okay, George, keep me informed on this mess. I have to brief the President in half an hour, and we still don't know when or how this attack on the bridge is supposed to occur. And the thing is, it's not just any old bridge. This one's an American icon. If it goes down, the United States loses a ton of worldwide respect we can't afford to lose."

Preston started out the door, and stopped to turn toward his assistant. "By the way, Jack said this accountant, whoever he is, also discovered the terrorists were scamming money out of the corporation and sending it somewhere. Have you heard any more about that?"

"No, I haven't. Only that the president of the company went ballistic and shut down all the bank accounts except payroll. Dan Roberts is on his way up to Boston now, so we should hear more later on today. I'll let you know as soon as we learn something."

126

"Phoebe, get in here! Where the hell is Milton?" Mac's voice echoed all the way to the computer room.

Phoebe leaped from her chair and flew into Mac's office on a dead run. "Yes, sir, I'm right here."

"Damn it, Phoebe, Agent Pallino just dropped a bomb on me. And another agent from some federal organization is on his way over here. Did you know about this? I mean, about what Fadhil's done?"

"No, sir. I know Milton got pretty excited about something he found. He tore out of here with Mr. Pallino before I could ask him about it. What did Mr. Fadhil do?"

"He damned near wrecked this company, that's what he did. He about stole me blind, by God." Mac leaned forward and put his face in his hands.

Phoebe came around behind Mac's desk and laid a hand on his shoulder. She wanted to give him a comforting hug, but wasn't sure it would be appropriate for a staff accountant to hug a CEO. "Oh, Mr. Mac, I'm sorry. I was afraid something bad was going on, although I never thought Mr. Fadhil would ever do anything like that."

Mac reached up and patted Phoebe's hand. He looked like he was trying to force a smile that wouldn't come. "Well, he did. I've lost more than money. I lost the man I would have trusted with my life. More than that, I trusted him with my *company*. God, I can't believe this."

Images raced through Phoebe's mind while she tried to think of what to say. She knew she should have done something to prepare Mac for all this and hadn't. There had been warning signs all over: Milton's insistence that sales and cash collections didn't match; discounts given when they shouldn't have been; unusual invoice numbers; smelly stuff in a vacated locker; and the attack on both her and Milton.

It all made sense. The wimp she used to looked down on had been right. The idol she'd looked up to turned out to be a scummy crook who'd hurt a nice man who trusted him. She leaned over and hugged Mac. "It'll be okay, Mr. Mac. I'm sure Mike and Milton can fix it." She patted his shoulder and could feel tears welling up in her own eyes.

Chapter 21

Dan Roberts waited for Mac McCleod to calm down. He'd witnessed emotional collapses before when people discovered they'd been scammed. Mac's ranting and raving had evolved into head-in-hands despair which lasted long enough to suggest the involvement of more than just money.

"Mr. McCleod," Dan said, "I know this is an ugly mess. But I need you to pull yourself together so we can complete our investigation. Can we talk now?"

Tears streaming down his cheeks, Mac raised his head. "How the hell could this have happened? He was a son to me. I'd made preparations to hand over my company to him. My *whole company*, damn it!"

"Yes, sir, I know. Believe me, you're not the only victim in this. I'm afraid I'll have to ask you some difficult ques—"

"I want to know how." Mac stood and slammed his fist on his desk top. "By God, I want to know how this could have happened without my knowing about it."

"So do we, sir. Ali Fadhil's technique was clever; although far inferior to the best we've seen around the country. That it could have been prevented is why I need to ask you some questions. Now, the fraudulent activities were discovered during what I understand is your company's first audit. Is that correct?"

"Yes."

"Is there a reason your company had not been audited before? I mean, since the scam has been going on for several years, prior audits might have mitigated the damage…or perhaps prevented any losses at all."

There was no response.

"Mr. McCleod?"

Mac wiped his eyes. *Mitigated the damage.* As though some heartbreak would have been acceptable if it weren't too much. "I heard you. We didn't need an audit until the bank required one. It's a privately held company and I own all the stock. I don't get it. We had everything in perfect shape. Our bank accounts all balanced, our inventory losses were minimal, and my people knew their jobs. We make good money." Mac glared at Dan. "So did my damned CFO, apparently."

"How involved were you, personally, in the day-to-day finances?" Dan's expression changed from compassionate to serious. "I have to ask even though I know you didn't participate in the theft."

"Hell, not enough, I guess. I trusted him. How much did he take?"

"About four million and change, according to our forensics exam. Did you review any of the accounting transactions during those two or three years?"

Mac shook his head. He stepped over to the window and stared out for a few moments, then turned to face Dan. "Only the summary reports Ali prepared for me. And, of course, his monthly bank reconciliations. They looked okay to me. So how did he manage to make off with so much and no one noticed it? You said it wasn't the slickest operation you guys had seen."

"Perhaps I should have said it wasn't as professional as it could have been," Dan responded. My associate is in the process of preparing a detailed report. You'll receive a copy as soon as we complete this investigation. The gist of it is that the company's copies of the sales invoices matched the cash deposit slips and both showed that your customers took their discounts. Yet, in fact, your CFO billed and collected the full amount with no discounts."

Mac shook his head. "And then what?"

"He then deposited the full amount into a bank account you apparently didn't know about, and transferred only the discounted balance as a deposit into your regular company bank account. He did the same in reverse with the discounts your company was supposed to receive from its vendors. There's more involved, of course. That's just the short version. I'm curious as to why you didn't become suspicious when you saw the deposits coming from a bank you didn't recognize, instead of directly from your customers."

Mac leaned back and stared at the ceiling for a moment before he responded. "Ali said we'd get a better interest rate if we maintained a minimum balance there until the next batch of customer checks came in. Then he'd make a lump-sum transfer to our regular bank account. I figured he knew more about that kind of thing than I did. Damn him. We'll recover, although it made a permanent hole in our employee profit-sharing fund. Damn it to hell. He hurt all of us. The FBI's after him, I hope."

"We'll get him. I'm sure you'll be called to testify."

Mac threw a hopeful glance at Dan. "Any chance we'll ever see any of that four million again?"

Dan shook his head. "Not unless you have one hell of a far-sighted clause in your insurance policy. Now, on another matter, are you at all aware of the Israeli connection?"

Mac frowned. "The what?"

"Israel. Apparently some of the stolen money was earmarked for political applications above and beyond the Golden Gate Bridge. Our forensics people just now uncovered a document referencing a plot, or something, against Israel."

Dan took his turn at the window overlooking the loading dock, stared out for a moment, and turned back. "Your employees said they knew nothing about that, so I suppose I shouldn't be surprised you didn't either. By the way, speaking of your employees, we've had to arrest two of them on suspicion that they served as accomplices. Personally, I think any charges will be dropped as frivolous. I just thought you ought to know about it."

Mac came out of his chair. "What the hell are you talking about?"

"Your receptionist, Trudy Foster, admitted to a sexual relationship dating back two years with Fadhil. Phoebe Denton admitted to having personally recorded many of Fadhil's transactions. She also acknowledged receiving instructions from him to provide as little assistance as possible to the auditor. Were you aware of all this?"

"No, damn it. I can assure you those two girls are completely innocent of any deliberate involvement in this scam of his. You can bank on that."

Dan hesitated for a moment, as though contemplating whether to suppress his thoughts or release them. "Like you banked four million on Fadhil's reliability?"

Mac glared at him in silence.

"Sorry, that was uncalled for. It's just that I'm having a tough time trying to understand how an executive who successfully guided his corporation through a competitive jungle could have been so oblivious to its financial footprints. Anyway, I agree with you, and I've already vouched for their lack of complicity. They'll be asked a few more questions, and will most likely be released this afternoon. Let me make a couple of suggestions before I leave,

130

Mr. McCleod. Do a thorough background check on your next CFO, and become more involved in the day-to-day operations. Please stay where we can reach you. We'll talk again."

Mac wiped his eye with the back of his hand and watched Roberts disappear through the door. His thoughts found their way back to the bright young University of California graduate he'd taken under his wing. He slumped into his chair and lowered his face in his hands.

* * * * * *

Milton turned in his seat to catch a glimpse of what other passengers were doing on the crowded United Flight 321 to San Francisco. "Mike, I wonder what all these people would do if they knew what's going on with that bridge."

"Well, a few of them probably couldn't wait to get there and watch. The rest would most likely demand the pilot find some other place to land. Don't worry about it. We have work to do. So grab something for us to eat while I dig into my stack of invoices."

Milton shook his head. "You sure you want to eat that stuff? Those little prepackaged snacks are only shadows of what I'm told meals used to be before airline customer satisfaction surrendered to earnings per share."

Mike offered an affirmative nod.

Flight attendants squeezed a beverage cart down the narrow aisle between rows of occupant-jammed seats. When the cart stopped by Milton's seat, he took two soft drinks, four snacks, and gave Mike half.

After the snack cart moved on, Milton leaned forward and poured himself into the task of examining more invoices, and Mike didn't appear to be getting anywhere in his effort to decipher the numbers on the RFPs he'd gathered from Ellie's files.

Mike shook his head. "Milt, these numbers don't make any sense, even when I match them up with the narrative in a beta-numeric style like you did on the invoices. I didn't have time to run them through our computer sleuths back at the office. Any suggestions?"

Milton closed his eyes for a moment, as though the question required some deep thought. "Okay, try this. Pair the first number with the first letter in the narrative, the second number with the second letter and so on. If that doesn't produce something then try some other configuration."

"Like what? This stuff is like an alphanumeric Ouija board."

"Oh, try pairing the first number with the first letter of the first sentence, the second number with something in the second sentence. You know, just kind of play around with it. By the way, these invoice messages are turning out to be mostly about money transfers. Still, I found a couple of invoices that make me think this whole bridge thing might get nastier than I thought."

"What do you mean?" Mike asked.

Milton handed one to Mike. "Well, look. This invoice refers to some kind of alliance between Fadhil and an outfit called MS-13. I guess they're going to be working together on it. Ever hear of an MS-13?"

Although Mike's jaw didn't actually drop, his stunned expression conveyed more than just bad news. His face tightened, and his surprise evolved into a look of consternation before he responded.

"Damn it. Are you sure it says that?"

"Absolutely. So, what does it mean?"

"It means the size of this whole mess just doubled. MS-13 is reputed to be the most violent street gang in the world. What kind of alliance is it?"

"Doesn't say. Only that money is available to pay them. Maybe that's why Fadhil went out there, because he's the money man. I guess the only good news is we just discovered where all that scam money of his will go."

"Nothing about this is good, Milt. What else did you find?"

"Not much. I'm almost all the way through these documents, and the only reference of any relevance is to some engineering assistant named Nahid accompanying Fadhil. Better get back to your RFPs. You only have six of them. Weren't there any more?"

"Probably, but I couldn't very well roll into Ellie's office with a wheelbarrow. And Nahid is a female name, by the way. Here, you work on these RFP's while I get on the cell phone and alert our San Francisco field office that we have big trouble."

Mike shoved his paperwork back to Milton, who dove into the RFP's with his usual zeal for working out complicated puzzles.

The flight attendant spoke over the intercom to call the passengers' attention to the overhead sign about fastening seat belts. Before she finished her announcement, Milton waved his hand in the air. "Got it, Mike. Hang on a minute while I work it through."

Minutes passed while the intercom barked out a series of connecting flights during the aircraft's slow descent. Milton turned to Mike with a look that signaled more bad news. "Okay, the rest of this stuff is mostly about Fadhil. But there's one repeated word that seems to be used interchangeably with Ellie, your wife's name. I'm afraid you're not going to like it."

"To hell with whether I like it or not. What's the word?"

"Nahid."

Silence... broken only by the grinding noise of the plane's hydraulics forcing the wheels into landing position. Mike's facial expression changed from puzzled to sad to angry resignation. His Snow White Ellie had turned into a witch who'd used him. At that moment he wasn't sure who he hated most: the wife who wasn't real, or the terrorists who were. A local weather announcement by the flight attendant crackled out over the intercom before Mike responded through clenched teeth.

"Okay, what else did you find?" Mike tried to ignore the aching he felt inside.

"Nothing. Look, I know how you must feel, Mike. I felt the same when I found out what Bremer did to me. I'm so sorry about Ellie. If there's anything I can—"

"You can stop referring to her as Ellie," Mike snapped, his eyes watering along with a tightening of his jaw. "Ellie's dead. This woman is Nahid, and that's her name from here on out, whoever the hell she is." Mike rubbed his glistening eyes with the back of his hand and turned away.

He struggled to suppress the memory of the most enchanting woman he'd ever seen. It wouldn't go away; the image of Ellie perched on the bow of his rented sailboat, shorts tight around her hips, dark hair blowing in the wind. He'd always known she was better than he deserved — a Helen he'd stolen from Sparta, a goddess who would become his queen of Troy. He hadn't seen the wooden horse outside the gates, and he cursed himself for it.

Silence prevailed again, interrupted by the soft thud of the wheels touching down on the runway. Mike slammed his right fist into his left hand. What seemed like a hundred memories of Ellie slashed and burned their way through his mind while the aircraft taxied up to the gate. The initial shock of it all now began to evolve into alternating feelings of hurt, anger, and betrayal.

* * * * * *

Two FBI agents from the San Francisco office met them at the end of the exit ramp. Mike made the introductions. "Milt, this is Wade Rollins, a long-time friend of mine from college. Wade, this is Milt Pringle, who broke the infamous code by himself. And I'll beat up anyone who calls him a bean counter."

Wade grinned and pumped Milton's hand. "So you're the guy who called this meeting. Nice to meet you. We've heard good things about you already. By the way, we received an email from our Boston office. Those two banks you couldn't get statements from are correspondent banks tied in somehow to a source in Saudi Arabia. I'll give you one guess as to where those funds skimmed from Metalcraft went."

"How can that be, Mike?" Milton asked. "I thought we closed that stuff down after September 11th."

Mike shook his head. "It happens. Remember the Riggs Bank scandal in D.C., and the infamous Bosnian Defense Fund fiasco where several U.S. banks operated as unwitting conduits for terrorist money? Now you and I have a scandal of our own."

Wade tapped Mike on the shoulder. "Mike, we also learned from your Boston forensics people that two of the six vendors involved in those coded invoices are phony post office boxes. The other four are real business entities in upstate New York. However, they don't do anything, as far as your field office knows, except operate as large storage facilities. They're apparently owned by a Mr. Benjamin. Does that name mean anything to you?"

"No. Never heard of him."

Wade remained silent for a few moments as though he were waiting for the right time to bring up the subject. "Mike, answer a couple of questions for me," he said. "How come it took so long to get to the bottom of this following Washington's initial warning several weeks ago? And does anyone have any idea when this alleged attack will occur?"

Mike paused and shook his head. "I hate to say this because I know it's exactly what Jack Marshall must be thinking right now. I guess the fault is mine for taking so long. If I'd been more tuned in to forensics I might have figured it out myself a hell of a lot sooner. As it is, I'm grateful that Milt did. So far we've found nothing in the clues we've uncovered that would identify

134

John Chaplick

the timing. Since the explosives have been missing for a couple of weeks from their storage at Metalcraft, I'm surmising the attack is imminent. What's most likely holding the bad guys up is the logistical problems in deciding how best to blow the bridge."

Wade pulled a piece of paper from his pocket and handed it to Mike. "Well, according to Milt's little write-up, this Fadhil guy began planning for it several years ago. Makes you wonder," Wade continued, "why no one at the company became suspicious in all that time."

Mike nodded. "Yeah, I thought the same thing. If you knew the company's CEO, though, you'd understand. He's not much into the day-to-day finances. He's more of a hands-on old fashioned manufacturing kind of fellow. The real problem was that he trusted that damned financial maggot like a son. Swallowed every bit of garbage his scumbag CFO fed him. Add to that the cleverness of Fadhil's coding scheme and you have at least one plausible answer to your question."

Wade grinned. "Okay. Well, we have a full day ahead of us tomorrow. There's a skeleton crew poking around up there on the bridge now. Of course, without a well-defined action plan, it's pretty much like looking for a needle in a haystack. I've called a meeting for tomorrow morning with every agency and bridge guru I can find. We'd damn well better zero in on an action plan then because I'm not waiting any longer. I'm sending our first team up onto that bridge on a full-court press before sundown tomorrow, whether we have a plan or not. You and Milt stay at my house tonight and we'll get started early in the morning."

Mike nodded. Maybe tomorrow's work would be intense enough to take his mind off the ache he felt inside.

135

Chapter 22

The San Francisco FBI Field Office agents called it a strategy meeting. It turned out to be more like a brainstorming session. The number of unknown variables had become so large no one could possibly have formulated a single strategy. Representatives from the FBI, DHS, CIA, the Highway District, the National Guard, and the local police force filed into the room — all asking if anyone had any ideas.

After the introductions and preliminary get-acquainted small talk, Wade Rollins stepped up to the podium and opened the meeting. "Okay, I'll give it to you straight and simple. Four terrorists have aligned themselves with God knows how many MS-13 local gangsters to blow up the Golden Gate Bridge. We have twenty-two policemen and six of our agents out there patrolling the structure and its access ramps right now. The rest of us will join them as soon as we can develop an action plan that makes sense."

Wade paused to scan the audience. "We don't know when the terrorists will strike, where on the bridge they'll strike, or what they all look like — except for their leader and two guys we think are his assistants. The file being passed around to you now includes their pictures and what little we know about the explosives. That's the bad news. The good news is, thanks to Mike Pallino and this young accountant sitting next to me, we know about the plot. The terrorists probably don't realize we know, or they would have blown the thing by now. That's a definite plus."

Wade stepped away from the podium with the mike in his hand and moved closer to the group, already shifting uneasily in their seats. "So, given the information we have, let's take this one step at a time. Pete here, from the bomb squad, has, I believe, correctly concluded that no one needs more than one or two people to plant a few bombs. Since our data indicates the involvement of a large international gang of criminals, we must conclude they plan to set off a number of charges. From Milt's decoding we know they're using HDX, or some variant of it. I don't have to tell you guys how bad *that* news is."

The rustle of people moving about in their seats signaled an increase in the apprehension level, and reflected the group's growing awareness of the dark possibilities.

Wade scanned the audience again as though to make sure he now had everyone's full attention. "As to determining where and how the explosives are likely to be placed," he continued, "we need to review how this bridge is constructed. It's a suspension bridge which, in this case, means it's hung from two thirty-six inch diameter cables, strung for about seven thousand six hundred and fifty feet over the top of two large towers anchored in the water. So, if you wanted to blow the bridge, the best way to do it is to knock the two cables off the towers. Or, sever all the hundreds of vertical suspender cables which hang from the main cables and attach to the bridge itself. Or, collapse the two towers. That's one hell of a lot of variables. Okay, talk to me all you experts. I need answers."

After a prolonged silence, one of the policemen spoke up. "Mr. Rollins, isn't there a fourth option? I mean, in the form of simply blowing the main span itself so that when it splits, the two halves will swing downward. That will put enough stress on the suspender cables to cause them to part, allowing the two halves to drop into the bay."

One of the District representatives stood and raised his hand. "That's a possibility, but we're pretty sure if that happened too few of the suspender cables would part to allow the broken span to fall. In fact, you could blow a large hole in the span and the cables would continue to hold up everything around the hole."

An FBI agent threw his hand in the air. "Wade, I thought of a fifth option which may be way out in left field. We all seem to be focusing on setting the charges on top of the bridge. What about approaching it from below by boat and attaching explosives to the base of the two foundations that anchor it?"

"Good question, Devon," Wade said as he moved back and forth in front of the group. "We've ruled that out for several reasons. One, the currents, wind, and tide forces are strong enough to make it too dicey to maneuver a boat close enough and hold it there long enough to set the charges. Two, the moss, slime, and sea algae covering the base of the foundation at the water level would make it virtually impossible for an attacker to gain enough footing to place the charges."

Terry Atkins, an agent who looked like he'd be as much at home in a barroom brawl as he would investigating terrorists, spoke up from a perspective which didn't surprise anyone who knew him. "Wade, why don't these Allah-seeking bastards just ram the damned thing with a boatload of this HDX? It worked pretty well on the U.S.S. *Cole*."

"We've thought about that, too, Terry," Wade replied. "Our terrorism experts and our bomb squad seem to concur on the reasons why not. First, the way the bridge is structured it doesn't present a large, solid wall of any kind. That means it's like a bunch of frames hitched together. Therefore there's no guarantee that ramming it would propel the force of the explosion in exactly the right direction. Second, they wouldn't need all these guys if they were just going to ram it."

"So, where does all this leave us?" one of the agents asked.

Wade paused, glanced around the room and walked back to the podium. "Okay, here's where we are. Attempts to blow the span or the foundation most likely won't work. In order to knock the overhead cables off their saddle joints, someone would have to climb five hundred feet from the roadway to the top of the towers. We'd spot 'em before they even began that climb. That leaves us with only one option, and that's to topple one or both of the two towers by zeroing in on them from the bridge span itself. Anyone have any idea whether or not this can be done?"

A specialist spoke up from the back of the room. "Yeah, it can be done. And it's the only way to go if these jihad people are working under a tight time schedule. Before I joined the bomb squad I spent most of my career dynamiting holes in masses of solid rock, working with highway construction crews. You need to collapse only one of the towers, although you've got to do it right."

An FBI agent in the back of the room raised his hand. "So, then why do they need all those gangsters if they're only going to blow one tower?"

"Well, maybe they plan to collapse both towers at the same time," another agent commented.

After a moment of awkward silence Milton put down the pad on which he'd been scribbling, and rose to his feet. He addressed the group with a not-surprising stammer, given that he'd never spoken to a large group before. "Gentlemen, I...uh...I don't know anything about explosives or bridges. I

138

mean, well…my job as an accountant has always been to make ends meet, not blow them apart, so—"

A roar of spontaneous laughter erupted from the group. It broke the heavy air of tension, and had the apparent effect of settling Milton's nerves.

"Well," Milton continued, "while I was listening to everyone, a horrible thought came to mind. What if the terrorists plan on placing enough explosives to pop a sufficient number of the suspender strands to drop the entire bridge span into the water all at once?" He sat down again and glanced at Mike.

A discomforting silence permeated the room while the attendees looked at each other, then at Wade, as if groping for an answer. No one seemed to have one.

The director of the Bridge Highway and Transportation District finally broke the silence. "Mr. Pringle, your horrible thought suddenly triggered one of my own. I hadn't made the connection until now, but last week one of my draftsmen, who worked on the maintenance and retrofit of the bridge, was murdered. We still don't know why. We think it may have been a prostitute, since the man had been seen several times in the company of an attractive woman. Anyway, we—"

"Was the woman tall, about five-eight, athletic-looking, dark skinned, and sexy?" Mike interjected. "With raven-black hair? And are any of your blueprints of the bridge missing, or out of order?"

"Ah… Mr. Pallino, I have no idea about the prints. The woman definitely fits your description, according to my sources. Why?"

Milton leaned forward and put his face in his hands on the table, as though he didn't want to see what might come next.

Mike stood, looked toward the window, then turned back to face his audience. He let out a deep sigh. "Guys, I hate to tell you this, but the terrorists have the blueprint, and they have a civil engineer who knows exactly where to place the charges. I'm convinced Milt's right. I believe they *are* planning to use a number of explosives."

Wade slammed his research documents down on the podium. "Damn it, Mike. Where are you getting all this? Who said anything about professional engineers or stolen blueprints? Look, if you know something we don't, you have an obligation to tell us. Well, do you?"

Milton raised his head and turned to face Wade. "I'm sorry, I neglected to mention this. My decoding actually did refer to a female engineer. The encryption indicated she was in possession of a blueprint. Sorry, I should have shared this earlier."

The second lie he'd ever told produced an expression of satisfaction on his face. Milton didn't look at Mike, didn't see the look of relief spreading across the agent's face, or notice his warm smile. Mike nodded in the direction of his accounting ally as if to acknowledge there were times when the truth should be bent a little, and occasions when an outright lie becomes the lesser of the evils.

The attendees huddled again. After group consensus appeared to have been reached, Wade dispatched them, in selected small groups, to their respective assignments on the bridge. Specific instructions were issued for each of them and for the twenty-eight men already out there. The overall framework of a strategy had been drafted. The specifics of when and how remained undefined.

Wade closed the meeting with a prophetic summation. "Gentlemen, we're about to play a deadly game of hide-and-seek on a giant erector set. Good luck to every one of us."

Mike scooped up his documents, stuffed them into a folder, and breathed a deep sigh. Jack Marshall had called him "the last of the twentieth-century dinosaurs who still couldn't spell forensics." Jack might have been right, he thought. Maybe this entire dilemma could have been solved long ago if Mike had only managed to climb out of his cocoon and embrace twenty-first century technology.

Chapter 23

Most of the pedestrian traffic on the bridge consisted of Wade Rollins' crew combing the structure like a colony of ants searching for food. The anxious teams on the bridge endured boredom, dampness, and bone chilling gusts of wind around the clock. Two days, and still no sign of terrorist activity. Below, the city's population went about its business unaware of the imminent clash of forces that would test the ability of the bridge, as well as the nation, to defend itself in an unprecedented kind of warfare.

An hour after midnight on the third day a dark colored SUV appeared at each end of the bridge. One entered the access ramp from the San Francisco side, the other from the Marin side, each followed by a fourteen-wheel truck, which stopped at the beginning of the entrance ramp in position to block any further access to the bridge.

Agent Bill Swank saw them first, two men leaping out of the SUV at the base of the northern tower — one of them with a rocket launcher slung over his shoulder, and the other with an AK-47. Firearm in his right hand, two-way radio in his left, he charged toward them while he barked the alert. Terry Atkins acknowledged the call and raced toward the vehicle at the other end of the bridge.

Within moments after Carlos' men rushed from the two trucks onto the bridge, the sound of gunfire echoed from one end to the other. The staccato of semi-automatic firearms accompanied muzzle flashes that punched holes in the dark like fireflies.

Milton's orders from Wade had been to leave the bridge immediately following completion of each of his runs as a food, water, and equipment bearer. His midnight run caught him in the middle of the firefight. Unable to get off the bridge, and with nowhere to go, Milton found Mike and struggled to keep up with him during their sprint toward the center.

"Stay behind me and keep low," Mike shouted at him.

Milton's breathing grew harder as they picked up speed. "Mike, I opened your case and retrieved the gun you took away from me before the flight. I have it in my pocket. What do you want me to do?"

"Keep it there, damn it. Don't even think about using it. If I'm hit I want you to drop down out of sight. Get behind a lamppost stanchion. Find a guardrail or something. The nearest damn cover available. You got that?"

A large man came out of nowhere before Milton could answer. It happened so fast the startled accountant barely had time to draw a gasp of air. Mike whirled and fired once into the man's chest. The man fell backward a few feet from them. A thin stream of blood trickled from the corner of his mouth.

"Move, Milt. Let's go." Mike jerked him away from the sprawling figure in the red bandana. By the end of the next hundred-yard dash the ache in Milton's side made him acutely aware of his inferior physical condition.

"Get down flat!" Mike screamed. He pushed Milton down beside a walkway stanchion. Exhausted, the frightened accountant dropped face down and never saw the two gunmen emerge from the shadows. Two quick shots from Mike's Glock made the dark figures disappear.

"Behind you!"

The warning shout came from an agent neither Mike nor Milton had seen. Mike spun around, dropped to one knee beside a prostrate Milton, and fired again directly over the accountant's head. Disoriented by the deafening sound, Milton groped for his glasses. The faceless form behind them fell backward. Milton recovered his glasses barely in time to see only the man's AK-47 spin to the pavement.

Mike pulled his young ally up by his collar and they continued their run. By this time the bridge was alive with gunfire and shouting. The whirling blades of two helicopters descending to lower SWAT teams onto the bridge added to the chaos. "C'mon, Milt, you're slowing us down," Mike bellowed. "I don't want you to get lost."

In the ensuing confusion neither of them had time to notice the bomb squads scurrying back and forth, disarming or tossing into the water whatever explosive charges they could seize. Absorbed in his two-way radio conversation, Mike didn't see the dark green SUV pull over behind him.

Caught in the crosscurrents of disorientation and fear, Milton froze while he watched the dark-haired woman leap out of the vehicle and charge toward him with her firearm leveled at Mike. Milton snapped back into a state of awareness, jerked the Taurus .38 from his pants pocket, and disobeyed rules for the third time in his life.

Still shaking, he fired twice at her dark form, missing both times.

His shots diverted her attention from Mike. She swung her arm toward Milton and fired. Milton arched backward, spun, and fell to the concrete, face down on his glasses which crumbled under him.

Mike whirled around again and faced Nahid. In one fleeting moment of desperation, a flashing image of a pretty girl running toward him in white shorts, on a marina long ago, clashed unbearably with his instincts as a federal agent. In the dim light, Mike wasn't sure, but he thought he saw an expression of shocked recognition in the woman's eyes just before he fired off the next shot. The bullet entered Nahid's cranium creating a small hole in her forehead, and exited through a larger one at the back of her skull, taking gray matter with it. Moments later, two other agents paused in apparent confusion at the sight of a tearful Mike Pallino kneeling over his beloved Ellie.

* * * * * *

The shooting had begun seconds after Ali dropped off the last team. He glanced over his shoulder toward the muzzle flashes and considered his options. He hadn't counted on having anything less than five minutes — plenty of time to run the SUV to the end of the bridge, out the unblocked exit, and be on his way. A quick stop to pick up his check, then out of the city, out of the country.

Ali pushed the accelerator to the floor. Rubber squealed and the SUV hit sixty at the same time agent Kowalski's shot blew out the right front tire. The SUV swerved, bounced over a short guard rail, and slammed against a stanchion. With the vehicle trapped between the edge of the bridge on the right and agent Kowalski approaching from the left, Ali elected to exit through the passenger door and make a run for it.

Footing made slick by the evening mist combined with poor visibility to eliminate any chance for solid traction on Ali's first step down from the vehicle. He slipped, pitched forward, and grabbed the only rail that stood between him and the dark waters of San Francisco Bay hundreds of feet below. While he hung struggling to get a good grip on the rail with both hands, he could feel the cold night air penetrate every part of his body. Ahmed had counseled him often that, to a member of the Mujahhidin, death is the ultimate reward. With the growing numbness in his hands, the words now rang hollow. His brain filled with visions of his imminent plunge. In seconds he would assess the accuracy of the rumor that a fall from the iconic bridge brings instant death, and drowning is never an issue.

With his body swinging helplessly in the wind Ali could see only the rail, and neither the falling Kowalski nor the bandana-clad man who shot him. Juan Mendoza leaned over and wrapped a large hand around Ali's left wrist only seconds after Ali's right hand relinquished its grip on the moist rail. With what seemed to Ali like the strength of two, the man hauled Ali to safety. Once on firm footing, a gasping Ali Fadhil rubbed his hands and turned to his rescuer. *"Gracias,"* he said, his sides heaving.

"Gracias a Dios, amigo." The man replied with a smile that revealed a row of mixed white and gold teeth. "Where is your woman?" he asked, and disappeared into the night without waiting for an answer.

Disoriented and unsure which end of the bridge had been his original destination, Ali ran toward what looked like the closest exit. Out of breath and still shaking, he felt lucky to slip through unseen at the San Francisco end. He hid, shivering, in a stand of coastal sage scrubs — as good a place as any to wait until dawn, when he could pick up the check and make his way to the airport.

Ali Fadhil hadn't felt so miserable since his Cairo days when he stood trembling in the cold beside his father, holding out his cup for coins that would ease the consciences of rich passers-by. He hunkered down in the sage scrubs and rubbed his torso violently in a futile effort to ward off the night chill that penetrated deep into his bones. His eyes glued to the bridge above, Ali listened to the gunfire and the low-pitched growl of the helicopter engines. With a little luck and the blessings of Allah, it would be only a matter of time before the deafening sound of explosions and the terrible wrenching of steel signaled the success of his work over the past three years. One way or the other his past was behind him, and dawn would bring a new life.

* * * * * *

A thundering explosion two hundred yards away interrupted Mike's bereavement. Concrete, steel, and shards of wire cable spewed out in every direction. The great bridge shuddered under its force, and then again under a second blast. For one horrific moment only the sickening sound of crumbling concrete and grinding steel could be heard. After a brief moment of silence an eerie whooshing sound drew attention to a thirty-foot section of the main span, twisted into a shapeless mass, plunging into the Bay.

The firefight continued until almost dawn on both sides of the ugly hole, from one end of the bridge to the other. By the time the terrorists surrendered, the death count amounted to twenty-four attackers and sixteen of the bridge's defenders, one of whom fell from the edge of the bridge, body unrecovered. The "erector set" configuration of the bridge localized the damage. Officials estimated one lane would be closed for almost a year, and that within three days traffic would resume in the others. The bomb squad announced they expected to find and disable any unexploded charges within twelve hours.

Thick early morning fog rolled in over the Bay. Its soft, white pillows obscured all of the iconic structure except the tops of its bright, orange towers, giving it the mystical aura it had always deserved. An integral part of a kaleidoscope of squawking gulls, mournful foghorn blasts, and Lilliputian tugs, the great bridge still remained majestically aloof.

The night surrendered to dawn, and the sun melted away the gentle white veil to reveal the grandeur of a colossus which, in a way, had been a participant in its own survival. In a panoramic contrast of forms and colors, the bright orange span stretched across a gray expanse of turbulent water. It connected an alabaster San Francisco at one end with the pastel-green hills of Marin at the other. Wade Rollins had been right. The "erector set" configuration of the structure had localized the damage. In the final analysis, the San Francisco Chronicle reported, the wounded bridge had won.

Chapter 24

Mike carried Milton to the ambulance and rode with him to the Orthopedic Trauma Center of San Francisco General Hospital. Attendants whisked the unconscious and bleeding accountant into the operating room where surgeons addressed first the hemorrhaging and then the damage to his internal organs. Mike notified Milton's parents and paced back and forth outside the operating room while the pulsing blue and yellow lights of electronic monitors inside recorded the surgeons' frantic struggle to save the young accountant's life. The horizontal pressure-waveforms on the screen tracked the deterioration in his cardiovascular system.

After an hour of frantic surgical effort, one of the assisting nurses came out of the operating room and approached Mike. She pulled her face mask down over her chin so she could talk, and tried to force a conciliatory smile. "Mr. Pallino, the chief surgeon asked me to tell you that this is going to take some time. We'll keep you posted on your friend's condition. In the meantime, why don't you get some rest?"

"Yeah, okay. I could use some shuteye. I'll find a chair somewhere and take a nap. Now, what's the prognosis? I need to know."

The nurse shook her head and gave up on the smile. "It's too soon to tell, sir. We're doing all we can." She turned away and disappeared into the OR.

Mike slumped into a chair, swamped by waves of guilt that he felt sure had waited impatiently to punish him ever since Jack Marshall issued his prophetic warning about Milt's involvement. Face in his hands, Mike sobbed uncontrollably until fatigue came to his rescue and eased him into a deep sleep.

Peaceful at first, his dreams gradually morphed into a macabre, paranormal state in which Mike saw himself standing on the edge of a cliff. He turned away from the edge to face a dense forest oozing a thick fog that

146

billowed in all directions. Three dark figures emerged from the fog and walked toward him in single file.

The first, a sad-looking old man with grease stains on his face and denim shirt, slowed in front of him, turned, but didn't stop. Mike recognized his father. "You left and never came home," the man said. "I waited for you as long as I could, then I had to close up shop and go." He walked past Mike to the edge of the cliff and stepped off. Mike felt a familiar pang of guilt in his chest. His mournful scream vanished into the emptiness.

The second, a beautiful woman, stopped to kiss him on the cheek. Mike could feel his attention being drawn from the sensuous lines of her long, blue evening gown to a dark, ugly hole in her forehead. She moved on to the edge of the cliff and turned back toward him. "I'm sorry," she said. She smiled, stepped over the edge, and disappeared.

Pillows of fog gathered around the feet of the third form. Mike strained his eyes to bring the slender young man into view. The man paused in front of Mike to adjust his thick, shattered glasses. He handed Mike a .38 caliber revolver, smiled, and said "I won't be needing this. Thanks for making me more than I was." Mike tried to force an apology. The words choked in his throat and blocked any sound. The young man turned away and followed the others over the edge.

Mike felt tears filling his eyes while unstoppable waves of guilt swept over him again. He raised his arm, placed the muzzle of the pistol against his temple, and contemplated the irony of the last head shot being his easiest ever.

Before he could squeeze the trigger he heard his name called out. The sound echoed from somewhere in the fog. He felt someone's firm grip on his firing arm. In silent protest Mike jerked his arm free and repositioned the steel against the side of his head. Again, the sound of his name rang in his ears. Louder, much louder and closer this time. As though in some bizarre response, the fog receded into the forest from which it had originated.

"Wake up, Mr. Pallino." The chief surgeon shook Mike's arm again. "The Pringle family is here. You need to wake up."

Mike woke, groped his way out of the chair, rubbed his eyes, and found himself face to face with a glaring Carter Bannister Pringle.

"Damn you, Pallino, how the hell did you let this happen? My son's alive and, by the grace of God, he's going to recover...or so the chief surgeon tells us. But no thanks to you."

Mike stared at the man for a moment, then turned, clasped his hands together in front of his chest, looked upward, and softly mumbled, "Thank you, God."

Angela Pringle placed her hand on Mike's shoulder. "What happened to our son was not your fault, Mr. Pallino. My husband and I have seen the early morning edition of the news. Perhaps Milton should never have been there, that's true. Now we understand how and why he was. The news media have reported him as a hero, along with you. We now realize this whole catastrophe has brought out a son we never knew. For that we thank you. Carter, Milton, and I will have to find the strength to move on. So will you."

Her husband's glare hadn't subsided. "She's right. Damn you, Pallino, I won't forgive you that easy, but she's right. You almost lost our only son, and nothing can change the suffering we've been through. You can at least do one thing. You can send me a complete write-up of this whole mess, and my son's role in it. I mean from beginning to end. And I want *your* version, not the news media's. Damn you to hell."

"Yes sir, I'll make sure you have it." Mike lowered his head again and turned away. He brought the chief surgeon in and stayed with Milton's parents for what turned out to be an hour's worth of detailed medical explanation about a slow recovery. He said another prayer, walked out, and took Wade Rollins up on his offer to drive him to the airport.

On the way Mike listened to his only cell phone message — a terse, angry call from his boss.

* * * * * *

At first Jack Marshall couldn't tell whether Preston Anderson's voice over the phone sounded angry or pleased. An interpretation of the Homeland Security head's tone could go either way. On the plus side, the iconic bridge was still standing, a fact which suggested grounds for acclaim. On the other hand, Homeland Security's protective measures, designed to prevent external attacks, had now been circumvented by a nearly-successful assault from within. Unable to see it coming, the FBI had relied on a nerdy accountant in an eleventh-hour salvage operation which left fifteen government agents dead.

"Tell me, Marshall," Anderson's voice came across calm and cold, "what exactly is there about the concept of inter-agency cooperation that you people in the Bureau don't seem to understand? Let me put that a different way. What kind of a damned jackass does it take to think he can stop a full-scale terrorist attack with nothing except a bunch of FBI clowns who can't even spell 'anti-terrorist intelligence,' let alone apply it?"

Jack rolled his eyes. "Yeah, yeah, Preston. I get it. You still think DHS is the anointed body divinely ordained to coordinate government defense of the U.S. of A. Well, guess what. It's been almost a month since Washington issued its holy proclamation about the Pakistan explosives. Know what happened during all that time? I'll tell you. Nothing, because every agency except the FBI stumbled around with its head up its ass. In the end, it was one of my agents who applied those 'anti-terrorist' measures of yours and rescued your hide from a disaster the DHS never would have been able to live down." Jack Marshall welcomed the long silence at the other end of the line even though he felt sure Preston would dredge up some kind of counter-argument.

"Jack, that's one hell of a rationalization. Especially since the guy who ultimately solved the mystery was a private-sector accountant no one ever heard of. And who was *not* one of your agents. By the way, we're all relieved that the young fellow is recovering. However, the big question bouncing around Washington is what a non-combatant was doing up there on the bridge in the first place."

Jack shook his head. He knew the question would never have been asked if that damned Pallino had obeyed orders. "Well, you can tell your friends in Washington that the accountant was, by necessity, an information conduit who simply got stuck there through no one's fault when the shooting broke out. So, if my agent hadn't the foresight to enlist the young man's involvement, the Golden Gate Bridge would now be starting to gather rust at the bottom of San Francisco Bay. Now, if all this sticks in your craw, then maybe it's time to take a page from the Bureau's book."

"I'm not going to dignify that with a response, Marshall. Okay, you win round one. Afterward, this whole thing better end with you dishing out appropriate punishment to the agent whose tardy response got all those men killed and almost snuffed out the life of that young accountant. We'll talk later. One more question, though. Did your boys ever round up the finance guru who I understand masterminded that shindig?"

Jack drew a long, deep breath. That part had all the earmarks of a bungle the FBI wasn't going to live down. "No. The man's either dead or still out there somewhere. We'll find him one way or the other." He hung up the phone, opened a file drawer, and pulled out the Washington memo that had first warned of the explosives. Feet propped up on his desk, the director turned the email over twice while he pondered the sequence of events since the apocalyptic little document had chunked its way out of his printer several weeks before. Preston had given him a hard time about how the whole affair had been handled, as had a number of his own counterparts in the Bureau.

In retrospect, there was no way the Bureau's reaction could have been any more effective. For one thing, neither the initial notice nor any of the subsequent ones provided enough information to pinpoint the anticipated location of the attack. Nor had its perpetrators been identified. For another, even the most up-to-date forensic procedures might not have unraveled the convoluted information buried in that accounting system…even if the gurus had known it was there in the first place.

All in all, then, Jack decided, Pallino had done the right thing by teaming up with a wimpy bean-counter to decipher that mess. In fact, as per Jack's prediction, maybe only a screwball like Pallino could have stumbled into a feasible solution. In the end, if Mike hadn't committed the unconscionable mistake of dragging the accountant up there on the bridge, this whole debate could have ended on a happy note instead of a cyclone of controversy. And Washington wouldn't be screaming for his hide.

Chapter 25

Mike walked into the reception area at Faraday, Ennis, Graham & Wilson with a slim hope that the people in Ellie's office bore him no particular animosity for having killed one of their own even if she was a terrorist. The young girl at the desk, and the two architects standing there, looked like they didn't know what to say. Word of Ellie's real identity, and her role in the plot to destroy the bridge, had filled every news medium's grist mill for the past two days.

Mike, like everyone else who had known her, expected Ellie to be offered a partnership in the firm. Why not? She was bright, beautiful, and competent. Everyone loved her. Now she was dead. He could feel the tension in the air the moment her associates saw him coming through the door. He sensed their unspoken reaction. By now they must have known he'd killed her in the line of duty. Still, he was her husband, the one who danced with her and kissed her under the mistletoe at the Christmas party. Then he blew her brains out through the back of her skull. He understood their silence.

"Good morning," Mike said, hoping to find an appropriate way to break the ice. "I'm Agent Pallino." He flipped open his wallet to flash his FBI credentials as though this was routine, no different from any other investigation. They nodded and seemed to be forcing conciliatory half-smiles.

"Yes, sir," the receptionist said, "would you like some coffee?"

He sensed from their reaction to the dark shadows under his eyes, and his look of sadness which deepened them, that maybe, in a way, they forgave him. That perhaps the innate feelings of compassion which bind human souls prevailed over the harshness of their actions.

"No thanks. I'm sorry, I'm required to search Ellie's office. I regret this as much as I'm sure you do. However, I need to confiscate her computer and any relevant records."

"We understand, Mr. Pallino," one of the architects said with a nod of acknowledgement. "If you need any help let us know."

"Thanks." He tucked the empty thirty-five-gallon canvas sack under his arm along with the folded-up little pull cart, and walked into her office with mixed feelings of nostalgia and sadness. He opened Ellie's screen and found one hundred and twenty unread messages. He skipped the advertisements, intra-office memos, and his own messages to her. He printed out sixty-four exchanges between Ellie and two unaccounted-for people named Ahmed and Behram, with no last names given. He'd let the Bureau nerds decipher those. Mike spent another hour satisfying himself that twenty-five of the entries were nothing more than routine business queries from customers and prospects.

The further he progressed through the last thirty-nine the more his jaw tightened. He wanted to curse out loud, to shove his fist through the computer screen. He took a deep breath and told himself it didn't matter anymore. Ellie's little extramarital affairs, so painfully documented in the amorous invitations from her various lovers, would have crushed him a few weeks before. Now they simply sliced away at his pride.

Mike scrolled through them again — easier to endure the second time and they might contain valuable information. The four CEOs might have been customers. Sex, he reasoned, has never been a bad business development strategy. Two CFOs and a tennis pro for God's sake! Those must have been purely carnal. Three purchasing department guys — probably successful RFPs again. Mike shook his head. The damned whore must have managed to screw her way to partnership candidacy at FEG&W. Unable to endure any further damage to his ego, Mike disconnected the computer and slammed his fist on the keyboard.

He stuffed the files into his canvas bag, secured the computer to the pull cart, and dropped back into the chair for a few moments of contemplation. He had never dreamed he could feel sadness, failure, betrayal, and anger all at the same time. The tears he'd shed during the past few days had dried up. Now, there was only an unforgiving emptiness.

He thought of Milton Pringle. At that moment he missed his meticulous sidekick more than he ever thought he could. Each had been strong where the other had been weak. Each had sympathized with the other's misfortunes. They'd made a good team. The knowledge that Milt would eventually recover only slightly curtailed Mike's feeling of unrelenting emptiness.

He reached for his picture that Ellie kept on the corner of her desk, and stared at the inscription which read, "All my love, Mike." He placed the photo face down, cupped his hands behind his head, and leaned back in the chair. He gazed at the ceiling while he tried to reconstruct what went wrong, what he might have done differently. Maybe there was nothing he could have done. Ellie had come with undisclosed baggage. Murky memories of her dark side floated through his mind, hand in hand with all the pleasant ones, as though good and evil had always been inseparable.

Looking for someone to take her fishing, she'd strolled down the marina at Marblehead just as the day came into its infancy, wrapped in the cool, pale dawn of a late New England spring. Mike had fallen in love before the sun reached its peak. He'd never suspected that she'd come into his life a pretty girl in white shorts, and leave as a terrorist on a dark bridge.

He glanced once more around her office, chucked her picture of him into the wastebasket, threw the sack over his shoulder, and walked out dragging the pull-cart behind. The firm's managing partner stepped out of his office to express his deep regret about Ellie. He offered his expression of sympathy about what he said he presumed Mike must be feeling. Mike thanked him, forced a brittle smile, and headed for the elevator.

He made a promise to himself. He would find Ali Fadhil and arrest him. No, kill him. Mike had fired the bullet which killed Ellie, there was no getting around that. Nonetheless, it was the sequence of events leading up to her death for which he blamed Ali and, as Terry Atkins described them, Ali's "Allah-seeking bastards."

153

Chapter 26

Ali Fadhil had packed away the persona of his past once and for all. His future belonged to Harvey Morgan, the man whose name he'd taken from an obituary years before He vowed to force all the memories of Ali Fadhil into the shadows of history. Harvey saw Rio de Janeiro, aside from its value as a fugitive refuge, as a place where his latent dreams could become real. He liked the city's translated name, *River of January*, which came from its discovery in that month of 1502 by Portuguese explorers. January: first month of a new year, first year of a new life for Harvey Morgan.

Rio had become a booming, crowded metropolis of eleven million people squeezed between the Atlantic Ocean and the Corcovado and Serra do Mar Mountains. A Mecca for tourists, business travelers, and expatriates from every corner of the globe — as good a place as any for Ali Fadhil to reinvent himself under a new identity.

Money, legal and otherwise, flowed in and out twenty-four hours a day. Harvey made this day an especially good one for Ernesto Villanueva, president of Banco do Nordeste do Brasil SA, strategically centered in the heart of the downtown business district.

A week had gone by since that night when darkness and pandemonium combined to enable Ali Fadhil to slip past the agents on the bridge. His complexion belied his Arabic origin and had made his escape easier. His three-million-dollar withdrawal from the Merrill Lynch account in San Francisco, deposited into Banco do Nordeste, represented broker Bill Kessler's loss and Ernesto's gain.

"It is a pleasure doing banking with you, Mr. Morgan," the beaming Ernesto said, "and welcome to Rio de Janeiro. Have you found a place to stay?"

"I've arranged an annual lease at the Guanabara Palace Hotel on Avenida Presidente downtown. I'm hoping we can do more than banking together, Ernesto."

"Yes, you spoke about such an arrangement during our first phone conversation. I'm prepared to continue that conversation, although I'm not at liberty to divulge my reasons right now. Let's adjourn into my conference room where we can get away from the phone and talk. I'd like to know exactly what you have in mind, Mr. Morgan. We can celebrate the beginning of our relationship with a glass of wine."

Ernesto's secretary brought in a vintage bottle of Merlot, smiled at Ali, walked out, and closed the conference room door behind her. While Ernesto struggled to open the bottle, Harvey wondered if Mac McLeod would miss the four million which had found its way into Harvey's nest egg at Merrill Lynch. A disbursement of one million from the account had been paid up front to Carlos Ramirez, a transaction which could not have been avoided. Harvey could now begin a new life, without the restrictions of Al Qaeda, and far removed from the bare-bones existence he'd known on the streets of Cairo. Ali had paid a high price for the luxury of starting anew, and the chilling memories refused to leave his subconscious unmolested.

He'd been lucky to grab a ledge of the bridge after the misstep during his sprint to avoid the authorities. Even luckier that one of Carlos' men had pulled him up before the force of the swirling wind against his suspended body could overcome his grip and blow him off. Still, his demons weren't through with him. They came to exact their punishment during his nightmares, in which he dreamed his grip failed, releasing him to experience every excruciating moment of a long downward spiral into San Francisco Bay. There, the nightmare allowed him to remain conscious while Great White Sharks severed his hips and legs, leaving the upper part of his torso bobbing on the surface.

Harvey blinked and tried to shake his head unobtrusively to bring his mind back to Ernesto. The banker seemed to be speaking to him from far away while he reached through Harvey's fog to hand him his drink. The moment Harvey held out his hand to take the wine the fog evaporated. Seconds after their glasses clinked together in a toast, Harvey managed to release himself from his goblins long enough to deliver his carefully prepared proposal.

"You know the banking business, Ernesto. My sources tell me you're well connected with the wealthy here in the city. I know investments. I know business. I have access to a licensed investment professional, and I see my three million-dollar deposit as only the beginning of a financial dynasty we could create together."

Ernesto snuffed out the latest in a long string of his daily cigarettes. "You have my attention. What are you suggesting?"

Harvey leaned toward Ernesto and spoke with an air of uninhibited confidence. "The formation of a limited liability corporation through which you and I can leverage our skills and associations to create wealth far beyond what either of us could possibly achieve separately." Energized by the prospect of leveraging money the way he'd always dreamed, Harvey sipped his wine and continued to engage his audience of one.

"Listen, Ernesto. Your wealth aggregation capability right now, although admittedly enviable, really extends no further than your ability to attract risk-averse depositors. They don't dare venture beyond money market accounts and CDs. You're missing the affluent investors still looking for the same kind of personal value enhancement that made them wealthy in their businesses. These people thoroughly enjoy the challenge of equity investing. They relish the excitement of it. However, they want to do it right, with investment counselors they can trust. Together, you and I can give them that."

Ernesto shifted in his chair, loosened his tie and reached to light another cigarette. "Go on. I'm listening."

Harvey took another sip of his Merlot. "We can make the LLC either an adjunct to your bank, or a separately-housed entity, depending on the prevailing banking restrictions in this country. We can offer our investors access to equities, fixed income securities, or the safety of interest-bearing bank instruments. More importantly, we can offer them a value-added feature they can't get anywhere else without paying a small fortune for it."

Ernesto put down his cigarette long enough to sample his wine. "And that would be?"

"That would be our commitment to move their money into the most promising growth equities in bull markets. We'll shift it back into less volatile securities, even bank deposits, during bear markets. All at nominal consultation and handling fees based on the size of their portfolios. Once we establish ourselves in this business, we can leverage our profits in far more lucrative endeavors, still consistent with our combined expertise." Ernesto stood, walked around his desk, and perched his rotund frame on the edge of it. The delicate procedure conjured up in Harvey's mind the image of an elephant on a tricycle. The scent of nicotine on the man's clothes attacked Harvey's nostrils as the overweight banker paused to refill their glasses before he responded. "Mr. Morgan, your introductory letter had already convinced me to bring in my attorney to sign our corporate documents. I had made up my mind to join you even before you came in to introduce the idea of a more lucrative venture. So tell me, how do we accomplish all this?"

Harvey smiled. It had been easier than he'd thought. Maybe the reasons Ernesto had been "unable to divulge" were behind the man's willingness to enter into this relationship. Regardless of the motivation, Ernesto would be Harvey's first partner. "We form a venture capital group. It will be dedicated to purchasing minority, yet managerially influential, interests in small-to-medium sized businesses."

Ernesto frowned. "And how do we find these?"

Harvey polished off the last of his wine and leaned in toward his prospect. "Easy. These will be entities which need second stage, or mezzanine, financing to continue on their growth curve. Two out of three of such businesses usually fail to produce an acceptable return. However, the third one historically returns a near-windfall profit, along with the annuities of quarterly dividends. I have some experience here, and access to some venture capitalists who have even more.

"Ernesto, there's big money out there for the taking. I can bring it in, but I need access to your upper echelon connections to do it. And I need the reputation of you and your bank to make the whole thing credible. I don't want you to respond right away. I can tell by your skeptical expression about windfall profits that you're a cautious man. That's good for a banker. However, there's a time to be cautious and a time to be bold. Think about it for a while." Harvey smiled again and shook Ernesto's hand. "You know where to find me when you're ready. I'm looking forward to our next conversation. Better yet, I'm looking forward to working with you."

On his way out through the lobby Harvey scanned the interior of the bank. He shook his head. There it stood, a modern, twenty-first-century structure committed to a nineteenth-century way of preserving wealth; a monument to mankind's conservative nature, which placed fear of losing ahead of the excitement of gaining. He smiled again and headed for a party at the Copacabana.

This would be the first on his long schedule of gala events where he hoped to establish a relationship with as many wealthy women as possible. Their current marital status would be of no particular concern to him with respect to the sexual component of the relationship. As to the business component, Harvey preferred married women. They were more mature, aspired to greater levels of wealth, and brought more assets to the table.

Chapter 27

Harvey knew she'd be there. Lani Reismann loved to party, particularly with him, and this was her kind of social gathering. His procedure for seeking out wealthy women usually began with subtle self-introductions designed to intrigue without enticing. During these preliminary approaches, Harvey limited his engaging cocktail conversations to inconsequential subjects in order to size up his targets before he committed himself to a more serious campaign. The Lani infiltration required a week to make her his lover, another week to solicit her business as a client.

The size of her inheritance made it worth the effort. In early 1945, her grandfather, Nazi official Guenther Reismann, sold his confiscated truckload of rare French and Italian art to the Vichy government. He crawled through the wreckage of the Third Reich with his fortune only hours before columns of Russian tanks clanked their way through the debris-strewn streets of East Berlin. After he died, Lani became the sole beneficiary of the Reismann estate — and the only exception to Harvey's rule that married women make better prospects.

The beautiful heiress caught a glimpse of Harvey making his way toward her through the crowd of revelers. She tilted her head back, tossed down the remains of her third Manhattan, chucked the empty glass into a flower pot, and rushed to throw her arms around him. Wherever Lani went, men turned to ogle, particularly at her long, sensuous legs, which several admirers claimed were valuable enough that they should have been insured by Lloyds of London.

"Darling, isn't this the best party ever?" she said with a noticeable slur. "I mean, it wasn't until you showed up. Now that you're here, it is." She pulled back, held him at arm's length and giggled. "C'mon, smile, you handsome thing. We're supposed to enjoy parties. Why the glum look? Hey, didn't the investments you sold me make enough money today?"

"They did fine, sweetheart. I'm a bit concerned about something. That's all. Let's dance."

"No, no. Not until you tell me what you're concerned about. Let's have it, time to confess to your favorite lover."

"You're my only lover." He assumed she knew it was a lie but probably wouldn't press the issue. "It's really nothing to worry about. The ghosts of my own paranoia, that's all."

"Ooooh, I love ghosts. Tell me about it," she purred. "Right now."

He let the staggering Lani lean against him while he steered her toward an empty couch in the corner, away from the orchestra and the swelling sounds of inebriated laughter. Harvey removed her shoes so she wouldn't wobble when she stood up, and stuffed them into her oversized handbag. He paused for a moment to prepare his confession. "Well, every now and then I swear I catch a glimpse of this guy. At least I think I do."

"What guy?"

"I don't know. He's like a shadow that follows me and then disappears every time I turn around quickly enough to get a look at him."

Lani climbed onto his lap and ran her fingers gently through his hair. "Why would anyone want to follow you? I mean, other than the two suitors I dumped so I could be with you." She giggled. "I think they're jealous enough to kill you, but they're not the kind who'd follow you."

Harvey hadn't told Lani, or anyone else, about Ali Fadhil. It had been only a month, yet it seemed like years. Al Qaeda, the bridge, Carlos' money, Metalcraft, and all the rest belonged carefully sequestered away in the past. His old nightmares about falling from the bridge had now been driven into exile by new ones. Recurring images of Mac McCleod leading an angry mob of heavily armed Salvadorans bent on his execution invaded his subconscious.

"It's a long story, honey. It comes down to some wealthy people I made wealthier, and now they want more. Come on, let's dance and forget about it. You're right. This is the best time to enjoy what we have." He lifted the tipsy woman from his lap and steadied her on her feet.

Lani kissed him on the cheek. "Okay. That's what I like to hear. First, go get me another Manhattan…or two. We'll drink to how much wealthier you're going to make me. Then let's go to bed after we dance for a while. I've reserved a suite for the night up in the penthouse of this simply marvelous hotel." She turned her head as though she were searching the room for something. "Oh, damn. Where did I put my shoes?"

160

"I put them in that Santa Claus sack you call a purse," he said. "Here, sit down. I'll be right back — with *one* Manhattan, or you'll be too drunk to know who's dancing with you, let alone who's making love to you."

After a few minutes of schmoozing with two prospective equity clients at the bar, Harvey returned to find Lani sound asleep on the couch. With the help of an amused bellhop, he carried her into the elevator. When they reached the penthouse, he put her to bed and tenderly tucked her in. At that particular moment, Harvey didn't really feel like making love, anyway.

By the time he returned to the party, it had escalated to a higher level of conviviality. The evening was still young and Harvey couldn't think of any reason not to respond to the invitational smile of the curvaceous blond who had been eyeing him from the bar all evening. He returned her smile and slid onto the empty stool she was holding for him with her outstretched hand.

"Well, it's about time you noticed me, Mr. Morgan," she said. "Are you surprised I know your name?"

"No. I also know who you are, Mrs. Gerhardt. Now Greta, where is your husband, if I might ask?"

"Oh, Conrad's out of town for a few days. Running a silver mine takes all the energy out of a man, so I forgive him." She took Harvey's hand, placed it on her exposed thigh, and leaned into him tight enough that he could feel her bosom against his chest. "I hear *you* don't run out of energy, do you Harvey?" she whispered.

In one deft movement Harvey removed his hand from her thigh. "It seems I never do with clients, Greta. Now that reminds me, I've been intending to talk with you about becoming a client. I'm sure my firm can help you and your husband become even wealthier than you are now. How would you feel about coming to my office tomorrow to discuss it?"

Greta reached up to place a hand on each side of Harvey's face. She stroked his temples gently. "I'd love to, Harvey," she said softly before she kissed him, "only after I've examined your expertise in bed. I'll tell you what, darling. You spend tonight at my place and I'll be in your office any time you want. Do we have a deal?"

Harvey flashed his client-comforting smile, paid her tab at the bar, and they headed for her place and an evening of "business development," as Ernesto would have called it.

Greta led him into a small cottage which appeared to be attached to the rear of her mansion. Harvey had never felt any reservations about making love to a married woman right in the bed in which she and her husband usually slept. He even found a sense of triumph in it.

* * * * * *

Greta opened the blinds just enough to allow the mid-morning sun to burn into his bleary eyes. Harvey kicked off the bed covers and sat up. He stretched his arms and blinked away the residue of a long, restful sleep. Mrs.Gerhardt sat completely naked on the edge of her bed, even more voluptuous than she'd appeared when they'd climbed under the sheets ten hours earlier. He felt remiss that he'd explored every inch of her sensuality in the dark without a full visual appreciation of her various dimensions.

"Greta, last night was an adventure I'll not soon forget. Tell me something. How did you manage to have this private little cottage of yours built right next to the main residence?"

She leaned toward him and ran her hand over his thigh, her exquisite breasts touching his knee. "It was a condition of my acceptance of Conrad's marriage proposal. I told him if he wanted me, he'd have to order construction of a little sanctuary I could call my own. He accepted my condition and now he's my beloved — and conveniently unknowing — husband. And for the record, I don't use my private domain solely for my extramarital affairs. I conduct all my business and social activities from here. So you can wipe that sly, male grin off your face."

Harvey slid from the bed and took a few minutes to dress before he turned to her with a serious expression. "Speaking of your business, Greta, why don't we talk about investing your liquid assets more profitably, as we discussed briefly last night? My value-enhancement methods are time-proven, and my portfolio management fees are minimal. I've never disappointed a client."

Greta dismounted her side of the bed with her usual sexual grace, and took her time easing delicate black panties up over a pair of sensuous thighs. She slipped into a blouse, curled up in an oversized armchair, and smiled at Harvey. It was a different smile, one that evokes images of a lioness preparing to spring out of deep yellow grass and sink her claws into an unwitting gazelle.

"You're not going to disappoint this one, either, darling. Before we talk finances, let's chat a bit about Ali Fadhil. You know, that smooth-talking

162

---

fugitive who's already conned half of Rio's wealthy women into becoming his clients and lovers at the same time."

Harvey felt a tightening in his stomach that shot like lightning into his chest. Visions of Mac chasing him with an angry crowd of Carlos' *guerreros* in tow flared up again. How could this woman possibly have known? If she knew, who else knew? And where did his slip-up occur? He could feel the jaws of an iron trap snap shut on his chest, squeezing the last drop of air from his lungs.

Greta cocked her head and rested her chin on her hand. "Oh come now, don't look so surprised. Did you assume I was as ignorant as all the others? Like your forever-inebriated blonde heiress? No, I have my information sources and I use them well."

She clapped her hands and giggled. "Look at you. All ashen in the face. Stop fretting. Your secret is safe with me. I have the connections to protect you…which has become quite a task lately. Did you know someone's already hot after your ass as we speak?"

Harvey slumped into the other larger-than-life armchair. His lips tightened. "I see. And exactly what is all this protection going to cost me? I assume we're talking about something more than unprecedented growth in the value of your portfolio. May I also assume you'll tell me who's hot on my trail?"

She jumped into his lap, wrapped her arm around his neck, and forced one of her breasts against his cheek. "Darling, my sources haven't figured that out yet. You'll be the first to know when they do. You needn't worry. We won't mention your real name again. Now, here's the deal. You do whatever it is you do with my portfolio when I turn it over to you tomorrow. I pay your standard management fees. And then, sweetheart," she kissed him on the forehead, "you pay *my* standard fees."

Harvey removed her arm from his neck and glared at her. "Explain, please." The tightening in his chest became more intense.

She exchanged Harvey's lap for a perch on the edge of the unmade bed, and flashed him a not-so-comforting smile. "Conrad's out of town on business every Friday and Saturday. You will show up here every Friday evening for cocktails and dinner served by my confidante. We enjoy each other in bed that night. We sleep in and share a late breakfast together, after which you spend Saturday morning regaling me with your computer print-out of my portfolio's exciting growth during the week. Then we kiss goodbye until the following Friday." She eased off the bed and stood in front of him. "Now," she cooed with a warmer smile, "tell me that's not a terrific deal for a con-man on the run."

Harvey stood, returned her smile, and came around behind her. He gently placed one hand on each side of her face and kissed her on the back of the neck. In the few seconds required for him to take up that position, Harvey Morgan reversed his thinking. His first instinct, which prompted his move behind her, had been to suffocate her. Afterward, he would turn the gas-stove burners on and set the little cottage ablaze. From that point on he would take his chances that the carnage would make it impossible for anyone to determine the exact cause of death. A possible suicide. Maybe even the victim of an enraged husband who had every right to be jealous.

Ali Fadhil's cooler thoughts prevailed. To kill her before she'd actually transferred her assets into his stewardship would constitute a job half-done. Until that transaction had been consummated, and a reasonable amount of time elapsed thereafter, compliance with her demands would have to be endured, regardless of the inconvenience. Keeping Greta happy in the interim, and identifying his pursuer as soon as possible, became, as of that moment, Harvey's main objectives.

Chapter 28

"Good morning, Mr. Morgan. Come in to my office. I have good news." Ernesto Villanueva motioned Harvey in with a wave of his hand and the same perpetual smile that seemed to say most news is good, and bad is only what you fail to make of it. "Banco Central do Brasil and Receita Federal do Brasil have checked your references at Merrill Lynch in San Francisco. They've approved the expansion of our services into the management of investment funds. They've also endorsed our entry into corporate acquisitions and mergers. There's more. A few days after the Reismann funds came under our management, six other families followed." Ernesto patted him on the back. "We're on our way, Harvey."

Harvey closed the door to Ernesto's office and sat down. "Well, I can see our investment management services are on their way, Ernesto. Unfortunately, our venture capital operation isn't going anywhere. I need you to agree to let me siphon off some of our clients' investment funds and plow the proceeds into young, high-return growth companies."

Ernesto settled into his chair and fumbled in his pockets for his cigarettes. A forced smile produced only a slight parting of his pudgy cheeks. "Ahhhh, Harvey, my friend. We've talked about this before. To redirect our clients' money without their permission is illegal. Even worse, these high-return companies of yours are also very high-risk businesses. And yes, I understand. You don't have to tell me again. High risk is the price one must pay for high return."

Ernesto pulled a pack of cigarettes from the drawer, lit one, and leaned forward toward Harvey to further emphasize his argument. "Still, I think the risk here is simply too high. Harvey, I don't want bad feelings to come between us. We can do what you want in this venture capital market as soon as we accumulate enough profit from our investment management operation to do it. Those will be our funds, and we can do whatever we want with them.

165

Right now I simply cannot condone the misuse of our clients' assets. I hope you understand."

Harvey stiffened and managed a half-smile. "Yes, of course, but I'm not talking about misuse, Ernesto. Look, our clients have given us freedom to allocate their funds wherever we think we can make the highest return for them. I'm simply suggesting that we channel a portion of these funds into a few privately-owned companies with high growth potential and no public recognition. The eventual returns don't get any higher than that. Our clients will be delighted."

Ernesto snuffed out his cigarette, reached over to his file cabinet, pulled out a computer listing, and laid it in front of Harvey. "I would accept such an allocation of our clients' money if we could show that these privately-held firms represented safe investments. Unfortunately, we can't make that claim. Look at this list. Three pages of companies exactly like the ones you're describing. All went bankrupt after two years. Please don't take offense, Harvey. I just cannot be a part of this redirection of our clients' money."

"Ernesto, that's fine." Harvey walked over to the credenza, poured himself a cup of coffee, and returned to his seat. He found Ernesto's refusal to allow entry to his clients disappointing. Nonetheless, there was no hurry. In the end, the scent of money would change the man's mind. "I want you to be comfortable with our relationship. The fact is, I already have access to funds sufficient to jump-start a venture capital business of my own. Perhaps you can join me whenever you're ready."

"Ah, Harvey, that's good. You never told me this. May I inquire as to the source of those funds?"

"High-risk investors seeking a challenge. As I once told you, there are all types of wealthy people with time and money on their hands. They've vacationed all over the world. They've sailed their yachts to God knows where and back. They've gambled in the casinos until they've lost interest in rolling the dice and trying to beat the house. Now they want to raise the bar to some real excitement. And nothing excites the rich like using their money to buy a stake in a high-risk, high-profit venture that will make them even richer. These people are perfect targets for what I'm proposing."

Ernesto couldn't contain a laugh. "And might I ask if these bored people might be women, by any chance?"

Harvey grinned. "You know me too well, Ernesto. Yes, four of them are. One isn't. I've printed out a brief profile on each one. Here, take a look.

Let's find a table where I can spread this out, and I'll explain exactly what I mean. Maybe you already know some of these people."

They moved to the conference room where Harvey spent the next hour outlining his carefully engineered approach to the five prospects, all of whom Ernesto recognized but didn't know personally. When he finished, Harvey folded up the document and stuffed it into his jacket.

The pleasant aroma from his two unfinished cups of coffee had failed to compensate for the acrid odor of Ernesto's cigarettes. Harvey waved a hand in front of his face to clear away the drifting smoke, and started toward the door. "Well, there you have it, Ernesto. I'm having lunch this afternoon with the one who isn't female. Want to come along?"

Ernesto shook his head. "I think not today, Harvey. Perhaps I'll join you some other time. Let's say, when you have lunch with one of the other four."

"Good choice, Ernesto." They laughed and Harvey slapped Ernesto gently on the shoulder. "Have to run. I'll see you later."

* * * * * *

Had the choice been his, Harvey wouldn't have selected La Terez as a place to have a business lunch. As if the noise and crowds weren't enough, almost nothing on the menu appealed to his tastes. Even so, it was Jose Varejo's favorite place. Harvey surmised that, judging by the line of people waiting to be seated, there were plenty of others who shared Jose's opinion.

Of all the names on his prospect list, Jose's ranked at the top. The successful executive ran a company that possessed all the financial ingredients necessary for Harvey to leverage Jose's wealth into an enviable fortune. Once accomplished, the result could be used to spread Harvey's reputation all over the continent. The month he'd spent cultivating the relationship with Jose had been a good investment of his time. Since Jose had agreed to the meeting, Harvey was not about to quibble over the location. He met his prospect at the door and offered a firm handshake. The waitress led them to a corner booth reserved in Harvey's name.

"Thank you for coming, Jose. I think what I have to show you will make this well worth your time."

"Ahhh, Mr. Morgan, whenever I can get a free lunch it's worth my time. I never let my wealth stand in the way of a gift. By the way, you didn't have to dress up in such formal business attire. I'm already impressed with your credentials. Around here we usually dine casually, like I'm dressed now. Why don't you remove your tie and get comfortable? Let's order and we can talk business while we wait."

Harvey deplored the service there. It came, to use one of Ahmed's expressions, "as slow as the end of a Russian winter." He removed his coat, loosened his tie, and waited until the sweet, stressed-out waitress delivered their martinis. A hard sell is best preceded, he knew, by the warming effects of a couple of drinks.

"Jose, my business is finding second-stage growth companies which need only a modest infusion of capital in order to become very large operations. Once they begin to use that capital to climb their growth curve, they quickly develop the capability to throw off large cash returns to their investors. Based on our conversations at the last couple of social events, I think I've found a perfect match for your interests." He paused to let his prospect ponder for a moment.

"I'm listening, Harvey. Go on."

"Embraco Corporation hasn't publicly announced it yet, but the board of directors has approved a so-called spin-off of one of its smaller divisions. I've researched the whole thing thoroughly, using, shall we say, some inside information. It's not really a spin-off in the usual sense of the term. They're actually dumping a small compressor division which hasn't met their profit objectives. Now, here's the—"

"Harvey, what makes you think I would offer to invest in an unprofitable reject that no one else wants?" Jose shook his head. "I thought I made my return-on-investment objectives perfectly clear."

Harvey leaned forward and lowered his voice, as if he were about to make a pronouncement he wanted to make sure no one else could hear. "That's precisely my point, Jose. In my business the highest returns are always made by investing in a solid winner that no one else knows about. This compressor operation is exactly that."

Harvey paused, held Jose's gaze, then sipped his martini before going on. "The head of it has already filed for incorporation with himself as CEO. Now, listen to this. He's also filed for patent protection on three new technologies for both his compressors and condensers. Technologies which will give him significant price and performance advantages…well beyond anything the industry has now."

Jose fingered his glass, electing not to raise it to his mouth. "And this, I suppose, signals an invitation to invest?"

Harvey spread his arms apart, palms up. "Of course. He's taking with him most of the key employees who worked on the designs for these improvements. My sources inform me that the parent company doesn't know about all this. Moreover, the employees who worked on them have all made arrangements to invest their own money in the operation once it's been severed from Embraco. Now, what does *that* tell you?"

Jose nursed his martini, and signaled the waitress to bring another for each of them. "It tells me there's some potential exposure to insider-trading litigation. Nonetheless, you have my attention. Keep going."

"Ahhh, there's no real exposure, Jose. No one will be trading in Embraco stock. We're talking here about investing in a brand-new corporation which, right now, has no market at all for its stock. It's a gold mine waiting to be discovered. It will, however, need capital. More capital than a few employees could ever provide. And that's where you come in." Harvey leaned back, waiting for a response while the waitress placed the second round of drinks on the table.

Jose paused again without showing any signs of enthusiasm. "How large a capital investment from me would be required?" It was the reaction Harvey had been waiting for, with or without accompanying emotion.

"I haven't finished running the numbers yet. On a preliminary basis, I figure somewhere between forty and fifty million Brazilian ray-als. For interested American investors that translates to about twenty-five million dollars. I'm looking at annual returns of ten percent by the third and fourth years, twenty percent in years five through seven, and upward of fifty percent afterward. I believe this will make you one of the richest investors in Rio de Janeiro, Jose. I'll email you my final figures, along with a complete report on this venture. I want you to think about it for a while, and then we'll talk again."

The waitress finally delivered their meal. To Harvey's surprise, Jose bowed his head to say grace quietly to himself before he picked up his fork. In a reluctant gesture of politeness Harvey lowered his own head, although he didn't really see the point. After Jose raised his head they said nothing for the first few minutes. Jose broke the silence.

"Don't use the internet for this, Harvey. Please deliver the envelope yourself, personally. We have too much at stake here. I'm optimistic about this and I want to talk to other members of my family about it after I receive your information. Then I'll get back to you."

They chatted for another hour while they ate and finished off the last round of martinis. After Jose left, Harvey leaned back and sipped his drink for a while. The mouse had sniffed the cheese. Maybe Ernesto's money wouldn't be necessary after all.

Harvey paid the bill and walked away without noticing the man who had been watching him from a booth across the room. The man rose, laid the equivalent of fifty dollars on the table, and followed Harvey out.

Chapter 29

Behram Naji endured the same discomfort he had suffered the last time he journeyed from New York to Nantaz via Tehran to meet with Ahmed. He found his superior wrapped in a veil of anger and depression. Naji suspected the meeting wouldn't be pleasant. They hugged each other with the same compassion that had underscored their friendship since they'd shared victory and defeat during the Russian campaign. Ahmed's face brightened only for a moment before his look of despair returned.

"It's good to see you, my old friend," Ahmed said. Ahmed's shoulders sagged in a manner Naji had never seen before, even during the darkest times they had endured together. "I regret to be meeting again under such unfortunate circumstances, Behram. The failure of my efforts to strike at the heart of our mutual enemy has cost me dearly. The credibility that took me years to build with the coalition is gone. Our president is furious with me."

Naji placed a hand gently on Ahmed's shoulder. "I'm sorry. We both had hoped for better. How are your other allies in the government taking it?"

Ahmed lowered his eyes and shook his head. "The entire upper echelon has barely managed to contain its disappointment. They're even asking how our president could have entrusted me with such a critical task in the first place. I can deal with the humiliation of all that. What I cannot accept is the realization that my favorite protégé had dishonored me and stolen from me. I've treated Ali Fadhil like the son I never had, against the advice of everyone who warned me not to trust him. They were right. Now my son, as well as the money, is gone." Ahmed turned away and locked his hands on the back of his neck.

Naji spoke barely above a whisper. "We've lost more than that, Ahmed. Whatever momentum the Islamic world might have developed toward the improvement of its untenable position has been stopped. What action do you plan to take?" He waited until his mentor turned to face him again.

Ahmed took a deep breath, as though he preferred not to answer the question. "Before a recovery plan of any kind is possible there must be punishment. It must be visible world-wide, not covert or isolated. I want to entrust the task of exacting retribution to you, Behram. I know you've disliked Ali from the beginning. For that reason it will be easier for you than for me."

Naji nodded. "What kind of retribution did you have in mind?"

Ahmed lowered his face into his hands again. "I can't find it in my heart to even think about the specifics. I'll leave it up to you. It's such a painful subject I would prefer not to know the method until it becomes public information. Just let me know when you've finished."

Naji nodded again. "I'll begin immediately. This will take some time, Ahmed. Since no one has any idea where Ali is, I will have to start with a visit to our *Mara Salvatrucha* contacts in San Francisco. They were the last to see him. Our only real hope of finding him rests with that source, as I'm sure you must know."

Ahmed looked up long enough to force a half-smile, which vanished quickly. "Yes. I've made arrangements with the New York MS-13 cell for your financing and documents of introduction. Don't waste any time. I want this resolved as soon as possible. May Allah go with you, my friend."

Behram Naji hugged his mentor, climbed into the jeep, and headed for Tehran. He shivered in the cold wind that penetrated bone-deep. His jacket drawn tight around him, Naji allowed his thinking to evolve unencumbered by any self-imposed parameters. He entertained — even savored — a wide range of free-floating ideas for Ali's penalty. A slow and agonizing death would be the preferred common denominator.

* * * * *

Toxic emissions from Hunters Point stung Naji's nostrils in much the same way they had assaulted the senses of Ali's small group. The same debris lay scattered everywhere, and the wind from the bay chilled him as it had Nahid. Only the junkyard's human occupants had changed. Carlos was dead. The gargantuan Miguel was dead. Half of Carlos' gang was either dead or in jail.

Chico Sanchez now ruled what was left of *Mara Salvatrucha*. He made it clear he welcomed the chance to kill anyone even remotely connected with

Ali Fadhil. Naji's skillful pleas alone kept him alive long enough to present his scribbled note of endorsement from the New York gang leader.

"Speak, you old Arab dog," Chico snarled at him after he'd scanned the barely legible document. "You have one minute. The moment I think you lie, the cold steel pressing at the back of your head will be the last thing you feel."

Behram Naji had been close to death too often to be frightened by the likes of Chico. He'd faced angry men's fierce expressions of hatred before. The surrounding circle of AK-47s pointing at him did, however, raise the threat of assassination to a higher level.

"We seek the same coward, and share the same desire for revenge." Naji spoke with a steady voice and a glare to match his adversary's. "I will find Ali Fadhil. Then I will kill him. I'm here now at my own risk because I need your help to track him down. Your counterpart in New York told me one of your men followed him to the airport. I need to know where he went from there."

Chico raised the bar on intimidation by thrusting the blade of a hunting knife up under Naji's chin, enough to draw a tiny trickle of blood. "Was this Ali one of your men?"

Naji tilted his head back just enough to allow him to answer without the movement of his jaw forcing the point of Chico's blade deeper into his throat. With every nerve in his body he could feel the intensity of Chico's craving for vengeance. "In all truth I must confess he was. I must also confess he was my responsibility."

Naji knew his next remark would either appeal to his captor's fixation on complete honesty, or perhaps drive the man to kill him on the spot. The fact that Chico hadn't done so already confirmed Naji's hope that his interrogator wanted to hear more. "And so, it must be I who avenges the loss of your men, for whose deaths I alone suffer the shame and responsibility."

In the ensuing silence Naji waited, resigned to the blackness of death which could come from either a hail of bullets or a quick slash of Chico's blade across his jugular. For a long moment no one stirred, as though time stood still. In his suppressed terror, Naji fantasized that perhaps they had already killed him. And now, much to his disappointment, the afterlife Allah often promised turned out to be nothing more than finding himself frozen in this position, forced to stare eternally at his killers.

With a movement carefully designed to emphasize its deliberation, Chico lowered his knife. The surrounding gangsters lowered the barrels of their AK-47s in macabre harmony with Chico's weapon.

173

The gang leader's words came as slowly as the descent of his blade. "My New York *cholos* warned me you would arrive as a brave warrior. They did not tell me you could speak so convincingly. So I have decided to let you live. This will be on one condition. You must bring us that man's head as proof you have killed him. If you fail to do this there is no place on earth you can hide. *Mara Salvatrucha* is everywhere. And then it will be your head which we will mount on the bridge until the sea gulls flock to pluck your skull clean. Do we have an understanding?"

Naji wiped the thin trail of blood from his throat with the back of his hand, and took his first deep breath in what seemed like forever. "Yes. Now, you said your *cholo* followed this man to the airport. What airline, and what was his destination?"

Chico crooked his finger and motioned one of his men forward. He whispered something to the *guerrero*, and turned back to face Naji. "Your man bought a ticket to Rio de Janeiro. We, unfortunately, lost the information that identified the airline." Chico turned back toward the heavily armed fellow he'd brought forward. "Is that not so, Xavier?" The man nodded in agreement.

Chico spoke to his men for a few minutes, sent them on their way, and walked Naji to his car. "Remember," Chico warned again, "we kill warriors as easily as we kill cowards."

They said goodbye without shaking hands, and Naji left for the airport. He slept in the airside waiting area until they announced the boarding of his flight to Rio. The gratitude he felt for Allah's preservation of his life more than compensated for the discomfort of the airport chairs.

* * * * * *

The moment his plane touched down on the tarmac of the Galeao-Antonio Carlos Jobim International Airport in Rio, Behram Naji felt completely alone. He found himself without contacts or Al Qaeda allies for the first time since he could remember. He recalled the confidence he had felt under Ahmed's leadership during the Russian campaign, and now he longed for the comfort and wisdom of his old friend.

His search for Ali Fadhil in a city of more than six million people promised to be a tiresome task. Naji had no access to Metalcraft's records. Electronic tracking was not possible for him in this unfamiliar place. It all

174

came down to his ability to follow his instincts along Ali's trail of women and money. First he had to find the trail. He knew Ali had to sleep somewhere. He had to eat somewhere.

Naji surmised Ali would have to do something with the money he'd stolen from Metalcraft. Ali's greed demanded a leveraging of that money into a multiple of the original principal. To live his kind of life he would require transportation, investment banking connections, and a cover of some sort. An expensive car and wealthy women represented likely components in the man's lifestyle equation.

Now that he'd sketched out the modus operandi of his quarry, Naji knew he had to eliminate the remote possibility that Ali had deceptively broken with his past and laid low in some ghetto where no one would expect to find him. In either case, he figured Ali had probably changed his name, and quite possibly his appearance.

Most of Rio's shantytowns, or *favelas*, were located in the city's North section, the *Zona Norte*. Hundreds of different-colored tar-paper-and-plywood shacks, crowded together like grave markers of the undead, formed a checkerboard pattern of paupers' castles in each *favela*. The shantytowns offered an unsuspected place to hide if disappearance from the face of the earth was the objective.

In the interests of maintaining a low profile, Naji rented a cheap room on the outskirts of the *favela* nearest to the downtown sector of the city. He shaved his beard, trimmed his hair, bought a pair of horn-rimmed glasses, and acquired two wardrobes. One designed to make him look like a businessman on vacation, the other to allow him to blend into shabby places like the *favelas*.

He spent his first day searching, with as much stealth as he could manage, through the four shantytowns closest to Rio. He spent the next day scouting some of the more economically disadvantaged areas of the city. He knew it had to be done, even at the risk of being spotted before he identified his target. At the end of the second day he felt satisfied Ali had not sequestered himself away, at least not in the most unlikely places. Naji kept his room, rented a Hyundai, and shifted his search to more affluent sectors of the city.

During the next two days his search combined a tour of the best restaurants, with resourcefully-contrived inquiries at the best hotels. At night he peeked into as many gala events as he could schedule, always careful to guard against the possibility his quarry might see him first. No sign of Ali.

175

On the fourth day he added stock brokers and investment advisors to his daily itinerary. Naji pitched them with a deceptively simple reason for his visit. He was Ara Narsekian, a wealthy American from San Francisco. The Armenian name would be consistent with both a dark countenance and a credible documentation of American citizenship.

Ara intended, he claimed, to find an advisor he could trust. Particularly one in whom other transplanted Americans had placed their confidence, and therefore could be used as references. The ruse produced a growing file of names and contact information along with brief, gratuitously offered background summaries. None fit the description of the man he was looking for. Ali Fadhil remained a ghost.

At the end of the week, Naji's quiet pilgrimage brought him to Banco do Nordeste do Brasil, and an interview with Ernesto Villanueva. Ernesto's face lit up.

"Ah, Mr. Narsekian. I believe I have just the advisor for you." The excited banker reached into his desk drawer and pulled out the new brochure his printer had made up only the week before. The single-sheet, two-sided document described the services offered by Harvey Morgan and his two licensed associates, along with a summary outline of their competencies in the investment field. "May I offer you a drink?" Ernesto asked.

Naji remained silent while he studied the brochure and tried to ignore the pungent odor of old cigarette smoke that clung to Ernesto's clothes. After a few moments he handed the document back to Ernesto and looked up with an expression of apology for not having responded right away. "No. Thank you. I can only stay for a few minutes."

"Yes. Well, as you can see, Mr. Narsekian, our Mr. Morgan meets your criteria perfectly. I don't need to emphasize this, except that you asked. You may be certain he's a highly trustworthy associate of mine."

Naji picked up the brochure again and studied it with more intensity. The narrative supporting Mr. Morgan's position appeared consistent with Ali Fadhil's business background. Then again, the description could have matched any of a hundred such profiles.

Naji forced a smile. "Usually advertising pieces like this show photographs, Mr. Villanueva. This one doesn't. Why is that, may I ask?"

"Ha! I asked the same question." Ernesto flashed a satisfied grin. "In fact, I had a marvelous photo of Mr. Morgan and his two associates all ready to go to the printer. I took it during one of their joint meetings with a prospective client. Harvey found out about it right before it went to print, and stopped it. He says photos are for hungry merchants and politicians. He says they're unprofessional for bankers and investment advisors. I couldn't disagree more, of course, but he's the boss in this investment branch of ours."

"I see," Naji muttered. "This Mr. Morgan seems like a modest man. Still, personal appearances are important to me when I have to trust the advisor with my money. Do you suppose I might have a glance at the photo you took?"

"I don't see why not." Ernesto reached into his desk again and handed his visitor a proof copy. "Harvey takes a much more impressive picture head on, of course. Even from this distance, you can see he comes across looking very professional."

Naji made every effort to hide his feeling of relieved satisfaction. It was Ali Fadhil, no doubt about it. His search had ended. The kill would be considerably easier than the search had been. Still, it had to be done carefully.

He handed the photo back to Ernesto. "Thank you, Mr. Villanueva, you've been a great help. I have a number of other sources to interview yet, but I'm impressed with what I've seen here. You're likely to see me again. I'm off to another appointment right now, so I'll say goodbye. I'll be in touch. Since I don't wish to be bothered by all the bankers I'm considering until I've made a decision, I trust you will hold our meeting in the strictest confidence."

Chapter 30

"You're on suspension, Pallino." Jack Marshall's voice dropped a decibel or two in volume, but the intensity of it remained as strong as ever.

Mike had hoped for a more agreeable reception from his boss, although he didn't really expect it. He lowered his gaze. "Yes, sir, I understand."

Jack shook his head. "No, I don't think you do. You can consider yourself damned lucky that boy survived."

"I guess I can't argue with you about that," Mike said. A wave of guilt surged into his mind from out of nowhere, accompanied by the haunting image of a muzzle flash and Milt hitting the deck. Mike felt, now more than ever, that his bespectacled sidekick would make a damned good CPA one day. Maybe this was all meant to be. "How long do you think the suspension will last?" Mike struggled to force out the question.

"Until the board of inquiry completes a full investigation. The findings will determine whether you'll have to resign, or if we can even reinstate you at a desk job somewhere."

Mike frowned. "A desk job?"

"Yes, a desk job. They're sure as hell not going to turn you loose in the field again. At any rate, it's out of my hands. I want your badge and your firearm turned in before you leave. Then I want you to go home and stay out of trouble. And *don't* talk to any of the news media. Is that understood?"

"Sure, Jack. But, damn it, a *desk job*? That's about the biggest waste of taxpayer money I can imagine. Can't you support me somehow?"

Jack leaned as far forward as he could manage and glared through narrowed eyes. "Let me explain the problem you've created around here, Pallino. Half the Bureau's top echelon is praising you for putting a positive spin on the FBIs image around the world. The other half is clamoring for your scalp. The American public thinks you're a hero. I don't."

Mike scowled. "Aw, c'mon, Jack. Name me one thing about this that's fair."

Jack rolled his eyes. "Damn it, life isn't fair, Mike. It just comes at you and you play the hand you're dealt. An innocent young man, who never should have been there, almost lost his life before it began. Moreover, there's still no sign of that Fadhil guy you went after in the first place. Right now my first instinct is to stick you in a forensics lab for the duration. Maybe I'll cool off a little later and reconsider. Then maybe I'll put in a good word for you. Now get out of here, and keep a low profile until I call you."

Mike almost made it to the door before his boss called out. "One more thing, Pallino." There always seemed to be one more thing. More often than not, a criticism Jack had forgotten to include in his reprimand. "I'm sorry about your wife on the bridge, Mike."

A sudden recollection of Ellie in her eye-catching evening gown at the last Christmas party flashed through Mike's mind. "Yeah, me too. I'm afraid I lost her long before the bridge."

Mike handed his badge and his weapon to Casey Dutton in the equipment room. "Keep these for me, Case. Maybe someday I'll get 'em back. They've been part of me for so long that giving them up kind of makes me feel like an unwilling organ donor."

Casey shook his head and forced a smile. "Yeah, I know, Mike. I think it stinks what they did to you. For whatever it's worth, the whole office is giving you a thumbs-up for what you did up there on that bridge. You're tops in our book, and we're sorry about the way Ellie used you and all."

"Thanks, Case. Who knows, maybe there'll be a silver lining to all this out there somewhere. See you around." Mike walked out and headed for an empty house again.

* * * * *

Dewey 'Bones' Rafferty showed up at Mike's place half an hour early, excited and hungry. It wasn't often an FBI agent invited a snitch from Back Bay to his house for supper. The emaciated-looking little man wore his best suit, which hung loose over his slight frame.

Over the years, Bones had garnered a corner on the market of underworld news. He knew about it anytime a drug deal went down. He knew every Ponzi scheme as soon as it hatched. Bones could be counted on to either be part of, or at least be familiar with, any big con going in the Boston area. He knew how to get anything on the black market.

Grateful for a source of reliable information, Mike had always taken care to protect Bones. At least enough to keep the skinny little man from going to jail when he trapped himself in his own scams. It was a *quid pro quo*. Bones fed Mike valuable information he couldn't have procured anywhere else. A couple of drinks, a hamburger, and an anecdote or two from Mike's Notre Dame football experience kept Bones loyal and talkative.

Without waiting for his guest to finish his meal, Mike came right to the point. "I can't get out of here, Bones, and I need some big-time help from you."

Bones choked down the last bite of his burger. "Yeah, I heard about you bein' suspended and all. That's a bummer, man. I mean, taking your badge and gun like that."

Mike shook his head. "Well, I'm optimistic about a favorable outcome from this investigation. The problem is that when I get it, I'll have to be ready to start hunting down a guy who needs to be found. I need you to get some things for me."

"Sure, what do you want me to do, Mike? I mean, maybe I should ask what *you* plan to do."

"I'm going to kill the scumbag responsible for what happened to Milt. The first thing I want is for you to get me a Glock and a Smith and Wesson .38. How long will that take?"

Bones grabbed a handful of potato chips while he paused to think about it. "Mike, it ain't none of my business, and I probably shouldn't say this. Look, you need to be careful, man. I mean, you wear a badge and kill a guy and it's self-defense in the line of duty. You kill a man when you got no badge and it's murder, man. One place you never want to find yourself is in the slammer with a bunch of cons when they find out you're an ex-FBI agent."

Mike stood and yawned. "Yeah, I know. Let me worry about that. Can you get the guns?"

"I'll get 'em. Take me a few days. How come you don't have one of your own?"

"I did but it made Ellie nervous having so many firearms around the house. I got rid of it and kept only the standard issue required by the Bureau."

"Okay, what else do you need?"

"There's a girl named Phoebe Denton who works at Metalcraft. You know where that is. I called her this morning. She went into this scumbag's office and found papers indicating he's been communicating with Merrill Lynch in San Francisco under the name Harvey Morgan. His real name is Ali Fadhil, although my guess is he'll never use that one again. Anyway, he's been scamming money from the company. I mean big money. I'm sure he invested it with that San Francisco brokerage, then pulled it out and fled the country. You look like you're still hungry, Bones. You want another burger?"

Bones flashed a wide grin. "Yeah, I guess I could use one, seeing as it's free."

Mike stepped over to the grill and brought him the last warm one. "I've a contact named Wade Rollins in the San Francisco FBI field office. He's combing through all the flights that left the country from San Francisco during the last few days. If he can tie this Harvey Morgan to one of those flights I'll know where my target went. I need you to pick up the file on this guy from Phoebe. I don't want her seen coming to my house. She's expecting you, so go there. As soon as I find out where Morgan went, I'm going after him. Badge or no badge."

Bones gobbled the burger as though it was the only food he'd had in days. He wiped his chin with the back of his hand as he went along. "Okay, Mike. I'll bring you the file and guns. Like I said, though, you better make sure you got authorization to shoot. Or, if you kill this guy before you're reinstated, you better hope they never find his body. Anything else?"

Mike scooped the last few dishes from the table and dumped them in the sink. "Yeah, I'll need a fake ID and an FBI badge in case the Bureau doesn't restore mine in time. I can't carry a weapon on the plane without those. Can you get them?"

"It won't be all that easy, but I'll get 'em. I gotta go. See you later. Just be careful, man."

Mike patted Bones on the shoulder, gave him a bottle of his best Merlot, and watched the loyal snitch drive away. He remembered watching Ellie drive away a few weeks before. It all seemed so distant now, like a bad dream from which he'd soon awaken and find everything okay again, just as it had been.

A satisfying career and what seemed like a perfect marriage. First, the marriage fell apart. Then he saved his country, and his career came apart in the hands of a damned board of inquiry. Now he was confined to his house, waiting to find out if he even had a job. It didn't seem fair. Maybe his mother had been right. Everyone should have two lives. The first to learn by, the second to enjoy.

Chapter 31

Harvey made no effort to conceal his irritation. "What do you mean he wanted a photo, Ernesto?"

"Just that, Harvey. This man came from San Francisco, like you did. He's an excellent prospect. I think we'll get him. However, he apparently prefers to know who he's dealing with, and asked to see that photo copy you wouldn't let me put in the brochure. He didn't want me to mention it to you, but I thought you should know. Anyway, as I said, he's a prospect who fits our client profile perfectly. I told you your photo would have been good advertising."

"Damn it, Ernesto! I didn't want to have...I mean, I didn't want our firm to have that kind of cheap publicity. What was the man's name, and what did he look like?"

"Ahhh...Narsekian, I believe. He was about your height and build, dark hair, cut kind of short like maybe almost a crew cut, and he wore glasses. Rather intellectual, I'd guess. Well-spoken, and claimed to be wealthy. Seemed like a perfect prospect for you, Harvey. I didn't give him your photo. He just glanced at it. I think he was very impressed."

"Did he say where he was going when he left?"

"No, only that he had other firms to interview. Is there something wrong?"

"Um...no. Just don't do that again. I mean with my photo. I'll let you know when I want to promote myself with a picture. Ernesto, this may sound strange, but if you see him again, I'd like you to take his picture without him knowing about it if you can. As I told you when we met, there are some people who want me to work exclusively for them, no one else. They'd go out of their way to try to do me harm. And this man may be one of them. I'm not saying he is, only that he may be. Can you do that for me?"

"Certainly. Where are you going? You seem so upset."

"I'm late for a luncheon appointment, that's all. And, yes, I'm a little nervous about all this, but not upset. Don't worry about it. I'll be back after lunch."

* * * * * *

Tired of waiting and ready to eat, Lani considered ordering her lunch whether Harvey showed up or not. If she'd even suspected she might have to dine alone, she wouldn't have turned down the offer from the guy who just walked across the room to proposition her. Lani blamed it on the blouse — low-cut in an angle across her breasts from her left shoulder toward her right underarm. She'd long since grown accustomed to being approached in bars and restaurants by men who couldn't resist the lure of an outrageously sensual woman who exuded an air of wealth.

Before she'd finished her first martini, Harvey joined her, kissed her on the cheek, and apologized for being half an hour late. The waitress laid a menu in front of him, smiled, asked him what he'd like to drink, and asked Lani if she wanted another martini. She nodded. Harvey ordered a Manhattan on the rocks.

"You're forgiven, darling," she said, "if you'll just stop looking so distressed all the time. What's gotten into you lately? You still think that guy you can't see is following you?"

"Worse. He's left me a note demanding I stop seeing you permanently, and another, three days later, saying he'd have me killed if we're seen together again. I thought you said your suitors weren't the nasty kind. Who the hell *is* this devotee of yours?"

Lani finished her first drink and put her hand on his arm. "Darling, I swear I have no idea who that could be. Didn't he provide any identification at all?"

"No. An unsigned little note slipped under my hotel room door. I think it's time you level with me about which of your former boyfriends are deadly serious about you and which aren't."

"Harvey, I meant it when I said there's no one I can think of who might be in love with me enough to go that far."

"That's not love, Lani. That's obsession. Now think back. Maybe it's someone from the distant past in your history of conquests. Take your time. Anyone come to mind?"

184

Before she could answer, the waitress delivered their drinks and asked if they were ready to order. Lani rattled off her choice as though she'd been waiting all day for the opportunity. Harvey shoved his menu back to the waitress without looking at it and told her to bring him the same. Lani placed her elbows on the table and lowered her chin to her cupped hands to think for a moment.

Harvey waited.

"Okay," Lani said after a long deliberation, "there was a suitor who owned a couple of hotels. This was, oh, two or three years ago, I guess. He proposed marriage to me twice...no, three times. He finally offered me one of his hotels if I'd agree to marry him. I told him I didn't need the money, and needed him even less. I thought that ended it until I learned later he'd threatened to expose the crooked dealings of my next suitor and ruin him if that fellow didn't drop me. Needless to say, the weakling did, which was fine with me. I didn't like him all that much anyway." She picked up her second martini and went to work on it.

"So where is this hotel owner now?" Harvey asked, with a tone of heightened impatience.

"I don't know. His name was Antonio Braggia. Someone said he sold his hotels and bought a few thousand acres of land somewhere. He was in the news last year, accused of hiring someone to kill one of his business competitors. They couldn't prove it so he got off." She leaned forward and put both her hands on his forearm. "What are you going to do, Harvey?"

"I'm not sure. I have another problem that has to be dealt with first. Then I'll go looking for this Braggia fellow. In the meantime, maybe it's best if we're not seen together in public for a while, Lani."

She patted his arm and smiled. "Oh, darling, I think you're overreacting. Oh, all right. If you think it's best."

The waitress delivered their meals and they ate in silence with only an occasional glance at each other. After they had finished, Lani emptied her martini, and they parted with another kiss. Harvey Morgan spent the remainder of the day changing accommodations to the Brisa Barra Hotel, where he registered under the name William Bristol.

* * * * * *

Because Antonio Braggia's cutthroat style of doing business destroyed a number of his competitors, he had enemies. Two bodyguards protected him twenty-four hours a day. His living accommodations included an inaccessible hideaway mansion constructed in the Serra do Mar Mountains, on the other side of Rio. His wife lived in town with a bodyguard of her own. Even she wasn't sure where her husband went when fear drove him into seclusion. Only his mistresses could come and go at will, as long as they were frisked by the guards, who considered the task one of the perks of the job.

From inside information provided by one of Antonio's bankrupt competitors, Behram Naji knew Antonio's whereabouts, and of his intent to have Harvey Morgan killed. He also knew Antonio's bodyguards monitored a motion-sensitive alarm system positioned to cover the mansion's exposed front and sides. Since the mountain wrapped its jagged cliffs tightly around the rear of the building, he guessed electronic devices would be useless there, and probably not needed anyway. For anyone else, the cliffs rendered the fortress impregnable from behind. From the perspective of an old mountain fighter like Naji, the rear approach represented Antonio Braggia's Achilles heel.

Naji would have preferred to take out the guards silently with his knife. Even decades after the Russian campaign, his skill hadn't diminished, only his strength — and he assumed the two apes guarding Antonio were young and powerful. Like a jungle cat stalking its prey under the protective cover of darkness, Naji crept up without a sound behind them while they busied themselves in the kitchen preparing a midnight snack.

He'd never had any use for silencers before. They were cumbersome, awkward to store, and time consuming to attach. It was too late now to wish he had one. He leveled his weapon, fired twice, and the guards slumped to the floor. In the wake of the deafening roar that reverberated through the house, Naji knew his chances of confronting Antonio in a surprise move had evaporated.

He could hear the hysterical screams of Braggia's mistress-of-the-day from the upstairs bedroom. He also heard a panicked Antonio trying to shut her up and lock his bedroom door at the same time. He had to assume Antonio had a weapon and knew how to use it. Having observed all the mistakes the Soviet Army made in Afghanistan, Naji had learned never to charge a well-barricaded enemy position without being prepared to take extreme losses. Storming Antonio's bedroom was out of the question. It might, he thought, be unnecessary anyway.

He didn't need to attack Antonio. Naji wanted only the man's agreement to call off the assassin he'd hired to take out Ali.

"Antonio Braggia," Naji shouted through the closed bedroom door after he'd ascended the stairs. "You don't know me, and my name is of no importance. All you need to know is that we both share a common enemy. I want him, not you. His name is Harvey Morgan. I know you've given an order to have him killed, and I know why. Your enemies have told me all about you. You may rest assured I am not one of them."

Naji paused, waiting for a response that didn't come. After a few moments he tried a different approach. "With all due respect to you and your reasons for wanting this man dead, it's of vital importance to me, and many others, that I kill him myself. I want you to call off your hired assassin now. If you don't have a phone in your room, I'll give you my cell phone."

Again, there was no reaction.

"Antonio," Naji went on, "we could begin an ugly gunfight right now, and probably kill each other and the woman. It's not necessary. I've killed your guards in order that you have no doubt as to the seriousness of my intent to be the one who kills Morgan. If you do as I ask, your own objectives will be satisfied with absolutely no legal exposure on your part. You win, I win. Do we have a deal?"

Naji had anticipated the long silence that followed, broken only by the terrified woman's uncontrollable sobbing. He waited.

"How do I know I'm safe after I make the call?"

Naji heard the kind of voice he figured could only come from a weak, frightened coward. He wondered how such a pathetic creature could have become so powerful.

"We have to trust each other, Antonio. I have no reason to harm you. If I did, we'd already be in the middle of a gunfight instead of a discussion. You have to trust me to be out of your life forever. I have to trust you to make the call without retracting it after I've left. You make the call, and you or your woman can watch me leave. You can't possibly lose."

Another prolonged silence.

"Tell me who you are," a shaking voice replied, "and why you want Morgan."

"Who I am is not important. His death is necessary to avenge the deaths of many of my people. To reveal my identity would only serve to compromise that. Now, do we have a deal?"

"Only if you can provide some form of proof you've fulfilled your end of the bargain." The tone had changed from frightened to assertive.

"I can assure you of that, Antonio. The discovery of a headless body will make front page news in *O Globo* and *Journal do Brasil*. It might even make it to *Correlo Braziliesne*. You won't lack for proof."

Following another not-unexpected period of silence, Naji could hear the man talking to someone. Only the words "Well, wake him up" were audible. Silence again, then some conversation in a language he couldn't understand — different from his English dialogue with Antonio. He assumed it to be Portuguese. Again he waited.

"Very well, it's been taken care of," Antonio said in a voice which now sounded indignant. "Now go, and please leave me alone. I put my life in your hands, and I expect that part of our bargain to be fulfilled as well."

"You're a wise man, Antonio. May Allah be with you."

Naji descended the stairs quietly, scanned the main floor again out of habit, and walked out into the darkness.

Antonio sent his mistress downstairs to confirm Naji's departure.

Chapter 32

"I did the best I could, Mike." Even though Jack's voice had lost its angry edge, Mike couldn't detect any warmth in it. He'd walked into Jack's office expecting the worst, and it looked like that might turn out to be exactly what he was going to get. "The board of inquiry voted to reinstate you," Jack continued, "although they specified that it had to be in a staff position. I did what I could on your behalf. I know it's not what you wanted. I'm sorry."

Mike turned his hands palms-up. "Aw c'mon, Jack. A staff zombie? How big a waste is that?"

"You'll have your badge and firearm back, but you'll be assigned a desk job. Probably something in Forensics Support. At least it's better than being dismissed. You'll draw full pay, be eligible for promotion, and all that. Except no field work. Look, why don't you take a couple weeks off? Go sailing or something. I know you love sailing. Then come on in and we'll see if we can find a position you might grow to like."

Mike shook his head. "So, the board thinks I'm good enough to sit behind a desk, but not good enough to do what I trained to do for the past five years. Is that the idea?"

Jack vaulted out of his chair. "Damn it, Mike, it was a close vote. Three to two. And I'll tell you something else. If the San Francisco office hadn't written up a glowing report on you and that accountant, the vote probably would have gone the other way. Now stop crying in your beer and be grateful you're still employed. Get out of here and I'll see you in two weeks. And don't leave the city without letting me know — even if you go sailing. I may need to contact you."

In the equipment room Casey greeted Mike with a wide grin and a pat on the shoulder. He returned Mike's firearm and badge. "I knew they'd never can you, Mike. Hell, Jack would have been down on his knees begging on

189

your behalf if they had. Welcome back. The rest of the guys'll be damned glad to hear it."

"Thanks, Case. They've made me an office weenie, but I'll consider it a probation period until they figure out it's a misallocation of resources and put me back out in the field where I belong."

Mike waved a thumbs-up, climbed into his Mercedes, and stopped off for a beer with Matt before he tried again to get used to a house with no one in it except himself.

* * * * * *

Bones showed up at Mike's door with Ali's file, a pair of handguns, and a forged badge that Mike no longer needed.

"Come on in, Bones. Did you have any trouble scrounging up this stuff?"

Bones handed Mike the file, laid the firearms on the hall table, and made a beeline for the fridge where he knew he'd find a leftover something or other. "Damn right I did, but this is everything. Any word on what they're going to do with you?"

"Yeah, they made me a staff grunt. They want to make sure the worst damage I can do is spill coffee on some lab rat's report."

Bones threw a collection of salami, pickles, potato salad, and cheese on a hamburger bun, and smothered it with mustard. He dropped his narrow frame, along with a small mustard spill, on Mike's leather recliner. "Jeez, I'm sorry, man. Those meatheads in the Bureau don't know it yet, but crime'll be hitting the ceiling now that you're not rounding up crackheads and Mafia anymore. That guy you're after, they been able to find where he went yet?"

Mike sat on a bar stool by the L-shaped kitchen counter, opened the file, and paused while he glanced through it. "No," he said without looking up, "they're still working on it."

"If you don't mind me asking Mike, are you really going to stay with the bureau? I mean, you don't seem like the kind to spend the rest of your life behind a desk." Bones wiped his chin with the back of his sleeve and dove into another salami sandwich.

Satisfied with the contents of the file, Mike tossed it onto the counter and turned to face his favorite snitch. "They can take their staff job and shove it, Bones. As soon as I get a call from San Francisco telling me where that maggot went, I'm on my way. I've two weeks to get the job done, assuming I find out where to hunt for him."

Bones gulped down another chunk of his culinary amalgamation and shook his head. "Okay, I'm gonna say this for the last time. And if you hadn't done so much for me I wouldn't say it at all. You need to be careful, man. You think you got it bad right now. You ain't even begun to know what trouble is until they pick you up for shooting someone without authorization. I don't care if the guy's a serial killer or a prince."

"No more lectures, Bones. I appreciate your concern, but I've made up my mind. Now, I have some lecture-type advice for you. Stay out of trouble. My successor, whoever he turns out to be, might not be as tolerant as I've been. Here's another bottle of Merlot. Go home and behave yourself. And thanks for everything. I won't forget it."

"Sure, Mike. Good luck."

Mike watched his old friend leave, and couldn't stop the returning memories of Ellie. He wiped the corner of his eye to clear off a tear he thought had dried up weeks ago.

* * * * * *

Mike's cell phone blasted out the familiar Notre Dame Victory March just as he finished the report he'd promised Carter Bannister Pringle. With judicious exercise of writer's prerogative, Mike injected the kind of flavor he thought a father would like to see in his account of Milt's joint venture with the FBI. He gave his closing comments a quick once-over, walked to the kitchen counter, and picked up the phone.

"Mike, it's Wade Rollins. I've traced your man to Rio de Janeiro, under the Harvey Morgan name you gave me. Better yet, I discovered he opened an account at Banco do Nordeste do Brasil to which he transferred several million dollars from his account at Merrill Lynch. Now, get this. He's formed an investment advisory joint venture with that bank. He's apparently dating some heiress down there. Now, tell me what you plan to do about it. I understand they stuck you on a desk job."

Mike pumped his fist in the air with the same gesture of triumph he once used to cap off his touchdown runs. "All right, baby, all right. Good work, Wade. Yeah, I thought the news about me being chained to a desk would travel fast. Anyway, I have two weeks' worth of what my boss calls rest and recuperation. I'm going after this creep to even the score. There's no place far enough away, and no hole deep enough for that sleazeball to hide."

"Whoa, old buddy. If getting even means you intend to kill him, you need a hell of a lot more than a badge. Surely, you know that."

Mike whirled around and punched the wall. "Damn it, I'll tell you what I know, Wade. I know it's an odds-on bet that this bottom-feeding maggot turned my wife into a high-priced whore. He caused the loss of my job and almost the death of the best partner I ever had…even if he was just a green-eyeshades accountant. Now I'm going to make sure this dirtbag regrets the day he slid out of his mother's womb."

"Aw, come on, Mike. Use your head. I can't believe you're about to throw the rest of your life away for some jerk who isn't worth the bullet it takes to kill him. Remember what they taught us our first week with the Bureau: passion and caution are bad companions…never fire when you're angry. Tell you what. Take your two weeks out here and spend some quality time with me, Helen, and the kids. We'll take you on a few tours of all the parts of San Francisco that don't blow up. We'll show you Napa Valley for the best Merlot you ever had. There are single women out here, too. Beautiful ones. Who knows, you might find your true soul mate. So, forget about this guy. He'll probably end up in a Brazilian jail, anyway. What do you say?"

"Thanks, Wade. Your concern and friendship mean a lot to me. Truly they do. It's just that this is something I have to take care of or I'll never be able to look at myself in the mirror again. Hell, maybe it'll all turn out okay. Maybe I can take you up on your offer afterward. I have to go. I'll keep you posted. Give my best to Helen."

Mike wiped Bones' mustard splotch from the recliner and slumped against the soft pillows. He thought about Wade's offer. Maybe he should have taken him up on it. Wade had it made with a wife and kids who loved him. They probably had a dog, and grilled hamburgers together like a tight-knit family should. Like the one Mike always wanted. Maybe he'd find a wife like Helen someday. Maybe buy the Contessa and take her sailing.

What the hell, first things first. Ali Fadhil.

Chapter 33

Naji knew the killing and decapitation of Ali Fadhil would not be difficult, simply unpleasant. Even for an old mountain fighter accustomed to violence. At least there would be some measure of satisfaction. Naji had harbored an intense dislike for the man from the moment he first met him. A jihad critical to Ahmed's future failed because Ali, through his own arrogance, had not taken proper precautions. That alone demanded punishment. Presentation of Ali's head to *Mara Salvatrucha* would preserve Naji's own — another important consideration.

The problem would be how to transport the head to San Francisco. None of Chico's *guerreros* would risk meeting him in South America to retrieve it for fear of capture by the *Sombre Negra*. Naji briefly considered transportation by car up the coast of Brazil, through Guiana, Venezuela, Panama, Honduras and Guatemala. Too long a trip. The dry ice required for preservation of the head wouldn't last. In any case, entry into the United States carrying a box with a human head would pose problems of its own.

The solution had to be air travel by private plane. It would have to be flown by a pilot who could set his plane down on some field in the U.S. where no one checks incoming baggage. The arrangements for that took longer than he had thought, and the price came higher than he wanted. Naji searched around until he found a pilot with enough connections to set up the flight. He made the deal, and waited in his car outside Banco do Nordeste for Ali to leave at the end of the day.

* * * * * *

Mike Pallino pulled his Mercedes up in front of Banco do Nordeste without noticing the man in the parked car near the driveway exit. He entered the bank and scanned the lobby for any sign of someone who might fit Harvey

193

Morgan's description. He made a mental note of the furnishings and the surrounding offices in the mausoleum-like structure before he approached Ernesto's secretary. After he introduced himself and showed his badge, she buzzed her boss.

"Sir, there's a federal agent from the United States here to see you," she said in an apprehensive tone.

"What does he want?"

"I don't know, sir. He wouldn't say."

"Send him in."

Ernesto squeezed his wedged-in hips from the chair and rose to meet Mike.

Mike flashed his badge and held out his hand. "Good afternoon, Mr. Villanueva. I'm Special Agent Mike Pallino from the FBI. I'll come right to the point without wasting time. I understand you have a Harvey Morgan in your employ. I'm here to take him into custody. Where might I find him?"

Ernesto looked stunned. "*Ai, meu Dios!* What has he done?"

"He's wanted for various crimes in the United States, Mr. Villanueva. Is he here, sir?"

"Yes, Officer Pallino. He's in the conference room down the hall, but he's with a client. Can this wait for a few moments? He will be finished shortly, and I would prefer not to alarm the client."

Mike shook his head. Alarm the client? Hell, he thought, if the client's not already alarmed he should be. "I don't see why not. In the meantime I'd appreciate it if you would bring me his personnel file and any related documents. I understand he's become a business partner of yours. Is that correct?"

"Yes, sir. You may wait in his office. You'll find his files there. However, I'll need a signed note from you stating that this is an official search before I can allow access to that kind of information."

Mike complied and scribbled out his own version of a search warrant, handed it to Ernesto, and made himself at home in Fadhil's office. Determined to dredge up his dim recollections of *Chapter Three: Evidentiary Materials*, Mike went through Harvey's file drawers with a vengeance. He pulled all the documents he deemed relevant to his plan to kill the man as a fugitive from justice, and stuffed them into a small canvas bag. He finished seconds before Ernesto ushered a surprised Harvey in and introduced him.

John Chaplick

"Thank you, Mr. Villaneuva," Mike said. "Please leave us alone, if you will."

Ernesto wiped a drop of perspiration from his brow, shook his head, and disappeared.

"What's this all about, Mr. Pallino?" Harvey's face showed anger where Mike had expected surprise, possibly even signs of sudden flight. "I've done nothing wrong, and you have no jurisdiction here."

"I do, and you're under arrest, Mr. Morgan. I'll bypass the customary reading of your rights because you have none here. Sit down. You *will* answer my questions unless you want to spend the rest of your life in a Brazilian jail."

"You're lying," Harvey snapped, still on his feet. "You're required to read me my Miranda Rights, and you can't arrest me without the consent of the Brazilian government. I know the law on this."

Mike grabbed Harvey by the necktie and pulled him close. He leaned toward his suspect with a glare that reflected the full measure of his accumulated anger. "Wrong, Morgan. If I can't arrest you, then I don't have to read you your rights. That's in the Miranda Law. The fact is I *can* take you into custody without reading you your rights because you're a damned terrorist under international law." Mike didn't really care whether Harvey knew it was a lie or not. He released his grip and Harvey stepped back, eyes wide. "Approval of both countries is automatic in the extradition of terrorists," Mike lied again, "and they have no rights. Now sit down before I knock you down."

Harvey eased into a chair. "What the hell are you talking about, Pallino? What terrorists?"

"I'm talking about an Al Qaeda weasel named Ali Fadhil. In the United States they'll execute you. However — and listen carefully — I can keep you alive and well down here in Rio, if you'll do as I say."

Harvey retreated a few steps and settled into a chair without taking his eyes off Mike. "I'm listening."

Mike leaned toward Morgan and spoke in a soft tone. "Look, we've both made our share of mistakes on this deal, but there's a way we can both benefit from them. I want you to be seen walking out of here handcuffed to me, as though I had arrested you. When we're out of sight of the bank, I'll remove the cuffs. I'll drive you to your hotel, and on the way you will give me some answers."

Harvey forced a weak scowl. "Yeah? Like what kind of answers?"

195

"Like the kind that'll convince me not to kill you. We'll have a few drinks in your room, and you will agree to transfer, into my bank account tomorrow morning, half of the Metalcraft money you stole. Once the deposit is confirmed, I'm out of here, and you're free to continue your illegal activities. You can explain it to your banking partner as a case of mistaken identity or something. And as far as I'm concerned, this meeting never took place. Now let's go."

* * * * * *

Half a dozen people, including Behram Naji, witnessed Mike exiting with his cuffed suspect moments prior to the bank's closing time. Rain-swollen clouds, which had darkened the skies all afternoon, burst. An accelerating wind swept the torrential downpour sideways. Mike shoved Harvey into the passenger side of his car, removed the cuffs, climbed in, and stepped on the accelerator. Tires squealed as the speedometer in the rented Mercedes climbed to sixty in a matter of seconds.

Five miles later Mike turned off the main highway onto a dirt side road where driving conditions had deteriorated from slick to muddy. Visibility had declined from poor to almost none in a matter of minutes, enough to obscure any view of the car following a quarter of a mile behind Mike's.

"Pallino, this is not the way to my hotel. Where the hell are you taking me?"

For the first time the arrogant man's voice sounded frightened. Mike declined to respond.

Three more miles and Mike wheeled the vehicle off the side road and brought it to a stop in a remote wooded area. He unbuckled his seat belt, pulled his .38, and leveled the muzzle at Harvey's forehead.

"Now I want straight answers, Fadhil. The minute I get the feeling you're lying, I spread your brains all over the side window of this car. Who is Nahid Medah?"

"For God's sake, Pallino, what difference does it make? She was just an Iranian whore they stuck me with. Why?"

Mike forced himself to remain calm. "How do you know she was a whore?"

"Because she screwed like a professional." Harvey unbuckled his belt and shifted uneasily in the passenger seat. "Where are you going with this,

Pallino? And what does this have to do with our little agreement to transfer money?"

Mike ignored the question. He clenched his teeth to stem the rage he could feel rising to the surface. "And you experienced her skill yourself? Tell me about it."

"You're one damned sick cop, Pallino. Okay, she was a sensuous bitch and the best I ever had in bed. She was also an accomplished assassin until some FBI flunkie blew the bitch's brains...whoa! Hold on. I'll be damned! You're the guy, aren't you? I heard it was her husband who ended up killing her. It was you, wasn't it? And now you think you're going to kill me and get away with it? You really *are* sick. Okay, before you pull the trigger, think about it, Pallino. Think about all that money that could have been yours. A million-and-a-half. More than you could have made in five lifetimes on a cop's pay. Now all you're going to get is a murder trial. Is it worth it?"

Mike's anger subsided. Never fire when you're angry, they'd taught him. Even close up. Wade's reminder rang in his ears. Calm down, focus, and squeeze the trigger with cold determination. "Yeah, you pathetic slime bag, it's worth it. Only they don't put a federal agent on trial for murder when he's forced to shoot a terrorist in self defense. After you're dead I intend to have the *Polica Federal* freeze your damned money until—"

The bullet that exploded the passenger-side window came from some thirty yards to the right of their vehicle. It entered Harvey's right temple, deflected downward through his left cheek bone, and lodged somewhere under the dashboard. In one swift movement Mike opened the driver's-side door and rolled out onto the rain-soaked ground to put the car between himself and the shooter. In a matter of seconds the driving rain washed the blood splatter from his face.

He snuggled up against the vehicle to get protection on at least one side, and glanced around to get his bearings. The steady downpour combined with the blackness of the sky and the onset of evening to prevent him from seeing the sniper. While he scrunched down in the mud trying to figure out who would want to eliminate Harvey, Mike felt a mixture of anger that someone had robbed him of the pleasure, and fear that whoever did it was a damned good marksman.

"I know who you are, federal agent. You can't see me, but I can see you." The voice came from a stand of small trees to the right of the vehicle. "Put down your gun. It's your prisoner I want, not you."

A series of thoughts raced through Mike's mind. The man was right. Mike still couldn't see him. He was obviously an experienced shooter to have been able to hit a relatively small target under such adverse conditions. A head shot, no less.

Maybe he was telling the truth about wanting only Fadhil. Otherwise, the man could have killed both of them. Fadhil probably had enemies...it made sense. A gunfight right now with such an adversary didn't. Best part, Fadhil was dead. A missed opportunity, but at least he now had no obligation to defend himself before a board of inquiry.

"I like your offer," Mike replied while he scrunched lower and tighter against the vehicle and scanned the trees again. "But how do I know you won't kill me as well?"

During the anxiety-ridden moment of silence that followed, Mike shivered in his soaked clothes. Maybe the shooter didn't have an answer and planned to kill him after all.

"I'll put your mind at ease, agent. You crawl back into your car, shove Fadhil out the door onto the ground. Leave him for me and you can drive away unharmed. Fair enough?"

Mike thought about it for a moment. The man knew his victim's true identity. Hard to believe when only a small handful of federal lawmen knew it.

"Okay, fair enough," Mike hollered back. "First, tell me how you knew this man's identity."

Mike realized he might have pushed his luck a bit too far, but an answer to his question might go a long way toward tracking the bridge jihad to a more specific source.

"I will tell you only that Fadhil's death represents the one objective on which both your people and mine can ever agree. Don't test my patience further. I'm not here to negotiate with you. Now, get back in your car and do as I say, or I will kill you within the next ten seconds."

Mike complied.

With one foot in a pool of blood and the other against Fadhil's rump, Mike reached over, opened the passenger door, and shoved the body out into the mud. He closed the doors and tried to wipe the bloodstains off the inside of the windshield with his wet handkerchief. He'd forgotten how blood smears, but managed to clear it — at least enough to be able to drive.

He revved up the engine, put the Mercedes in gear, pressed the accelerator, and turned back for one more attempt to catch a glimpse of the assassin. All he could see was a dark form approaching with a machete in one hand and what appeared to be a wooden box in the other.

Mike never looked back.

* * * * * *

Naji laid the box of dry ice on the ground and hovered over the body of the man whose failure had set back — by he couldn't even guess how many years — Islam's ascent to its rightful place in the world. He stared down at the corpse for a few moments before he knelt and went to work with the machete. He placed the head in the box, turned, and carried it back to his car. The body, he figured, would be discovered in a few days. Sooner if the federal agent reported it.

He didn't hurry. Naji knew weather conditions would postpone the flight to San Francisco until the next day. He laid the box in the trunk and slumped into the front seat of his car without turning on the ignition. He leaned back and watched the rain pummel the windshield while he contemplated the events of the last two weeks. Presentation of the box with Ali's head would honor his bargain with Chico. News reports of the corpse's discovery would fulfill his promise to Antonio. Ahmed Yasin would be avenged, although revenge would come at the price too painful for him to bear. Still, Naji had warned Ahmed a long time ago not to rely on Ali Fadhil. Naji knew that both he and Ahmed had done everything that could be done. In the final analysis, Islam's dream of ultimate triumph would have to wait.

Chapter 34

Mike savored a satisfying feeling that the bridge ordeal was over, along with the accompanying tension of struggling to discover the source and timing of a disaster so imminent and yet so invisible. For a few rare moments of optimism he imagined a brand new life ahead of him. Still, the past wasn't completely buried and he knew it. Mike stared at Jack Marshall's message on his iPhone. The fugitives who rigged up the car-deaths of those two Metalcraft employees had been neither captured nor identified. Milton's attacker was still on the loose somewhere. In Jack's customary style, the terse little memo said "find them." Mike clicked off, shut the thing down, and cursed it. Okay, fine, I'll go round up Bones and get started, but first things first — a visit to the boat I'm going to buy at the marina, then a trip to visit Milton at his new digs in Boston.

Mike arrived at the marina, parked his car, and walked toward the dock where the Contessa was moored. No better time to buy it. He'd earned the right. He'd pay whatever the old man asked. Well, maybe not without at least some measure of negotiation. Except for a dog, he'd have about everything he really wanted. Especially now that Jack had broken the rules and restored him to field service again.

Mike glanced around. The old man was nowhere to be seen. The Contessa looked like it hadn't been moved even for a test run. Mike smiled. Maybe there still hadn't been any takers at twenty-some-odd thousand. Now he could wheel and deal for a lower price… maybe something like fifteen-to-sixteen thousand. He stepped aboard for a last look-over before the man returned. One quick glance fore and aft to make sure no one was working on her, and he started down the steps into the cabin.

She didn't see him coming down, and he didn't see her making her way up. The inevitable collision left the girl flat on her back and Mike on one knee, scrambling to recover his balance.

"Holy Mary Mother of....who the hell are you?" he snapped as he bent over to help her to her feet. He could feel she was small and light. She reminded him of skinny little Phoebe back at Metalcraft, only prettier and more filled out.

She glared at him, pulled away, and struggled to stand by herself, as if to make it clear she didn't need his help. "I'm Susie Crockett. Who are you? And what are you doing on my boat?"

"What the hell do you mean *your* boat? I came here to buy this boat. I've been planning it for years. My name's Mike Pallino."

She reached down to smooth out her slacks. "Well, Mike Pallino, you're an hour late. I just bought it from that sweet old man who runs this place. By the way, you don't happen to be an experienced sailor, do you?"

Mike pounded his fist against the bulkhead and threw his hands in the air. "Yes, damn it, not that it's relevant. I was afraid something like this would happen." He tilted his head back and looked straight up. "There must be someone up in the great beyond who doesn't like me. Maybe it's Fadhil."

She smiled in a sweet, innocent way that only served to further irritate him. "Why don't we both sit down, Mike Pallino. Perhaps we can work out a business arrangement. I get the feeling I've seen you before. What do you do for a living?"

Mike's glare softened. He had to admit the little boat-thief looked pretty in her navy blue open-at-the-top blouse and white slacks. Her feet were small and delicate, even in those flat blue shoes shaped like ballet slippers. Her blonde hair curled around her ears and tumbled down her shoulder.

"A business arrangement? Hell, kid, you don't look old enough to do business. In answer to your question, I'm an FBI agent."

She sat down on a small, built-in wooden life jacket case and glared at him. "I'll have you know I'm twenty-three, a graduate of Indiana University, and I don't like being referred to as 'kid.' Well, are you interested or not?"

Mike leaned against a bulkhead and studied her. He wondered what business could there possibly be if she'd already completed the transaction. "Okay, I'll bite. What did you have in mind?"

"First, apologize for calling me a kid."

"Damn it, you're an irritating little...okay, I apologize. So, let's have it."

"Well, for starters, Mike Pallino, I need to learn about sailing. I'm from Indiana where they really don't have any ocean. I—"

"Yeah, I know. I spent four years in South Bend."

201

"Well, I've wanted to sail all my life. I was thinking, maybe you could teach me, and we could work out some kind of joint ownership. You know, sort of as compensation for your teaching services."

Mike rolled his eyes. "You gotta be kidding. I could spend the rest of my life providing instruction and it wouldn't come near paying for half of this boat. What *did* you pay for it, by the way?"

"Twelve thousand. Now here's the prob—"

"*Twelve thousand?* I'll kill that old man. How did you manage to get him down to that?"

She put her finger on her chin. "Well, I kind of had to bare my soul. It was a little embarrassing. I'm stuck with some pretty heavy college loans, and I'm looking for a job here in Boston. The trouble is they're not hiring any English majors. I think he felt sorry for me. But, here's my problem. My father gave me five thousand for the down payment and cosigned on the loan. However he made his future payments for the boat contingent upon my learning how to sail it. He said he'd finance it for one year and, if I hadn't found a job by then the deal was off. That's where you come in. I figure you could teach me. Then, if I can't make enough to continue the payments after a year, you could help in return for my giving you a half interest in the boat. So what do you think?"

Mike's jaw dropped. He shifted to an upright position, spun around, slapped his forehead, and turned back to face her. "What do I think? I think you're some piece of work, Susie Crockett. You buy a sleek little craft you don't know anything about, can't sail it, can't pay for it, and you don't have a job. You know what? I think I'll simply wait until you default on the loan. Then I'll walk in, pay off the balance, and this boat is mine for ten thousand less than that old man wanted from me. Now, what do *you* think?"

She cocked her head to one side and looked up at him. "I think that's not a very nice thing to do. Especially for a federal agent. Aren't you supposed to protect people?"

Mike threw back his head and laughed. The girl's bold innocence took him by surprise, and he realized he hadn't laughed that hard in a month. "Fair enough, young lady. Okay, why don't I take you to lunch and we can discuss this convoluted 'business' arrangement? Come on, let's disembark before your first installment comes due and the bank finds out you've knowingly made a fraudulent representation of your financial resources."

She followed him to his car, smiled at him, and asked, "You're not going to arrest me, are you?"

"I probably should, but I won't. Get in."

* * * * * *

The waitress came around, announced they were all out of menus, and told them to order from the list of sandwiches and burgers hand-written on the wall. Mike apologized for the limited offering, and explained that none of the restaurants within a mile or two of the marina were any better.

"I'll have two cheeseburgers," Susie said. "One to go, one for here."

"I'll have the same," Mike said. "Only I'll eat both of them here."

He studied the pretty girl across the table from him, and decided he had to ask. "Why don't you eat them both here? The other will be cold by the time you get it home."

"Oh, the second one's for Charles. He doesn't care if it's cold."

"I see. Charles sounds like a very easy-to-please boyfriend."

"Oh no, Mike, he's my dog. A black Lab."

She hadn't called him by his first name until then. He felt glad she did, although he wasn't sure why. "I've always wanted a dog, but never found the time to commit to it. In fact, until now, I haven't committed enough to a lot of things I've always wanted." He stroked his chin and pointed at her. "Hey, I believe we've met just like you said. You're the girl with the dog that was so friendly down at the marina some time ago. Forgive me for not remembering."

She gave an affirmative nod, cast a furtive glance at Mike's left hand, and looked up at him again. "You're right. It's good to reconnect with you. Now, I didn't see a ring, so I assumed you're not married."

He felt a slight tightening in his throat. He remembered the mixed emotions he felt when he'd chucked his wedding ring into the basket next to Ellie's desk, along with her picture of him. "No. Not any more." Then he wished he hadn't put it quite like that.

"Divorced?"

"No."

"Oh. I'm sorry. Your wife must have died. Was it cancer?"

"I'd rather not talk about it. Here's the waitress with our lunch. Let's chow down."

Mike devoured the two burgers in the time it took Susie to mince her way through one. Except for a brief exchange about her college curriculum, they didn't talk. He paid the tab, waited while she stuffed the Charles-burger into her purse, and they walked out together. They remained silent until Mike let her out by her car at the marina.

"You don't eat much do you?" he said. "I mean, you look like you could afford to put on a little weight." Again he wished he hadn't phrased it quite that way.

She raised her head and stiffened. "I eat plenty. In fact, I'm very full-figured. Anyway, it's better than being overweight."

Mike tried to stifle a grin. "Okay, I'll take your word for it. We didn't talk about that business arrangement like you wanted. I don't mean to sound intrusive, but how about dinner tomorrow night? I mean, unless we figure out something before the end of the month, the loan sharks will be after you and you won't need any sailing lessons."

"You're on," she said, with a wider grin than any she'd offered so far. "Only I have a better idea. Let's pack a lunch and you take me out on my boat for my first lesson. Are you game for that?"

"Susie Crockett, you are one presumptuous lady. Okay, meet you on board the Contessa at six tomorrow. You pack the lunch, I'll bring the drinks. You might want to go light on breakfast."

She tilted her head again the way he's seen her do it before. "Why?"

"Let's just say I want to make sure you can handle the movement of the boat without getting queasy on your first voyage."

He ignored her quizzical look and watched her drive away. This time he didn't think about Ellie. He realized that, for the first time in weeks, he hadn't thought about her. In fact, from the moment he crashed into Susie, he hadn't thought about Jack, the bridge, Milton, or any of the ghosts that had chained themselves to his every waking moment. Here was a delightful young woman who liked dogs. She even liked sailing— at least for the moment. He smiled at the thought of how different she was from Ellie. Then he eased into his Mercedes and headed to visit the young man who had changed his opinions on just about everything.

* * * * * *

Carter Bannister Pringle didn't exactly welcome Mike with open arms, but he didn't snarl at him either. "Come on in Mr. Pallino. You're probably surprised to find me here in Milton's apartment, but his mother and I are helping Phoebe clean up the place and make sure Milt gets used to moving around by himself. The two ladies are out shopping. They'll be sorry they missed you. Have a seat. I'll get Milt and then leave you two alone. By the way, I received your write-up on his role on the bridge. Well phrased." The man's expression remained as deadpan as his greeting.

No longer bandaged and trussed up, Milt hugged Mike who grinned and returned the squeeze as enthusiastically as he could without stressing his friend's healing torso. "Milt, it's great to see you up and about. How do you feel?"

I'm fine, Mike. Ready to get back to work. Did you know Mac McLeod hired me as his Chief Financial Officer?"

"Yeah, I heard. That's the best news I've had other than you getting well again. Now you can clean up your predecessor's mess. Bet you're gonna love that." They both broke into a robust laugh, and Mike felt the rekindling of a friendship he'd wondered if he might have lost. "Say, how are you and Phoebe getting along? Your dad said she was here helping out."

"More than that, Mike. We're going to be married. I'm counting on you to be my best man. Its six months away, but you'll be getting your announcement in a month or two. I'm also going to take another shot at the CPA exam. Keep your fingers crossed for me."

Mike grinned. "I have no doubt that you'll pass it. If you don't, I'll have Jack Marshall vent his wrath on the AICPA. That ought to cure them." Their outburst of laughter brought Carter Banister back into the room to check on them. He shook his head, grinned for the first time Mike could remember, and withdrew to the kitchen.

Mike spent the next hour relating the chain of events after San Francisco. Milt shook his head and reiterated his sorrow about the Ellie/Nahid outcome. They chatted and consumed beers for another hour before Milt showed signs of needing to rest. Mike expressed his regret that he'd missed Mrs. Pringle and Phoebe, then bid his friend goodbye. He paused before getting into his car and turned for a glance at the waving Milton. He somehow knew it would be one of those enduring friendships forged strong in the kiln of hard times.

Chapter 35

The muted red glow of sunrise gave the sky an orange hue. Six-fifteen and she'd already broken Mike's first nautical rule — never be late for an embarkation. He'd completed his pre-cruise check of the engine, sails, lines and navigation equipment half an hour before. Now, he paced back and forth at the end of the marina, wondering if the strange girl with all that chutzpah and no money had stood him up for their first date.

A deep, guttural bark interrupted his thoughts. He turned to see Susie and her big black Labrador making their way toward him. Mike wasn't sure what attracted him most — the long awaited presence of a dog that Ellie had forbidden, or the sight of this pretty girl with her tight, white shorts, a red blouse, and long blonde hair that bounced with each step. He remembered the first time he took Ellie sailing. She'd come running toward him on a marina like this, on an identical early morning, dressed much like Susie. He felt an unexpected twinge of returning sadness.

"Hi. Sorry I'm late," she said. Her engaging smile washed all thoughts of punctuality and everything else from his mind. "I was so hungry I forgot what you told me yesterday and dived into my first steak and eggs breakfast in a long time. I don't know, maybe it was just a reaction to your silly comment about my needing to put on weight. Anyway, I thought I'd bring Charles. I hope you're not mad at me."

"Nope, not at all. I love dogs. Is the lunch bag hanging over your shoulder for us or for him?"

"It's ours. Are we ready to go?"

Mike bent down to give the dog a friendly rub behind the ears to initiate their friendship. "Yep. As soon as you and Charles step over those lines onto the deck I'll cast off. Put your stuff over there on the life jacket box. I'm going to assume Charles won't get excited and jump over the side. If he gets nervous we can always secure him to the base of the mast or something."

He loosened the lines and revved up the diesel. Water churned, and the growling inboard pushed Contessa's bow slowly outward from the dock and away from its mooring. In the still of the morning, Massachusetts Bay unleashed a sudden gust of wind that drove a sea-salt aroma into their nostrils, a gentle reminder of the ocean's unpredictability. The boat gained speed as it moved past the breakwater toward the open sea, and Mike could feel his tension easing.

The seas were two to three feet with a slight chop under a mild, but gradually freshening wind by the time he cut the engine. He pulled on the halyard to set the sail, and the great white sheet billowed as the wind filled it. The craft continued to pick up speed, and Mike could tell from her unsteady balance that Susie had already begun to feel its movements.

She sidled up to him. "Can I help with the sails?"

"Maybe. Let me see your hands."

"What?"

"Your hands. Hold them out so I can see your palms."

She extended her arms, palms up. Mike frowned. They were soft and as white as her cheeks.

He looked at her with a mild grimace. "I guess I should have believed you when you said you didn't know anything about sailing. I can tell you've never hauled on a rough, wet line to raise a sail or spinnaker."

"What's a spinnaker?"

Mike rolled his eyes. "Never mind. You watch the scenery and let me finish raising the sail. You'll get a better view on the port side. When you feel like it you can roll up those other lines I left lying loose on the deck." He turned and flashed a grin. "Maybe it'll get some calluses started on those tender paws of yours."

"Okay, the right side is starboard, left is port, right?"

"Very good. Any more questions so far?"

"Yes. I can't see land anymore. How do you know we're not lost this far out?"

"We don't need to see land. I know exactly where we are."

"Yes, but if you can't see anything, how can you be so sure?"

"Susie, we have GPS, a compass, a well-charted map, constant communication with the Coast Guard, and I've been here before. You're starting to look a little uncomfortable. Stop worrying and enjoy the sea. Look at Charles. He seems as happy as a dog can be."

"I'm not worrying. Does this boat have a keel?"

"Of course. A very large one. Why?"

"Well, my stomach says this boat is rocking and swaying more and more. Isn't a keel supposed to smooth things out a bit?"

"The keel *is* providing stability. And a boat doesn't rock and sway. It pitches and rolls. Can you relax a little more?"

She put her head in her hands and knelt on the deck. "I don't think so. I think I better go lie down. I'm not feeling all that well."

Mike shook his head. "No. Don't lie down. That's the worst thing you can do when you're feeling seasick. Just makes it worse. Stay up here and on your feet. Move around. Stop staring at the horizon. You need to correct the instability your inner ears are feeling."

"There's nothing wrong with my ears," she snapped. "And the horizon is the only thing that *is* stable right now."

"No, Susie. Let me explain." He moved away from the tiller again and put a hand on her shoulder. "It's all relative. Look, you're standing on a moving platform. Everything not on that platform will appear to be moving, especially the horizon. Do you understand?"

She glared at him. "Fine. So what do you suggest?"

"You should focus on something that's already on this boat. Like the cabin, or mast base. Even Charles. Then what you see will appear to be stable."

She stepped back with her arms akimbo and glared at him. "Mike Pallino, that sounds like a lot of nautical mumbo jumbo. Oh, never mind. I trust you so I'll do it." She paused and put her hand to her mouth. "Excuse me. I think I'm about to lose my breakfast." She ran to the port side and leaned over before Mike could stop her.

"No, Susie, not on the windward side. Do it on the leew—oh, for God's sake."

His warning came too late. She let it all go and, at that particular moment, Mike could see the Atlantic breeze was not the only element blowing back into her face. He grabbed her and held her with both hands until she finished. He wished he'd been there to restrict her breakfast to black coffee and burned toast. He sat her down, wiped the vomit off her face with a saltwater-soaked rag, and put his arm around her while she put her head between her knees and cried.

"It's okay, Susie, it's okay. I think you'll be fine now. You're shivering. Take off your wet blouse."

She forced herself to sit up straight, wiped her eyes, and glared at him. "I'm fine, now, and I won't sit here naked."

"Damn it, I'm giving you this so you won't be naked." He removed his denim shirt and handed it to her. "Here. Put it on and hand me that blouse. It stinks and it's not keeping you warm. I have to get back to the tiller. We've wandered off course. Just stay here and rest for a few minutes. I'll swing the bow around and try to smooth-out the ride a bit."

Mike turned away after he made sure she put on the blouse. Still, he could sense her eyes scanning his frame while she admired his smooth movements. He felt a sudden conflict of emotions he'd never experienced. On one hand, he wanted to take her down below, lay her on her back on one of the two narrow little bunks, ravage her and let the Contessa wander with the currents. On the other, he felt a strange sense of responsibility for this ingenuous young lady so far away from home. Not to mention the second thoughts she might develop after learning she'd had sex with a man who had blown his wife's brains out a few weeks before. His cravings would have to wait.

By the time the sun reached its peak a few minutes before noon, Mike figured they'd had enough for one day. He turned the bow toward the distant shoreline and allowed the boat to run free with a following wind on the quarter. Half an hour later Contessa glided into its slip and bumped gently against the dock. Mike wrapped another spare shirt around her and helped her step out with Charles in tow. For one fleeting moment they looked at each other as though each had discovered a new world with only the two of them in it.

She brushed a few strands of her wind-blown blonde hair from her forehead. "Did you and your ex-wife have any kids?"

Startled by the question, Mike paused before he responded. "No. I wanted kids but she didn't, I guess."

"I'm sorry." She smiled and put her finger on her chin. "Well, if you did someday, what would you name your baby?"

Mike threw back his head and laughed. It felt good to laugh again. Maybe someday soon he'd be able to tell her what happened to his wife that night on the bridge. "Susie Crockett, you sure ask direct questions. Hell, I don't know. Depends if it's a girl or boy, I guess."

"Okay. Say it's a boy."

Mike paused, hands on his hips. "I'd name him Milton."

Susie drew her head back. "You're kidding. Isn't that kind of a sissy name for a tough FBI guy's son?"

"Hell, no. Not for the Milton my kid would be named after. Anyway, it's not subject to negotiation. Look, you better get going. I'll call you tomorrow."

As if in mutual acceptance of a temporary restraint, they smiled at each other and she thanked him for the ride. Susie left with their uneaten lunch, and Mike stayed to tighten the Contessa's mooring lines while he resurrected old thoughts about kids, backyard barbecues, and dogs. He almost told her about his new assignment to go after the guy who attacked Milton that evening at Metalcraft. Then he'd thought better of it. Now he wished he had. He realized he hadn't had any lunch. He knew he was long overdue for a double cheeseburger.

Chapter 36

Mac McLeod dressed up for the first time anyone at Metalcraft could remember. He even tidied his office by replacing the two solid-metal folding chairs with two metal ones with cushions. He figured it wasn't every day a partner from Potter, Moore & Bremer came to visit him. He wanted to make a good impression.

Aubrey Moore brought a young auditor with him, both wearing the kind of tailored suits Mac would never have bought for himself. Aubrey smiled and reached to shake the CEO's hand. "Good morning, Mr. McCleod. I'm Aubrey Moore and this is Tom Reardon. I'm the acting managing partner of PM&B for the time being. I'll be responsible for your audit. Tom will complete the work remaining at the time of Milton's injuries. We're truly sorry about all you've been through, although we're glad to hear that you've offered Milt the CFO position. I think he'll be a real asset for Metalcraft."

Mac waved them in and came around his desk to shake their hands. He pointed toward his new deluxe seating accommodations. "Please sit down, gentlemen. Call me Mac. Everyone else does. Yeah, it's been a zoo around here. We're all still in a state of shock. I've been kind of wiped out about the money, about almost losing Milt, and the trouble caused by my damned former CFO. Agent Pallino insists he knows nothing of Ali's whereabouts. He did say Milt's boss will most likely end up in jail. Is that right?"

Aubrey nodded. "Yes, except that Paul's wife is dying of cancer so they'll probably allow him some time with her until she passes…probably only a matter of days."

"I'm sorry to hear that. I can't say I'm not damned angry about that man's involvement in this whole thing. Even so, no one deserves to suffer a loss like that."

Aubrey shook his head. "We're all upset about what Paul did. Anyway, Tom here was originally assigned to your audit. He'll wrap it up. You're going to need some major upgrades in your internal control procedures to prevent anything like this from happening again. Tom will help you set those up, and he'll walk you through them."

With Mac's secretary away at lunch, Trudy took time out from her receptionist duties to bring in a pot of coffee for everyone. Black, as usual. Mac fought back a smile at the sight of Tom's unsuccessful attempt to pretend he could keep his eyes off her. Mac pulled a file from his drawer, drew out a letter from the bank, and handed it to Aubrey. His expression turned serious.

"Mr. Moore, this is the bank's original agreement to extend an expansion loan pending review of our audit results. I'm afraid this disaster of ours is going to ruin our financial statements as well as any chance of getting that loan. Is there anything you guys can do?"

Aubrey sampled his coffee without registering a complaint about the absence of cream and sugar. He scanned the letter and handed it back to Mac. "I'm not in a position to promise anything. A lot will depend on what Tom finds, and what your financial statements look like upon completion of his audit."

Mac lowered his face in his hands. "Damn it, that's what I was afraid of. Whatever he finds is going to be four million short of what it would have been without Ali's scam. So, does that mean we're all wasting our time on an audit that'll turn the bankers off no matter what?"

Aubrey managed one of his rare grins. "Not at all. As tragic as your four million dollar loss was in terms of its impact on your historic financial results, I doubt that it will impair your future cash flows to any significant extent. Since the bank's interest will be in the ability of your future operations to meet the debt service requirements, I'm optimistic. Tom will run some proforma numbers for the bank."

Mac gulped down the last of his coffee. "Some what?"

"Proforma financials. That is, statements of your last four years' operations as they would have been without the impact of Mr. Fadhil's fraudulent activities. Depending on those and the audit results I think you stand a good chance of working out a loan agreement with your bank."

Aubrey pushed his coffee aside as though he had no intention of ingesting more than one swallow. "Now on another matter, the bank will insist on your hiring a competent and reliable chief financial officer. As your auditors, PM&B will endorse that requirement. Agent Pallino said you have a young lady who is generally familiar with Metalcraft's financial operations — at least enough to hold things together until you find a CFO. Is that true?"

"Yes. Phoebe Denton. She's young and hasn't much experience, but she learned a lot from Milt. From this whole ugly mess, I think. Young Mr. Reardon here can give her some guidance. By the way, I've hired young Milton as my CFO as soon as he recovers." Mac turned to Tom and managed a full grin for the first time in several weeks. "Phoebe may not be as exciting as Trudy to look at, Tom, but she's pretty bright. You'll enjoy working with her." He pushed the coffee pot in Tom's direction.

Tom blushed and waved off the invitation. "Yes sir, I'm sure she'll be a much- needed help."

Mac's expression turned serious again. "Mr. Moore, I'm still concerned about those people who put my CFO up to all this. I'm especially concerned about the ones who killed my two employees. Not to mention the attacker who barged in here and tried to kill Milt. I asked Mike about it but he seemed reluctant to respond. Do you know if the FBI ever rounded up any of them?"

Aubrey shook his head. "Well, I've become involved in this investigation only because I'm Paul's partner and they needed to pick my brain. I'm told they haven't caught anyone yet. I've also been told they've assigned Agent Pallino to pursue the matter. I've spent more time than I wanted talking to him about Paul Bremer's role in this. I came away with the distinct impression Pallino's determination to track down the ones responsible for the attack on Milt went well beyond his professional obligation."

Mac frowned. "How do you mean?"

"I'm reading between the lines, of course, but I believe Mr. Pallino took a real liking to Milton. Took him under his wing, so to speak, and felt more responsibility for the young man's injuries than he probably should have. Makes me think the agent's commitment to finding the attacker has become more a vendetta than an objective search."

Mac pointed his finger at Aubrey and shook it. "Hell, a damned vendetta is exactly what's needed to round up those murderous snakes. Think about the message it sends if they get away with it. I hope Mike nails 'em."

"At any rate," Aubrey said, ignoring the comment, "Tom will start first thing tomorrow. Let's hope that sometime in the next few years you'll be able to take Metalcraft public. I'm glad to have met you, Mac. We'll keep in touch and I'll personally keep track of this audit and everything that results from it."

Mac grinned and breathed a sigh of relief. "Good. I feel better already."

Aubrey smiled. "Talk to you later."

Mac walked them through the reception area to the door. He wondered, as he watched them leave, how different everything would have been if he'd brought someone like Milt in three years sooner. Still, he couldn't suppress the feelings he had for Ali. Competent, bright, and skilled at reaching out to the financial community, Ali had seemed like everything Metalcraft needed to secure its future in a global market.

Mac slammed his fist on the table top and shook his head. What was there about blowing up a damned bridge, he asked himself for the third or fourth time, that could have enticed the man away from all that Metalcraft could have offered him? From all Mac could have offered.

* * * * * *

Aubrey Moore and Trent Potter accompanied the two FBI agents into Paul Bremer's office. One of the agents read Paul his rights. The other reiterated the agreement made between the agents and Aubrey that handcuffs would not be necessary.

Aubrey wrapped an arm around Paul's shoulder. "Paul, we want you to know how sorry we are about all this. We also understand your monetary motivations, although I have to tell you we'll never really comprehend how you could bring yourself to become directly complicit in such a treasonous act. We'll make sure the proceeds from your partnership buyout will be used to provide the best care and comfort possible for Edna. Trent and I and our wives will be with her right to the very end."

The agent ushered Paul toward the door. Paul nodded and forced a smile.

"Any remaining funds," Aubrey continued, "will be escrowed in safe, interest-bearing securities. The principal will, of course, be restricted until the completion of your prison term. However, all interest earned will be available to you upon request during your term. We'll visit you as we're able and we'll make sure you have whatever comforts are allowed. We'll act as advocate witnesses for you during your trial. We're all truly sorry about this."

Paul walked between the agents, then stopped and turned to look down the long hall toward his office. "I'm grateful to both of you," he said, "as I always have been. I only wish I could try to explain things to Edna. I don't want her present at my trial. She's suffered enough already. I've had a wonderful career here, and that's the part I'll always remember."

One of the agents tugged at Paul's arm. "We need to move along, Mr. Bremer."

Paul managed another half-smile. "Okay. But, for the record, I'm pleased that Milton Pringle's okay and getting the respect he deserves. He's a fine young man and deserved a lot better than what I gave him. I used him, for which his parents will never forgive me, nor would I expect them to."

He turned to Aubrey. "However, I want you to make sure they know I had no idea events would work out the way they did. Please do that for me."

The man who had built PM&B turned to throw one last glance at the partnership photographs on the wall before he walked out with the two FBI agents. He wondered who the firm's future partners might be. Tom Reardon would certainly be one of them. Paul knew the standards for partnership promotion would be high because he'd set them that way. Milton Pringle would make it to the top, someday. Not at PM&B, but perhaps somewhere else. Certainly somewhere else once the accounting world learned that Milt's Metalcraft audit findings had broken up a terrorist conspiracy.

Paul Bremer took his last walk down the hall.

Chapter 37

The waiter brought in a pitcher of beer, two glasses, and a bowl of pretzels. He set them on the table between Mike and Bones Rafferty. "Will there be anything else?"

Mike smiled and shook his head. "No, that's fine. Just keep the nearby booths empty for a while as usual so we can have some privacy."

"Yeah," Bones added, "and remember, if anyone asks, we were never here."

The waiter nodded, pocketed the two twenties Mike slipped him, and walked away.

Bones had already devoured his first handful of pretzels, washed it down with half a glass, and had begun working on his second. "Mike, I swear I didn't know that those guys who killed the two Metalcraft employees were doing anything that you'd be involved in. If I did I'd have told you about them."

Mike filled his glass and grabbed a handfull of pretzels before Bones could empty the bowl. "Forget it. Neither did I at the time. After that thing on the bridge I never would have guessed the bureau would assign me to go after those killers. Maybe someone figured I knew more about the case than anyone else. I don't know. Anyway, tell me what you know about them before I waste a lot of Bureau investigation time that may not be necessary. No, wait. First convince me this beer joint is still a secure place where what we say here stays here. Or that we were here at all. I don't recognize that kid who waited on us. I thought Jake owned the place and worked it solo."

"Don't worry about it. The kid's Jake's son. Family business, and they ain't about to squeal on a customer. We're okay. Besides, we're in Saugus, far enough from Boston that it's out of the loop. The Boston grapevine doesn't grow this far out."

Mike nodded while he savored his first few gulps of beer. "Good. Now, you said 'those guys,' like there's more than one. The Boston police have a fragile lead on only one suspect they think might be involved. No leads at all on the people who set up the attack on Milt. The attacker's supposedly dead. Rumor is that someone up in New York became real upset about his failure to put Milt out of business before he could break the code. Anyway, that trail came to an end. So talk to me."

"Yeah, okay. Look, word on the street is it was two separate hits. I mean the Milton contract was an out-of-town arrangement. Came out of New York. The two who pulled off the car wreck were locals. Maybe hired out of New York. No one knows."

Mike leaned toward Bones and lowered his voice. "Okay, so where the hell can I find these guys?"

Bones paused to finish off his second beer and load up number three. "Mike, I know they're auto mechanics. Damned good ones, too. Had to be, in order to rig that car so it would spin out of control at the right time. Then those same guys — or maybe someone else, I don't know — they finished the job by killing those two kids in the car and makin' it look like they were drunk. But the two guys who rigged the car ain't too bright, I can tell you that much."

Mike frowned. "Why do you say that?"

"A guy named Tank Kruski owns a bar on the South Side. Word is that the two guys you're lookin' for hang out there...it's called Tank's Place. A few too many drinks and they were heard dropping hints about what a smooth job it was. I mean, like leaving no evidence except a burned-out car. But after the honchos in New York killed the guy who attacked your friend, these clowns went into hiding. No one's seen 'em since."

Mike polished off the last of his drink, glanced around, and leaned forward, as though he still didn't trust the owner or his kid. "What are their names?" he whispered.

"Don't know. That's one thing they were pretty tight about. The bar owner might know, though. He probably won't give out any free information, seeing as they were customers. I don't know, Mike. You're going to have to go in there yourself if they're still in town. I mean you gotta be real quiet, because if they get even one sniff a federal agent's looking for them, they're gone, man."

Bones scooped up the rest of the pretzels. "I'm afraid that's all I can tell you, Mike. Except if you go in there don't get hot-headed like you did with that guy in Rio. You got lucky on that. Word on the street has it that you could have been in big trouble if that shooter hadn't popped your man before you did, and saved your ass."

Mike cursed the underground information network under his breath, and glared at his favorite snitch. "Bones, I sure as hell hope you're not going to lecture me about that the rest of my life. Because if you are, I'm going to find a way to throw you in jail."

He slid a hundred-dollar bill across the table at Bones as compensation for his info-dump. He laid down enough to settle their bar bill and another twenty for the waiter. "I have to go, Bones. Thanks. If you find out any more, let me know."

Bones put up his hand. "Wait a minute. You ain't going in there after them looking like a cop, are you?"

"No. I'm going to look like one of Tank Kruski's regulars. Don't worry about it. See you around."

* * * * * *

Mac McLeod leaned back in his chair and enjoyed the first feeling of real comfort he'd experienced since the scam had unraveled. Simply knowing Tom Reardon was on site wrapping up the audit produced a sense of relief. Aubrey seemed like a good man to have on his side, too, if Metalcraft ever needed someone who could authoritatively address the Securities and Exchange Commission.

The sound of his phone broke the reverie. He picked up thinking how nice it would be to have one of those electronic intercom things he could buzz people on like other CEO's have.

"Mac, it's Mike Pallino. How are you doing?"

"Pretty well, Mike. I miss Milt. Guess we both do. I'm looking forward to getting him back as my CFO someday after he heals up. In the meantime they're pulling the loose ends together on our audit as we speak. Anyway, it's good to hear from you. What's up?"

"Well, Phoebe tells me you're working hard to get back on track with your customers. I have an idea you might like to hear on that score."

219

Mac pushed a pile of engineering specifications aside. "I'm open to suggestions. What's your idea?"

"Well," Mike said, "I'm thinking you might need some marketing push if your expansion loan goes through. You know, to jack up sales enough to pay off the loan...or something like that. You're the businessman. You'd understand more about it than I would. I know a delightful — and highly intelligent — young lady who might help your advertising and sales promotion campaign get started. Are you interested?"

Mac took a sip from his coffee cup and winced. He expected the last batch at the end of the day to be a bit strong, but this one tasted like Trudy had drained her engine oil into it. He pushed the cup of mud aside. "You bet I am. We're operating at full capacity now, but you're right, we'll need to grow fast once the loan goes through. Who's the lady, Mike?"

"Her name is Susan Crockett, a friend of mine. She graduated cum laude from Indiana University with a degree in English. She's bright, pretty, and ambitious. She can talk a banker into extending a signature loan to an unemployed alcoholic. I think you'll like her."

"Send her over. I'd be glad to interview her. By the way, I heard you've been assigned to the case about my two murdered employees. Any truth to that?"

"Yes, but I don't want that to get out, so keep it to yourself. And tell whoever you heard it from to do the same."

"Sure. When can I expect to hear from this dynamic lady of yours?"

"I'll ask her to call you right away. I'm sure she needs a job. Be careful, though. She'll try to take over your company by buying you out with your own money."

Mac laughed. "My kind of girl. Sounds like she's already done a number on you."

"Yeah. It's a sweet number, though. I'll talk to you later, Mac."

* * * * * *

Mac McLeod's secretary ushered Susie Crockett into his office and made the introductions. She and her boss exchanged grins while they observed Susie's expression, which signaled disbelief that a company president's office should be so stark.

Mac came around the desk and shook Susie's hand. "Have a seat, Miss Susie Crockett. I'm pleased to meet you. Mike Pallino told me you could walk on water and, from the looks of you, I believe him." He turned to his still-smiling secretary. "Marie, bring us some coffee, please."

Susie glanced around the diminutive space once more, forced a smile, and sat down. "Well, I'm afraid Mike stretched things a bit, Mr. McLeod. I'm an English major without much actual business experience, but I'm creative and resourceful. Mike said that's what you needed."

Mac drew his head back. "Oh, he did, did he? Well, we don't run a pretty ship around here, Susie. We focus on being damned productive. Pardon my English. What else did Mike tell you?"

Susie crossed her legs and shifted in her chair, as though she'd already concluded it had been designed by someone who placed simplicity ahead of comfort. "Oh, he told me a lot of things about what's needed around here. I'm confident they can all be built into the marketing program I'll develop for you."

Mac paused to take the tray from Marie, and pushed the cream and sugar toward Susie. "Marketing program, eh? Okay, tell me how a young English major without any actual business experience is going to be able to put a marketing program together for a seventy-five-million-dollar company."

Susie threw one of her captivating smiles at him, uncrossed her legs, and leaned forward. "Well, Mr. McLeod, I'm a fast learner and I know that your expansion plan is going to need strong marketing support. For example, you don't have a market research function, which you'll need to identify the needs and demographics of your yet-to-be-identified new markets. Furthermore, you may need an extensive business-to-business advertising campaign to pave the way for your breakthrough. Now, do you even *have* a formally structured marketing department, Mr. McLeod?"

Mac straightened up and arched his eyebrows. "Well, by God, Mike told me you were an assertive young lady. He forgot to mention bold and aggressive. Okay then, the first thing I want my fast-learning marketing director to learn is to drop the 'Mr.' and call me Mac. Then I'd like to know how your study of great authors allowed you time to learn that much about business."

Susie sipped her coffee, shifted in her seat again, and glanced around the room again. "Yes, sir. Well, I earned a minor in business — a requirement imposed by my father who refused to finance my tuition unless my curriculum included something more 'useful' than English. I didn't like it very much, but now that I'm here, I think I will. Of course, the first item of business will be for me to arrange for a much larger, more impressive office for you. First impressions are important, you know. Especially for the president of a company."

Mac stared wide-eyed at her for a moment, then threw back his head and laughed. "Damn, Susie Crockett, I think you and I are going to get along like gangbusters. Good. You start tomorrow. Now, as to salary, how does fifty thousand a year with bonus options sound to you for starters?"

Susie gulped. Even her father hadn't made that much until recent years. Still, she thought, this wasn't a time to appear overwhelmed. She sat upright in her chair and smiled at Mac again with as much of an air of self-assurance as she could muster. "I think that would be quite adequate, Mac. As long as my bonuses are commensurate with increases in sales."

Mac shook his head and gave out with a grin so wide it looked like he'd been saving it for this occasion. "Fine, Susie. I'll see you in the morning. By the way, I suggest you come in through the manufacturing floor every now and then. You know, just to get a feel for the place. And don't bother to dress up so much. I wouldn't want to see grease stains on a designer dress. We're pretty informal around here. I'll introduce you to the other employees first thing."

* * * * * *

After Marie walked Susie out, Mac sat alone and chuckled quietly. It felt good to spend some time with upbeat people like Susie who could make him forget his troubles...at least for awhile. Still, he couldn't help thinking about the downside — once again he'd put himself in the position of having to trust someone else with functions he'd once handled without any help when the company was smaller. He'd trusted Ali, and that had worked out badly. Still, the worst was over and things could only look up. He'd lost a son. Who knows, maybe he'd gained a daughter?

Mac straightened the array of papers on his desk, locked the files, and walked down the long hall to the manufacturing area. A half-hour before closing and activity on the shop floor had begun to wind down. Hands on his hips, Mac listened and scanned the area, his senses alert for sounds and movements that might signal something less than the kind of smooth operation he'd come to expect over the years. Reassured, he waved to a group of six machinists who'd known him since the old days.

"Hey, Mr. Mac," one of them yelled, "when are you gonna come down here an' get some oil and grease stains on yer shirt again?"

Mac grinned. These were people he could trust. No one ever stole or scammed here. "One of these days, Charlie, one of these days. You guys know where my heart is."

He reached into a box of spare machine parts, picked one out and turned it over in his hand like he used to do during inspections. He took a deep breath, returned the part, and walked out to his car. Some memories are good, he thought, and some are bad. But on the shop floor they're always good.

Chapter 38

Tank Kruski had to be the largest human hulk Mike had ever seen, aside from that three-hundred-plus-pound Purdue tackle who had decked him ten minutes into the last game of his junior year. The dim lighting in Tank's Place made Mike's two-week-old growth of beard look even darker. His long hair hung down over the collar of his beat-up leather motorcycle jacket emblazoned with the words "High Plains Drifter." His only real concern at the moment was that someone might steal the Harley he'd parked outside while he made himself busy staking out two killers on the inside.

"You look like you're ready for a refill," Tank said. He leaned over the bar to pour before Mike could answer.

From his seat at the end of the bar Mike scanned the other patrons. Two of the more inebriated customers were involved in an intense argument about the effectiveness of the Red Sox farm club system. Tank's L-shaped bar accommodated enough customers to promote conviviality, while tables filled the remaining space for people who wanted more privacy. A one-hundred-gallon tropical fish tank built into the wall behind the bar threw off some extra light and added a bit of décor.

After Tank mediated the argument he returned to Mike. Elbows on the bar, Kruski leaned forward and grinned. "You're kind of becoming a regular customer here. I get the feeling I've seen you someplace before. Mind if I ask where you're from and what line of work you're in?"

Mike had stationed himself there off and on for several days waiting for an opportunity to get into a conversation like this without raising suspicion by initiating it himself.

"Sure, I don't mind." He sipped his beer. The object was to drink slowly and not too much at each swallow, to avoid becoming inebriated during the long stakeout stints at the bar. "Cheyenne, Wyoming. Did some coaching. Tried to get a bike repair business going but it went belly-up and left me damned near broke. Started up a car repair business and did pretty well until the landlord jacked up the rent. So, I said to hell with it and hit the road. Did some odd jobs here and there, working my way East. Saved up some money from before, but I could use a little more." He ignored Kruski's "someplace before" comment.

"Yeah, you looked like you been on the road when you first came in. You got a name?"

Mike took another swallow. "Cole. I been waiting around and listening, hoping maybe I could connect with someone who looked like he might be able to give me a job. I'm a pretty fair auto mechanic. Can't go knocking on doors, though. I got a record. They told me this was a place where car and truck people come and wouldn't ask a lot of questions if I hit 'em up for a job. If you know what I mean."

Tank grinned, reached over, and gave Mike a friendly pat on the shoulder. "Yeah, I know what you mean. You're not my only customer in that boat. I won't even ask if you got another name. Cole's good enough. I might be able to help you, though. Couple of my old customers work for an auto repair shop. They haven't been in for awhile, but I'll tell 'em about you next time they show up."

He turned away and made the rounds, keeping the other patrons happy while he listened to their sad stories as though he gave a damn. Tank never let anyone's glass remain empty for more than a few seconds.

Mike nursed his beer while he tried not to listen to a whiner three seats from him, telling anyone who would listen what a bitch his wife was. Welcome to the club, Mike thought. He wondered how long he'd have to work this charade before Tank's two guys happened to come in again. Susie hated his beard and long hair. He'd become tired of her asking when he'd planned to clean himself up. He drained the beer, paid the tab, walked out, and cranked up the Harley.

* * * * * *

Another week passed without any helpful leads from either the Bureau or the Boston police, and Mike had almost reached the limits of his patience. Worse, he was running out of credible background lies to tell Kruski. A former high school football star, Tank admitted he had difficulty believing his newest customer's insistence that he'd never tried out.

"Cole, a guy built like you would have made one hell of a running back. Maybe even a defensive back. You said you never played. How come?"

As much as Mike wanted to share gridiron stories with the friendly giant, he knew it would be risky. The wrong comment at the wrong time might allow anyone familiar with Notre Dame football history — or the televised Heisman interviews — to connect Cole to all-star Mike Pallino, beard or no beard. That would finish any chance of finding the guys he was after. Might finish himself as well. In fact, his failure to make it through tryouts in the pros might have been an advantage here, where people seem to have better recall about professional players.

"Wanted to, but my old man had me working so many hours in his garage fixing cars I never found the time."

"Ahhh, that's a bummer, man. I sure could've sworn I seen you someplace, though. Anyway, after you left the other day the two guys I was telling you about came in. I told them about you looking for a job. One of them seemed interested. Said he'd be in tonight to check you out. So, do I get a commission if they hire you?"

"Damn right. Soon as I bank my first paycheck. Or what's left of it after I fill up your cash register buying beer. What are the names of these guys?"

"One of them is called Bear, but that's gotta be a nickname. The other calls himself Marlon, I think. Don't know their last names."

Tired of scraping his rump on a barstool, Mike took his jacket off and laid it on the seat as a cushion while Tank served another customer. He waited for Tank to wander back after he finished sharing a sick joke with a couple of guys — something about the pope and three nuns in a French whorehouse.

"What's the name of the repair shop," Mike asked, "so I can sound intelligent when they check me out?"

Tank swiped an old, gray-colored washrag over the top of the bar from one end to the other — a superficial attempt to clean a surface on which alcohol stains, cheese dip, and cigar ashes had been ground-in since who knew when. "Ahhh, let me think. If I'm not mistaken, it's called 'The Car' something...no, 'The Bike 'N Car Barn.' That's it. And speak of the devil, here come your boys. I'll introduce you."

Aside from their identical white tee shirts bearing the repair shop logo, they looked like Mutt and Jeff opposites. Marlon, so skinny he would have made Bones Rafferty appear overweight, and Bear, with dimensions that

226

matched his name. Marlon's scrawny hand almost disappeared in Mike's. Bear flashed a mean grin while he tried to intimidate Mike with a grip that probably could have crushed most of the hands he shook. He must have realized his mistake a moment or two after Mike responded to the challenge by squeezing the man's hand white. Bear jerked it away with a wince that elicited a wide grin from Tank.

"So, Tank tells me you're a grease monkey," Marlon said as he eyed Mike up and down. "Said you work on motorcycles, too. Said you could turn a busted bike into a real kicker. That true?"

Mike took a second or two to dredge up what few slang terms he could remember from his high school summer jobs fixing cars in his dad's shop, repairing a bike or two in between. "Yeah, cars are my specialty, but I've worked on a few hogs that were basket cases. Managed to nurse a couple of 'em into first-class lane splitters. Problem is, I need a job where people don't make a big deal about your past. Done a few things with cars that got me in trouble."

Bear grinned, still trying to shake the circulation back into his fingers. "Yeah, we understand. Listen, Cole, if you can turn a wrench like you shake hands our boss can use you. No questions asked about where you been, only what you can do. C'mon, let's have a beer and talk about it."

They talked for two hours, during which Mike came to realize Bear worked as the lead mechanic at Bike 'N Car Barn, but Marlon possessed the brains and the money-making talents. Marlon proved he also knew how to save money by offering Mike an hourly wage so low any shop could have turned a profit on it. Mike accepted, glad to get his foot in the door after having become a professional bar-fly. One last beer and the three of them called it a night. While he watched Bear and Marlon admiring the Harley, Mike figured the three of them had probably consumed enough alcohol to ensure Tank's profit for the day.

* * * * * *

By the end of his first week Mike knew it was plain for everyone to see he wasn't a natural. He had to think about almost every step in the process of getting a busted bike up and running. He finished the job, though, which was apparently good enough.

Marlon approached him with a grin. "Hey, my man, it's Friday night, Happy Hour. Let's clean up and drain a few at Tank's. I want to talk to you about a promotion. Bear and I'll treat you to a burger on the way and your first beer when we get there. Let's go."

Tired of grease, oil, and repairing hogs, Mike decided he'd become close enough to these guys to solicit the kind of information that could put them away. He needed documentation, though, and he didn't have recording equipment with him. He couldn't risk hiding a device like that on his person until the right opportunity came along, for the same reason he couldn't carry a firearm. It would be an open invitation to discovery. He needed time to retrieve the recorder from his rented locker half an hour's drive away.

"You talked me into it," Mike said. "Meet you there in forty-five minutes. You guys get started without me, and I'll stop and finance my own burger on the way." He slapped Bear on the back, and fired up the Harley.

His round trip took him a little over an hour, during which Bear and Marlon had managed to polish off the first pitcher by themselves. Tank deposited another tray of beer, chips, and a glass for Mike just as Mike sat down to join them. Tank grinned. "Hey, you guys just want to be alone here in a corner, or is my underarm deodorant so strong you can't sit at the bar?"

"Ahhh, we got private business, Tank," Marlon said, "and we need quiet. No offense."

"Yeah, just kidding. Wave at me when you're ready for a refill."

Marlon grabbed Tank's shirt sleeve and whispered to him. "Yeah, and I think we're gonna move over a few tables, okay? I think that guy in the corner can hear us, and we don't need any eavesdroppers. I don't much like the way he keeps sneaking a peek or two in our direction."

They changed tables and Marlon didn't waste any time. "Cole, you been here a week and done a good job. Not as good as we thought you'd do, but we figured you're probably a little rusty, that's all. Now here's the thing. We need to promote you from bike work to car work. You probably noticed we aren't doing any high-tech auto work. You probably thought that was kind of weird for a place that advertises it."

Mike took a small sip from his glass. He thought if he could work it so they drank two for his one he'd have an easier time soliciting information from them. "Yeah, I wondered about that. Figured it was none of my business, though."

228

While he bent over to pick up some chips he intentionally dropped, Mike reached unobtrusively into his pocket to make sure the recorder was on, and to check the Smith & Wesson strapped to his ankle.

"Well, truth is that's really why we hired you. Now this is just between us, and I don't want it to go any further. We did a car set-up that went bad a while ago. Now the cops are poking around town looking for guys who have enough expertise to pull a job like that. No evidence, mind you, and they can't pin it on anyone. Problem is they been checking out car repair shops all over the city, so we had to back off doing any complicated auto stuff for awhile. We don't even want to be seen doing normal repairs. It's costing us money. A lot of money."

Marlon chugged down his beer and poured another. Not to be outdone, Bear kept up with him. Small talk dominated the conversation until they'd emptied both pitchers, and Tank restocked their supply. Mike continued with his half-swallows while Marlon grabbed another handful of chips and leaned forward, as though he wanted to be absolutely sure his next remarks would be private.

"That's where you come in, Cole. We got a backlog of orders a mile long we don't dare touch. We need you to start fixing those cars and bringing some cash in here. I figure you're not the best mechanic in the world, but you're good enough to fix up the stuff we got lying around. Sure, the cops will get around to us sooner or later and might even pull you in for questioning. Tank said you got a record. Anyway, you done your time or whatever, and you're clean. So they'll have to let you go. Bear and I'll make it worth your while, Cole. Don't worry. We'll see you get more than your normal share of the money. So how does that sound?"

Marlon and Bear seemed engaged in a contest to see who could contribute the most toward draining the pitcher. Mike set his glass down on the table and brought his hand up to his forehead, as though he were thinking hard about the proposition. "I don't know. I guess I could handle it, but you guys would have to make it worth the risk. I mean, if the cops haul me in for interrogation, they just might find a reason to keep on my tail. I don't need that."

The conversation stopped until after Tank delivered another round of drinks. Marlon waited until Tank walked away. "Sure, we understand. Don't worry, you're gonna do real good when you get those cars fixed and we get paid."

229

Mike leaned back in his chair and stared at the ceiling. He tried his best to look like a man deep in thought. "Okay," he said, still staring at the ceiling, "tell you what. I like the sound of this. I'm going to have to have a good story, though. When the cops ask me why I'm doing all this car work by myself, I don't want to get tangled up in something that conflicts with what they already know."

Mike lowered his gaze and fixed his eyes on Marlon. "So I need to know what really happened on that car job you said went bad." Mike knew he'd just gambled two hard months of uncomfortable patience and careful stalking on that question. It had as much chance of blowing his cover as producing evidence sufficient to support a conviction.

Without saying anything, Bear and Marlon each chugged another full glass in their continued race to the bottom of the pitcher. After an excruciating period of silence, Marlon glanced at Bear, who offered an affirmative nod.

Marlon looked around again to assure himself of complete privacy, and spoke in a slow, soft voice. "Okay, here's what happened. This guy came down from New York and made us an offer we couldn't refuse. I mean, this deal would pay us more than we'd make in the car shop in ten years. All we had to do was rig up this car so it would spin out of control after a certain number of miles. Not all that easy to do, but not a big problem. Now—"

"Who was this New York guy?" Mike interjected.

"Don't know. Didn't ask." Marlon downed the rest of his beer, but Bear had moved one ahead of him by then. "Anyway, the hard part turned out to be attaching the triggering mechanism to the explosive this guy brought us. I'd never seen anything like it before. It looked like your run-of-the-mill plastic device, but it wasn't. The guy told us this thing would be different. He said it would blow without leaving any evidence. That way the investigators would have to assume the car flamed from the accident alone."

"Sounds pretty slick," Mike said.

"Yeah, you can say that again. So me and Bear followed the instructions, jimmied the steering mechanism, and attached the explosive to the timing device. It triggered the bomb the instant the car started to spin out. Somehow this guy from New York talked these two employees of some company to drive somewhere together in this damn car. Don't ask me how. Anyway, the thing went off like we engineered it to do and should have killed these—"

"What company did you say it was?" Mike asked.

230

Marlon paused. "I think the guy called it Metal something. The problem was—"

"Wait a minute, I've heard of a company called Metalcraft," Mike said as he took another sip and tried to make it look like a gulp. "Is that the—"

"Yeah, that's it. Now the problem here was the blast killed one of these two poor slobs but not the other. So, way we heard it, New York sent a hit man to finish the job manually himself, if you know what I mean. Pretty messy. And then they wouldn't pay us because they claimed we screwed up installing the mechanism. Bear an' me we were gonna go after this guy. I mean, we're talkin' big bucks here. Figured it was worth a try."

Marlon belted down another few gulps in what was shaping up to be a futile effort to catch Bear.

"Then we found out they killed this other guy for messing up a hit inside the company. We figured the smart thing to do was lay low for awhile 'til it all blew over. We sure could have used the money, although it ain't worth dyin' for. And these people, whoever they are, get real serious about punishing screw-ups no matter who's at fault."

"Yeah," Bear interjected, "and we weren't about to take any more chances."

Marlon nodded. "Right. Now, the flames didn't hide the fact the car was rigged, but all the cops know is maybe it wasn't the crash that killed those people. All they can do is try and find out who in town had the capability to do that kind of set-up. So, that's the story. You in or not?"

Mike forced a smile. "Okay, count me in. I can fix your cars, but I'm not doing any bomb-rigging."

"No, we're out of that business," Marlon said. "You just get busy on that backlog of repairs and start bringin' some cash in for us."

The conversation turned to laughter and about an hour's worth of shared anecdotes on the subject of motorcycles. Truth and accuracy became less and less important as the contents of the pitcher disappeared. Before Tank could load them up again, Mike paid the tab and they wobbled out.

Marlon and Bear slapped Mike on the back and welcomed him as their newest auto mechanic.

Mike could hardly wait to turn the recording over to Jack Marshall and savor the arrest of Marlon and Bear the next morning. The Metalcraft murders mystery would be solved.

Mike watched Marlon and Bear stumble into their car. He straddled his Harley and grinned at the prospect of rubbing Jack's nose in a successful wrap-up of a case that never once pretended to comply with Jack's concept of proper protocol.

Before he did anything else, Mike realized he had to urinate. There seemed to be no sense in going back into the bar. A perfectly good bush waited for him a few steps around the corner of the building, and the task required neither indoor facilities nor light. He dismounted, walked into the shadows, and relieved himself of some of the evening's intake.

Out of the corner of his eye, he saw the man rush out of the bar and jump into his car. The man never saw Mike. Tires squealed, and the vehicle tore out a few seconds behind Bear and Marlon, heading in their direction. Something about it didn't look right. The guy in the corner who had glanced over at them two or three times hadn't looked right either.

Mike put the bike in gear, spun it out onto the road without turning the headlight on, and took off after the car. He maintained a safe distance behind until the car accelerated, pulled out into a no-passing zone, and began to close the distance between itself and the car Bear drove, with Marlon in the passenger seat. Mike's instincts grasped the evolving picture a second before his brain did.

A puzzle that should have come together one piece at a time over the past month while he loitered at Tank's bar flashed into his mind in one high-definition digital blast. Why hadn't he seen it? The contract that had called for the assassination of Milt's mugger for his failure also had Bear and Marlon's names on it for the same reason. Mike could have kicked himself.

He jammed the Harley into high gear, reached down for the Smith & Wesson, and prayed he could reach the trailing vehicle before it pulled up parallel to Bear's for a couple of shots through the driver's window. Visions of Ali Fadhil's assassin scoring a perfect hit through the passenger window from thirty feet away in the rain ran through Mike's mind. By comparison, this hit would be child's play — close range, dark-but- perfect weather, targets too drunk to take evasive action, and time for as many shots as the shooter needed to finish the job.

Mike realized he couldn't make it in time. A second before the assassin lowered his passenger side window for the kill, Mike took aim through the man's rear window. A clean head shot was out of the question because the headrest would be in the way. Even so, the shooter would have to lean at

232

least a bit toward his passenger window for best position. That would be his Achilles heel.

Mike fired four times, moving the barrel slightly from left-to-right after each shot. He hoped one of the bullets would crease his target's skull. Worst case, the volley would distract the man until Mike could pull alongside and finish the job.

The would-be assassin's car lurched, side-swiped Bear's vehicle, and sent it skidding off the right side of the road into a patch of thick brush. The ricochet effect spun the shooter's car out of control off the left side of the road, over an embankment, and into a tree. Mike heard a loud, dull thud, accompanied by the sound of crunching metal. A bright flash lit up the night, followed by a muffled explosion. Flames began to lick at the lower branches of the tree.

Mike hit the brakes, jumped off his bike, and raced down the embankment toward the shooter's car, Smith & Wesson in hand. He tried to open the jammed driver's-side door, but quit after a few tugs, and smashed the window with the butt of his firearm. He pulled and squeezed the unconscious driver out through the window moments before the flames curled their way to his feet. Mike dragged his bleeding captive away from the car, and cuffed him to the rear wheel of the bike. After he frisked him, Mike ran toward the spot where Bear's car had left the road. He could feel the recording equipment beginning to itch inside his shirt.

Still three-sheets-to-the-wind and holding up a weaving Marlon, Bear waved at Mike. "Hey, Cole," he slurred, "what the hell are you doing here? Did you see that? Some damn jackass tried to run us off the road. I thought I heard shots. What the hell happened?"

Mike shook his head. "Some jackass *did* run you off the road. Fired at you once or twice, too. Are you guys okay?"

"Yeah, guess so. Don't know if our car'll start. Or even if it does we're pretty much stuck in that bush. Why you here, though?"

"I saw that nosey guy in the bar take off like a hungry dog after you and Marlon. Figured he wasn't going after you just because you didn't leave a big enough tip. Lucky for you guys he doesn't shoot any better than he drives a car or you'd both be dead by now."

Marlon rubbed his eyes and showed signs of re-entering the world. "You can let go of me, Bear. Who was that guy, Cole? And where did he go?"

Marlon's question posed a problem. Mike wasn't ready to reveal himself as an FBI agent until the next morning when he'd arrest Bear and Marlon with two other backup agents at his side. He couldn't let them near the shooter because they'd wonder how Cole-the-drifter came by a pair of police handcuffs and an official-looking handgun. Worse, the man might regain consciousness and blow Mike's cover right on the spot.

"Ahhh, he hit a tree and knocked himself out. At least I think that's as bad as it got. He might be the one you guys told me about. You know, the reason you two laid low for a while. Anyway, you two better get back there and try to get your car on the road. I'm going to call the cops and see if I can get me some brownie points for collaring the bastard."

"Yeah, good idea," Marlon added. "You take care this guy doesn't jump you, Cole. See you tomorrow."

"Maybe that'll go in my favor when they pull me in for fixing your cars. I'm thinking maybe you two guys better stay out of sight. I mean before you end up with more publicity than you ever wanted. If you can't move your car, at least you can stay under cover until I help the cops drag this guy downtown. I'll see you tomorrow at the shop."

Marlon nodded. "Yeah, that makes sense. Nice touch about the brownie points, by the way."

Mike rode downtown in the ambulance with the wounded man and two of the four patrolmen who'd responded to Mike's call. The medic patched up the hole in the would-be assassin's right cheek. The man refused to talk. Mike figured the man's identity and where he came from was someone else's problem.

For now, Mike felt a sense of satisfaction that the Metalcraft case looked just about wrapped up. Except for all the scumbags who financed Ali, and the sharpshooter who took him out.

Before he could savor the satisfaction, his mind formed an unwanted flashback to the dream he had about the three people at the edge of the cliff. The image of his father and Milton hurt the most, and Mike could feel a familiar sadness sweeping over him again.

Chapter 39

Mike found Jack Marshall not exactly smiling, but at least he wasn't scowling. Mike eased himself into the chair in front of Jack's desk and decided to wait until his boss announced his reason for summoning Mike in. Maybe things were looking up for a change. Anyway, Jack hadn't pounded his fist on the desk yet. Mike remained silent while Jack poured two coffees and shoved one of them toward Mike — a rare event.

"Pallino, I can't say I'm pleased with the way you engineered this whole thing. Anyway, I'll admit I'm damned glad you got it done. Have you heard the news?"

"No, sir. We arrested the two mechanics and turned the shooter over for interrogation, but that's the last I know of it." Mike reached for his cup, half expecting Jack to lean forward and take it back.

"Well, they'll be proposing a heavy sentence for your beer-drinking friends. The big news, however, is the gunny who tried to kill them turned out to be the same guy who popped Milton's mugger for screwing up. Came out of the same New York terrorist cell Ali Fadhil had been tied into. Word on the street is we've scared the hell out of everyone connected with that cell. It's virtually disappeared. Or at least gone underground for a while. Which means you're back in everyone's good graces." Jack grinned. "For the time being, anyway. You've still some vacation coming. What are your plans, if I might ask?"

Mike gulped a mouthful of his coffee. "Jack, you're probably not going to believe this. I think I'm getting married."

"What do you mean you *think*? Haven't you asked her yet?"

"I did and she accepted. That's the good news. The bad news is I haven't told her about Ellie and what happened on the bridge. After I tell her about that she may change her mind."

Jack leaned back in his chair, sipped his coffee, and paused for a moment while he looked Mike over. "Mike, I've never met this girl, and I never knew a whole lot about Ellie. Only what I saw of her at the Christmas parties. What I do know is you're a good man, and you deserve better than what happened to you. If this new girl turns you down for doing your job, you send her in here to me and I'll straighten her out."

Mike threw back his head and laughed. He couldn't remember ever having laughed with Jack Marshall before. "Thanks, Jack. I just might, except I'm afraid you'd scare hell out of her."

Jack grinned again. "Mind you, I'd be obligated to tell her what a stubborn S.O.B. you are. But I'd let her know she'd be crazy to pass up a good thing. Anyway, get out of here and take some vacation. You need it."

Mike walked toward the door and paused to glance back in anticipation of Jack's customary epilogue. It never came.

* * * * * *

Mike knocked on the door of Susie's apartment half an hour early. He didn't want to be late for dinner at O'Malley's and risk missing part of the Red Sox game afterward at Fenway Park. Wrapped in a bath towel and a surprised look that turned into a wide grin, she opened the door and waved him in. Charlie plodded over to him, wagged his tail, and licked Mike's outstretched hand. He gave the big dog a strong rub behind the ears.

"Hey," Susie said, "are FBI agents always early when they nab someone?"

"No, only when they think the 'someone' might steal a boat and skip town. Hey, Mac says you're doing well at Metalcraft. I knew you'd like working with him." He handed her a bouquet of yellow roses.

She flashed one of her flirtatious smiles. "Oh, they're beautiful...and so are you without the beard. By the way, thanks for the recommendation. Mac thinks the world of you and I'm sure it's because of you I got the job. And are you doing this so I'll have to let go of my towel to take the roses?"

Mike returned the smile. "No, I hadn't thought of it that way, but now that you mention it, I like the idea. About time you showed me your place. Nice apartment. Here, I'll put the flowers in that tall glass on the table."

He felt an unexpected twinge of sadness, even before his eyes had completed their sweeping glance around her living room. A moment too late he turned away. He hoped she hadn't noticed.

Susie cocked her head. "What is it? You look like you just saw a ghost."

He turned back and forced a smile. "It's nothing. An old memory, I guess. They come and go. You finish dressing. We don't want to be late for the game."

She pulled an Indiana University sweatshirt over her head to cover her torso and wrapped the towel around her waist. "I'm not doing anything until you tell me what's wrong. Did you see something in here that reminded you of a bad time?"

He eased his frame onto the couch. "I don't know. I suddenly realized your apartment looks like Milt's. Some things can't be explained, I guess."

She sat down next to him and wrapped her arm around him. "Look Mike, Milton's going to be okay. You can stop worrying about him. You miss him a lot, don't you?"

"Yeah." He turned away and wiped the corner of his eye. "There's always a day in your life you'd like to live over. To do it differently, I suppose."

Susie studied him for a moment before she spoke. "I read the interview you gave the newspaper about him and that night on the bridge. You have to stop blaming yourself. It wasn't your fault."

"Yeah, it was. He took a bullet for me, Susie. Or at least he diverted a shot that would have been aimed at me. I never should have allowed him to come. I should have sent him home. I'd given him a gun and he wanted to help. The more I think about it, the more mistakes I realize I made. Look, I'm sorry. I wanted this to be a fun night for us. Damn it, I'm sorry. I didn't expect this to happen."

"It's okay, honey." She held him tighter. "It's okay. Maybe it's better if we just stay here tonight and talk it out. Listen, I have some news that'll cheer you up. Mac told me he's offered Milt the CFO position at Metalcraft. He chose Milt over a bunch of impressive resumes the auditors gave him. He said anyone who digs in like Milt did would be the perfect candidate for the job."

Mike succumbed to a widening smile. "That's great, Susie. I agree with Mac's assessment. I'll bet Phoebe will be happy about it, too. Gives them a chance to reconnect."

Susie gave him a knowing look. "I think they've already done that, Mike. Word is that Phoebe made a beeline for San Francisco and camped out on a lounge chair beside Milton's bed until they released him."

"Yeah, I forgot to ask him what took so long for them to let him out."

"There were complications, Phoebe said. She sold the hospital a big fib that the FBI had assigned her to stay by his side and collect all the information he had about the terrorists. Looks like the hospital staff bought it."

Mike shook his head and grinned. "Okay. Anyway, I'm fine now. Thanks for listening. Right now, go get dressed. You'll like O'Malley's. The food's awful and the service is worse, but it's fun. Get into something comfortable. We don't exactly have box seats at Fenway."

"Okay. How about feeding Charles while I throw on some clothes? I'll be ready in a few minutes. Pour yourself some wine. Bottle's on the table and glasses are next to it. I have another surprise for you. I'll tell you when we get to O'Malley's."

Mike poured some yucky-looking pellets from a large dog food bag with a label that promised good health and a coat of thick, shiny fur. Then he turned and scanned the room with a three-hundred-and-sixty degree sweep in a matter of seconds. No particular reason, it was just a reflex action from his training — to remember as much as he could of what he saw: second-hand unmatched furniture; a couch, two armchairs, an end table with the wine on it; a small piano that looked more like a toy; pictures of people Mike assumed were Susie's parents; her bachelor's certificate from the University of Indiana and a photo of a teenage boy hung on the wall. The boy's face looked familiar. Mike stared long and hard at it for a few minutes but couldn't place it. He wasn't sure whether to attribute the discomfort he'd begun to feel to the sight of the boy, or to his inability to identify him.

"Okay, how was that for fast?" Susie bounded into the room and swung her hip into his with enough force to tip him off balance.

"Who's the kid in the picture?" His eyes glued to the photo, Mike recovered his balance and ignored what he took to be her playful attempt to flirt with him.

Susie's eyes turned to the photo. Her smile vanished and he sensed he'd raised a subject she didn't want to talk about.

"That's my older brother. He got into some trouble and left home five or six years ago. We haven't seen him since." She put her hand on his shoulder without taking her eyes off the photo. "Mike, I should have told you this. It wasn't fair to keep it from you. I wasn't completely truthful about why I came out here."

He saw she'd begun to cry, and wrapped an arm around her. "Okay, so why did you come if it wasn't to fulfill your sailing dream like you told me?"

Susie wiped her eyes and blew her nose before she looked up at him. "I came to find him. I know he's here in the Boston area somewhere. I learned that from some reliable sources, and please don't ask. Mom and Dad have almost given up on him. Now, here's the surprise I said I'd tell you about later. Mom and Dad are coming out here next week — ostensibly to help me look for Marlon, but really to check you out since I told them we're engaged. I'm really sorry, Mike. I should have told you all this before."

Mike put his hands on the sides of his head. "Whew! Susie Crockett, you do have a knack for blowing me away. Now I suppose you're going to confess you're interested in me because I'm with law enforcement and might be able to help you find your brother, right?"

"No. Never. In fact, I wanted to find Marlon myself before he got himself into more trouble. *Please* believe me."

Mike shook his head. "I believe you, but I'm afraid I have some bad news for you. It didn't hit me until you mentioned his name, but now I'm reasonably sure I can place the kid in the photo. If he's who I think he is, your brother's already in a hell of a lot of trouble."

He placed his hands on her shoulders and looked her straight in the eye. "Susie, I'm not sure how to tell you this. The other day we picked up a guy named Marlon for his accessory role in an attempted murder. He's a few years older now, but he bears a close resemblance to the boy in that photo. He's not using Crockett as his last name, of course, but I'm going to ask you to come down to the police station and confirm all this. Are you up to it?"

Susie put her face in her hands, and wept, as though she already knew what she'd find.

Mike knelt beside her. "Susie, this isn't going to be easy, I know. Look, the name Marlon may be simply an unfortunate coincidence in this case. If so, we can walk away and start looking for the real Marlon, your brother. You okay with that?"

She lifted her head, wiped her eyes again, and stopped crying. "Yes. Guess we'd better forget about O'Malley's and the game. Let's go."

He nodded, and they turned their backs on dinner and Fenway Park.

* * * * * *

Mike had called in a request to set Marlon up in a room to avoid Susie's having to see him behind bars. The closer they approached the room, the more Mike could feel her tremble, an unexpected reaction from a girl who'd appeared so self-assured. His thoughts of what she must be feeling conjured up images of Milton when the young accountant learned he'd been betrayed by the boss he idolized.

Mike's own past flooded back, like a tide he thought had ebbed away. The muzzle flash, Milton going down face-first, his own mixed emotions as Ellie's head snapped back under the force of the bullet from his gun. The moment the officer opened the door Mike wanted to turn away, but couldn't.

Susie and the undernourished-looking Marlon hugged each other and broke into tears. Mike rolled his eyes. Damn it. He'd spent two months in a successful effort to track down and put behind bars his prospective brother-in-law. Jack Marshall had it right. Life isn't fair. It just comes at you and you play the hand you're dealt. Mike cursed under his breath, and felt like slamming his fist into the wall. He took the name of the Lord in vain twice, and didn't care what his always-reverent father up there might be thinking about it.

Still wrapped in Susie's arms, Marlon turned to face Mike. "Hey, you lousy traitor. I'm having a tough time thinking of you as anything except Cole the hog-fixer. I see you met my sister. Damn your ass, if you've done anything to her I'll kill you."

"He hasn't done anything, Marlon," Susie said. "Mike's been wonderful, and we're going to be married."

Marlon pounded the wall and scowled. "Oh, that's just great. And here I was thinking jail time is the worst thing that could happen to me. Wrong. The worst is finding out I'm gonna have a Fed for a brother-in-law. I don't know whether I should thank him for savin' my life, cuss him out for puttin' me in here, or hate his guts for pulling the wool over my sister's eyes."

"Marlon, I'm caught in a place I never expected to be," Mike said. "If I'd suspected Susie was your sister I'd have told the bureau to find another agent and take me off the case." He could picture Jack Marshall flying into a rage with a request like that, coffee cup bouncing all over his desk. "As things stand, the best I can do now is testify on your behalf that you were dragged into this mess by a bunch of people who had more than rigged cars in their crosshairs. I can't get you off, but I think I can have your jail time cut short. And by the way, I love Susie and I'll take good care of her."

Marlon glared at him. "Yeah, okay," he said after a long pause that seemed like it would ever end. "I guess you had to do what you had to do. I'll leave it at that for the time being. Maybe someday I'll be able to say no hard feelings, man." He turned to his sister. "Susie, I hope you know what you're doing marrying this two-faced guy."

"Yes, Marlon. I really, really love him. *Please*, I want you to come back to the family when this is over. Mom and Dad have suffered enough. And so have I. They'll be here next week. I think we should all make up. Okay? Please?"

Marlon patted her on the top of her head in big-brother fashion. "Yeah, we will. I'm damned sorry about all this. Guess I just had to find out who I am. I'm not sure I like what I found. But what the hell, I think I know where I'm going now. You and this cop take care of each other, and tell Mom and Dad to hang in there. You got that?"

They hugged each other again before the bailiff told them the time was up.

Mike and Susie didn't speak until they reached his car. She broke the silence. "I don't feel like sleeping in my apartment tonight. I'd like to sleep on the boat. Could we do that?"

"Sure, no problem. Sleep at my house if you want."

"No, I prefer the boat. I'll pick up some things at my apartment first, okay?"

"Fine. Let's get a bite to eat after that and we can both check out the sleeping accommodations on board."

She looked up into his eyes with an anxious expression. "What do you think will happen to him, Mike?"

He shook his head. "Not sure, Susie. I think he's facing accessory-to-murder charges. Under the circumstances, I believe the court will be as lenient as can be expected, but it's not looking good. I'll do what I can, but don't expect too much."

Susie gripped his hand and smiled. "Thanks. By the way, I decided on a name for our boat."

"Okay, what would that be?"

"*Hoosier.* We both went to school in Indiana, so it works. What do you think?"

Mike grinned. "I like it fine. *Hoosier* it is. It's a fitting name for an Indiana family that's getting back together, as well. Maybe we can find a way to sail it along the Wabash someday."

Susie laughed and squeezed his hand tighter.

He turned to face her. He took her free hand in his and kissed the top of her head. He knew that his images of death, destruction, infidelity, and terrorism would resurface, uninvited, for a long time to come. Then he hugged her again and vowed to begin a new life filled with dogs, backyard barbecues, and maybe a son named after a young accountant who'd changed a federal agent's life forever.

Made in the USA
Charleston, SC
07 August 2015